A Run
For The
Money

Murder Ink Press

Austin * New York * Boca Raton

ALSO BY STEPHEN G. YANOFF

FICTION:

The Graceland Gang

The Pirate Path

Devil's Cove

Ransom on the Rhone

NONFICITON:

The Second Mourning

Turbulent Times

For more information,
you can visit www.stephengyanoff.com

A Run
For The
Money

Stephen G. Yanoff

authorHOUSE®

AuthorHouse™
1663 Liberty Drive
Bloomington, IN 47403
www.authorhouse.com
Phone: 1 (800) 839-8640

Published by AuthorHouse 05/13/2016

ISBN: 978-1-5246-0850-7 (sc)
ISBN: 978-1-5246-0851-4 (hc)
ISBN: 978-1-5246-0849-1 (e)

Library of Congress Control Number: 2016907680

Print information available on the last page.

This book is printed on acid-free paper.

This book is dedicated to three marvelous women, each a winner in her own right ...

Janice Baum

Susan Marquess

and

Christine Nickles

ACKNOWLEDGEMENTS

There are a number of incredible women (and several men) who made this particular book a pleasure to research and write ... My beautiful wife, Patty. My loving mother, Hazel. Rachel Zell, Rebecca Yanoff, Goldie Delilah Zell, Gladys Deatrick, Thelma Wilson, Margaret Bell, Joyce Booke, Ann Dodson, Sally Hooper, Marie Petit-Homme, Jill Mirostaw, Maria Sequeira, Hermelinda Garza Perez, Feliciano Acosta Perez, and Yanet Vazquez.

I would also like to acknowledge Dr. Lara Hochman, a wise and wonderful physician.

Finally, a tip of the hat to Thomas M. Mannion, one of the most entertaining and knowledgeable handicappers in the world!

Remember, Lady Godiva put all she had on a horse
and she lost her shirt!

W. C. Fields

CHAPTER ONE

The park ranger announced to the group that they were standing on hallowed ground, close to where General Thomas "Stonewall" Jackson had been mortally wounded by his own troops. He warned the mesmerized tourists that the general made frequent appearances, and if any among them were brave enough to stay until dark, they might catch a glimpse of his ghost riding across the battlefield in search of a missing limb. When some of the tourists snickered, the ranger went on to patiently explain why Jackson had a restless spirit.

On May 2, 1863, Confederate pickets had accidently shot him at the Battle of Chancellorsville. The incident had occurred in total darkness, as the general and his staff were returning to camp. Under a moonless sky, they were mistaken for Union cavalry by a squad of soldiers from the 18th North Carolina Infantry Regiment. Shots rang out, and despite frantic shouts from Jackson's staff, a second volley was fired. The general, on horseback, was hit by three bullets – two in the left arm and one in the right hand.

Several officers were killed during the melee, which lasted for several minutes. Darkness and confusion prevented a prompt identification – and also delayed the provision of immediate care for the wounded. When the smoke had cleared, figuratively and literally, the injured were removed on stretchers, but during the evacuation, General Jackson rolled off his stretcher and landed on the ground. Incoming artillery rounds were to blame, but due to the severity of his injuries – and the subsequent delay – Jackson's left arm had to be amputated.

As fate would have it, he survived the surgical procedure, but died of complications from pneumonia on May 10, 1863.

Among his last words, uttered in delirium because of a dose of opium, were orders to two of his subordinates.

But his last words before dying were: "Let us cross over the river and rest under the shade of the trees."

The park ranger paused for effect, then added, "Any questions?"

A blonde woman raised her hand. "I have a question. Where is the general buried?"

"General Jackson was buried in Lexington, Virginia."

"All of him?"

"I beg your pardon?"

"I thought his arm was buried separately."

The park ranger hesitated, choosing his words carefully. "Did you drive through Chancellorsville?"

"Yes."

"Did you see a sign for the Wilderness Tavern?"

"By the traffic light?"

The ranger nodded. "That's where the cut off Jackson's arm. The surgeon had no choice. The arm was badly mangled, the bone shattered. Back then, severed limbs were thrown in a pile and then cremated, but Jackson's chaplain, Reverend Lacy, couldn't abide with that, so he retrieved the arm. Later that evening, he walked down the road to his brother's plantation and buried the limb in the family plot behind the garden."

The woman, who spoke with a slight Austrian accent, nudged the man who was standing beside her. "I told you."

The park ranger smiled. "Would you folks like to see the gravesite?"

The entire group expressed an interest, so the ranger led them on a thirty-minute hike that meandered through a series of soybean fields. Eventually, they reached a tree line, and ten minutes later they caught a glimpse of a large roof. Before long, they arrived at a vacant house, a remnant of a bygone era. Without a word, they passed through an ancient garden gate and into a clearing that was encircled by large trees and an aging post-and-wire fence. Scattered before them was an array of venerable tombstones, one of which bore a simple inscription:

"ARM OF STONEWALL JACKSON"

The ranger knew what they were thinking – that it was odd for a limb to have its own gravesite – so he reminded them of Jackson's exalted status in the Confederacy. The arm had once belonged to the South's most brilliant commander, the general that Robert E. Lee referred to as his "right arm." Stepping aside to allow for photographs, he went on to tell them that Jackson had gained triumph in the Shenandoah Valley, displayed uncommon valor at Sharpsburg, and routed the Union force at Chancellorsville.

During the lecture, the blonde woman reached for the arm of her male companion and pulled him back toward the vacant house. They stood on the front porch, shaded from the midday sun, and shared a bottle of water. Neither of them said anything for a moment, and then, with some difficulty, Irene Kaminski dragged over two rocking chairs.

She looked over and gave Adam Gold a long, searching look. "Well, what do you think?"

Gold frowned. "What do I think about what?"

"The gravesite."

"Interesting."

"That's it? Just interesting?"

Gold took a deep breath, as if what he had to say was going to be physically painful. "If you've seen one grave, you've seen them all."

Kaminski did not avert her gaze. Adam Gold was a top notch insurance investigator, but he could be too skeptical for his own good. If the truth be told, he'd been reluctant to make the long drive down from Manhattan, believing it to be a waste of time. After a lengthy silence, Kaminski spoke softly, as if she were wary of her own thoughts. "Did you notice the ground? There was fresh dirt on the grave."

Gold thought about that for a bit, then said, "Maintenance work."

"Maintenance my eye. Somebody dug up that arm."

Gold looked at his boss to see if she was being serous, which indeed appeared to be the case. He found it hard to fathom that the president of a major insurance company could believe such claptrap. Under normal circumstances he might have laughed, but there was nothing normal about her statement – or the situation in which he found himself. "Did we drive six hours to talk about stolen body parts?"

"More or less." She reached into her purse and took out a letter. A thin smile crossed her lips. "Your next assignment."

There were times, like now, when Adam Gold's world seemed to be spinning out of control. A woman named Melanie Dupry had purchased a kidnap and ransom policy from the Anchor Insurance Company and had filed a claim on behalf of her employer, The Sisters of the South. From what he was able to decipher, the organization, based in Richmond, was responsible for protecting and preserving the graves of some famous Confederate generals, including Thomas "Stonewall" Jackson. Incredibly, she was claiming that grave robbers had stolen Jackson's arm and were holding it for ransom, demanding five hundred thousand dollars for its safe return.

Predictably, she wanted the Anchor Insurance Company to cough up the dough.

Gold muttered a few choice words, then shook his head. "When did we issue the policy?"

"Six months ago."

"What limit?"

"Two million."

"Any deductible?"

"Nope."

Gold rubbed his chin thoughtfully. "How do you suppose they came up with half a million?"

"They only stole a quarter of Jackson's remains."

"So they say. Maybe we should have a chat with the park ranger."

Kaminski made a face. "The park service is supposed to be protecting these sites. I don't hold out hope for a straight answer from them."

Gold figured as much, and he was willing to concede the point, but he wasn't quite ready to fork over half a million dollars. Not by a long shot. Wracking his brain, he tried to recall the insurance definition of *kidnap*, which was not a far cry from the legal definition: The crime of unlawfully seizing and carrying away a person by force or fraud, or seizing and detaining a person against his or her will with an intent to carry that person away at a later time.

In Gold's view, the law covered a whole person, not a portion thereof, and he made that point emphatically. "I think we should deny the claim."

Kaminski reminded him that the definition of "kidnapping" was difficult to nail down with precision because it varied from jurisdiction to jurisdiction. Most state and federal statues defined the term *kidnapping* vaguely, allowing the courts to fill in the details. The state of Virginia was no exception.

She went on to tell him that kidnapping laws in the United States were derived from the Common Law of kidnapping originated by courts in England. In the beginning, the crime was defined as the unlawful and non-consensual transportation of a person from one country to another. During the twentieth century, states began to modernize and redefine the definition, eliminating the requirement of interstate transport.

To muddy the waters further, the insurance industry now had its own category of kidnap and ransom, often referred to as K&R Insurance. Most policies covered the perils of kidnap, extortion, wrongful detention, and hijacking. In general, a policy would reimburse a loss incurred by the insured, but it would not pay ransoms on the behalf of the insured. Typically, the insured would have to lay out the money, incurring the loss, and then seek reimbursement from the carrier.

Although she had worked hard to maintain an aura of unflappability, Kaminski's façade was beginning to crack. The veins stood out on her neck, a sure sign the stress on her was mounting. "The terms and conditions of our policy are typically vague. They do not state that a covered individual must be alive. Nor do they require an entire body to be kidnapped. Furthermore, our form clearly covers the peril of extortion."

Shifting nervously, Gold said, "Houston, I think we have a problem."

"A big problem." She went on to tell him that criminals extorted over 500 million dollars a year in kidnap and ransom payments. Every year over 1,000 professionals and executives were kidnapped – and that number was growing. The size of ransom demands was also growing. Prior to the 1970s no one was demanding as much as one million dollars, but in today's world demands often exceeded ten million dollars. The combination of political unrest, poverty, and lawlessness were the main reasons that kidnapping – and ransom demands – were on the rise. "The odds are stacked against us. Most kidnappings are carried out in order to obtain a ransom, and in most cases a ransom is paid. To be honest, rescues are rare, mainly because the authorities in most countries are concerned about the safety of the victim, not the capture of the perpetrator."

"Well, I suppose that's a good thing."

"Yes, but it can have a serious effect on a company's bottom line. Even if we recover the ransom, which is also rare, we get stuck for expenses."

Those expenses included hostage-negotiating fees, lost wages, ransom fees, consulting fees, and death and dismemberment fees. In many cases there were also personal financial losses, medical and dental costs, rest and rehabilitation costs, travel and accommodation expenses, family counseling costs, and legal considerations, including judgments and settlements.

"In other words," Gold said, "heads they win, tails we lose."

"Precisely."

"I still think we should deny the claim, but if you disagree maybe we could offer a partial settlement. You never know. They might take the money and run."

"I don't think so. Our insured is a very determined woman – and she's well-connected, politically. If we try to play hardball, we could end up chatting with the Insurance Commissioner. I don't know about you, that that's not on my bucket list." A pained expression crossed her face.

"I've never known a commissioner who didn't dream of higher office. They usually want the governorship, so they bend over backward to please their constituents. We end up looking like an out-of-state bully."

"We could hire a PR firm."

"Do you know what that would cost? More than the damn claim. Besides, we have a rate increase pending in Virginia. I don't think it would be a good idea to alienate the powers that be. Do you?"

"No, I suppose not."

"I'm afraid we're stuck between a rock and a hard place."

Gold had a good idea what that meant. It was time to saddle up and move out. "I reckon you'll want a preliminary report?"

"More than that. I want a complete investigation. I want to know who the bad guys are, how they work, and where they live. In other words, I'd like a shot at getting our money back."

"I just hope I don't get shot," Gold muttered. "I'll be mixing with bad company."

"I realize that, but we have no choice. We have to catch these ghouls. Trust me, Jackson's arm is only the beginning. We could be looking at a slew of claims."

"There are other policies?"

"Two or three generals and a very famous colonel."

Gold shook his head. "I don't understand our underwriting philosophy. K&R Insurance is high risk. We're a standard lines company. Why do we bother with such a volatile class?"

"Because, as they say out west, there's gold in them thar mountains. Did I get that right?"

"You're within range."

She missed the joke and went on. "You may not like the class, but K&R insurance generates a lot of income – over $200 million in annual premiums."

"How many claims per year?"

"I'm not sure, but I do know that the F.B.I. investigates 300 to 400 kidnappings per year. About one-third of those involve a ransom."

Gold let all this sink in for a moment. *Here we go again*, he told himself. *Why couldn't I have found a safe, sane, regular job, with an office and a company car and a pleasant, predictable future?* Somehow he managed to flash a smile devoid of even the slightest trace of warmth. "When do I start?"

"You're halfway there. Next stop, Richmond."

Gold rubbed his temples and stood, staring out, at nothing. "Let the games begin."

She reached out and squeezed his hand reassuringly. "Better than dealing with the Insurance Department."

Gold fixed her with a cold eye and said, "I don't know about that. Better the devil you know than the devil you don't." He shook his head, wondering what he was getting into this time. "What a way to start the summer."

"Think of it as a learning experience. Who knows where you'll end up."

"Yeah, that's what worries me."

CHAPTER TWO

Irene Kaminski had no intention of tagging along with Gold, but she was happy to give him a lift to Richmond. On the way to the capitol, she revealed that she'd had some underwriting experience with K&R coverage, and that earlier in her career she was regarded as something of an acknowledged expert in the field of high risk insurance. Kidnap and ransom policies had been introduced by Lloyds of London, in response to the 1932 kidnapping of the Lindbergh baby. The United States had been one of the leaders in reported abductions, but that dubious honor now belonged to Mexico, which recorded 72 kidnappings per day. Columbia and Brazil ran a distant second and third.

"Speaking of Lloyds…" The words trailed off as she glanced at Gold, who was still trying to wrap his mind around 72 kidnappings per day. "I never told you about my trip to London."

"Well, I know you've been busy."

"What else is new."

Gold lapsed into silence. He had been bracing himself for a conversation like this for some time – ever since he decided to hide the truth about Thomas Hargreave's death. In time he said, "How was the memorial service?"

"Very touching. There was a military band and a gun salute." She exhaled sharply, revealing a crack in her professional demeanor. "Thomas had served in the British army. He was stationed in the Falkland Islands."

Looking solemn, Gold said simply: "Yeah, I know."

She seemed a little surprised. "He told you about this military service?"

"Briefly."

"I'm surprised to hear that."

"Why?"

"Thomas was a private person. He rarely opened up to strangers." She looked at him, her eyes moving slightly back and forth as she seemed to search his face for something. "He must have liked you."

"What's not to like?"

She almost smiled, but then she remembered what they were talking about - the tragic death of a dear old friend. "You'll be happy to know that he's been nominated to receive the Queen's Commendation for Brave Conduct."

"You don't say."

She reached over and squeezed his thigh. "Thank you for writing a letter to Scotland Yard. Your eyewitness account was very helpful."

"Well, it was the least I could do."

"You're a *mensch*."

Gold managed a weak smile. "I have my moments."

She tried to return the smile, but her face darkened suddenly and a single tear raced down her cheek. "Thanks to you, Thomas will be remembered as a dedicated officer, a man who never shirked his responsibility and died in the line of duty."

This was followed by more silence, Gold drumming on the dashboard with his fingers. Finally, he said, "I guess Scotland Yard never heard from their French counterparts."

"There was no official report."

"That's odd."

"I think I know why." She glanced at him fleetingly, then turned her attention back to the road. "Their lead investigator resigned from the force."

"Captain Jarnot?"

"The loss of the Gobelin Tapestry was more than she could handle. I heard that she had a nervous breakdown."

Gold looked out his window, examined his fingernails, and finally directed his gaze back to Kaminski. "That's a damn shame," he said softly. "She was a good cop. A little high-strung, but a first-rate officer."

"They say she was obsessed with the tapestry. Do you think that was true?"

"Obsessed is a pretty strong word. Let's just say that it was very important to her."

"Well, it was important to me, too, but I didn't let it ruin my life."

"If I remember right, you were in a bad mood for several weeks."

"True, but I got over it." She sat quietly for a moment. "I wonder what happened to the tapestry."

Gold looked up almost whimsically toward the roof. "Ah, now, let me see." He thought for a moment. "Maybe it was taken to a pirate lair in the Caribbean."

Kaminski ran a hand through her thick blonde hair, sighed, and slumped back into her seat. "I think you've got pirates on the brain."

"I'd rather deal with pirates than kidnappers."

"Well, don't worry yourself. These clowns are not really kidnappers, not in the traditional sense of the word. They're more like grave robbers. Low-life body snatchers."

"That makes me feel much better. For a moment I thought they might be sick individuals." He laughed cynically. "I still think we're making a mistake. We should let the park service handle the investigation. They're trained for this sort of thing."

"You think so?"

"I've never heard of any lost bodies."

She slid off her glasses and put them on the seat beside her. Gathering her thoughts, she aimed a glance at Gold, whose expression was a picture of melancholy. "Ever hear of Abraham Lincoln?"

"Rings a bell."

"Would you believe that somebody tried to steal his corpse?"

"Recently?"

"No, but that's beside the point. The point is that somebody *tried* – and that they almost got away with it. You need to brush up on your history."

"So it seems."

Marshalling her thoughts, she calmly described how robbing a grave was not that difficult. Everyone was vulnerable. Presidents, potentates, and paupers. It didn't matter where the person was buried or how much security there was. History had proven that, with enough planning, bribing, and luck, any corpse could be stolen.

Truth was, the Lincoln heist had been foiled at the last possible moment. If she remembered correctly, a Chicago counterfeiter had concocted the scheme in order to free one of his associates. The idea was to the steal Lincoln's body – or what was left of it – and hold it for ransom. The gang intended to demand $200,000 in cash and a full pardon for their colleague, who was serving a ten-year sentence in the state penitentiary.

The date for the grave robbery was set for November 7, 1876, which coincided with election day in Springfield, Illinois. The robbers reasoned that Oak Ridge Cemetery would be deserted at night, so under cover of dark, a gang of four men sawed the padlock off the iron door of Lincoln's tomb, pried the marble lid off the sarcophagus, and attempted to lift the heavy wooden coffin. They were only able to move the five hundred pound coffin about fifteen inches. One of the robbers, a man named Lewis Swegles, was ordered to bring the horses and wagon up to the tomb. Instead, Swegles, who was a paid informant of the Secret Service, alerted the eight detectives who were in hiding.

The comedy of errors continued when a detective's gun accidently discharged, alerting the tomb robbers and allowing them to escape out the east gate of the cemetery. Nevertheless, they were captured in Chicago ten days later, tried and found guilty, and sentenced to one year in Joliet State Prison.

"One year?" Gold said, raising an eyebrow. "Jesus, that's just a slap on the wrist."

"I couldn't agree more, but from what I remember, that was the maximum allowable sentence. Three years later, the Illinois legislature revised the statue on robbing graves, and I believe the penalty was increased to ten years in prison."

Gold shook his head, in awe of her encyclopedic memory. "Jesus, Irene, you know more about American history than I do."

Kaminski smiled and rubbed the bridge of her nose. "You know the old saying. Those who don't know history are destined to repeat it."

"Who said that?"

"I'm not sure. It was either Edmund Burke or Victor Wong."

A thin smile crossed Gold's face. "Ah, yes, the man of a thousand phrases."

Kaminski's expression grew somber." Do you know why I told you that story?"

"To pass the time?"

She fixed him with a flat, unamused glare. "To remind you that we can't rely on the park service, or any other bureaucracy, to protect these graves or catch the bad guys. Sometimes we have to be proactive, and it's my belief this is one of those times."

Gold scratched his jaw with a road map, pondering her statement. "Are you telling me to take the law into my own hands?"

"No, of course not. I'm just suggesting that you might have to break a few rules. You know, get down and dirty."

Gold stared at her for a moment, dissecting the words, trying to decode the shaded message. *Down and dirty?* Jesus, great choice of words. He grimaced and somehow managed to smile at the same time, realizing that he was about to get down and dirty in more ways than one. "Here we go again," he muttered. "Down the rabbit hole."

She paused a moment before saying, "I think you'll find this case intriguing."

"Really?" Gold found that amusing. "What's so intriguing about a bunch of grave robbers?"

"Didn't you handle the Presley claim?"

Rather than answering, Gold gave her a quick once-over, frowned, and shook his head. He knew something was up the second he looked at her face. "Yeah, that was my baby. What about it?"

"They almost stole Presley's body."

"Who's *they?*"

"Grave robbers."

"For real?"

Kaminski, eyes narrowed to slits, nodded slowly. Her tone was businesslike as she gave him the details. In August 1977, just two weeks after Elvis Presley's death, the police were contacted by an informant who had infiltrated a group that planned to steal Presley's 900-pound, steel-lined, copper-plated coffin and hold his remains for ransom.

A police task force was dispatched to the grave at Forest Hills Cemetery in Memphis, and sure enough, they encountered three men, including the informant, snooping around Presley's mausoleum. The men were questioned, but no tools or explosives were found, so they were only charged with criminal trespassing.

Since no actual crime was committed, other than trespassing, and no evidence was found at the scene, all charges against the men were dropped. Of course, if they had been successful, the body would have fetched a pretty penny.

"How many pennies?" Gold asked.

"One billion."

"I'm sorry I asked. Please translate."

"Ten million dollars."

"Big bucks."

"I'd say so." She couldn't help but smile as she watched Gold rubbing his forehead, putting it all together. The man moved cautiously, but always in the right direction. "The moral of the story is simple. Some folks are worth more dead than alive…or almost as much." Very gingerly, she reached under her seat and pulled out a brown paper bag. She placed the bag between them, proffering it as if it were a gift.

"What's that?" Gold asked.

"A .38 Smith & Wesson. You left it in your desk."

"You think I'll need it?"

"You never know about rabbit holes. They might contain other varmints."

CHAPTER THREE

The city of Richmond was not part of any county and was therefore considered to be an independent city, which was somewhat fitting in light of its past. "The River City," as it was known down South, was where Patrick Henry uttered the famous words, "Give me liberty or give me death." During the Civil War it had served as the capital of the confederate States, and like many Southern cities, it still retained a fair amount of antebellum charm.

Kaminski had never been to Richmond, so she was surprised by its proximity to Washington – just two hours south – and relieved to discover how easy it was to get around. The city was laid out on a grid system, which made for smooth navigation despite the fact that many streets in the oldest sections of the city were very narrow and one-way.

The most noteworthy street was arguably Monument Avenue, a long thoroughfare that stretched from the city center to the west end. All along the avenue were statues of Confederate heroes, familiar names from a bygone era: J.E.B. Stuart at Lombardy Street, Robert E. Lee at Allen Street, and Stonewall Jackson at the Boulevard.

Gold had read somewhere that Richmond was sometimes referred to as "a city of neighborhoods," and it was easy to see why. Leaving I-95, they drove through a dozen neighborhoods, each bearing its own distinct look, flavor, and identity. The most populous, and arguably the most interesting, were the Fan District, the Museum District, and the downtown area, which included Shockoe Bottom and Shockoe Slip.

The Shockoe area was just east of downtown, positioned along the James River. Driving through, they saw it was bounded by I-95 and bisected by railroad lines. One of the oldest parts of the city, it was the very spot where several hundred thousand people were sold into slavery.

It was also home to the Sisters of the South, the organization dedicated to preserving the more noble aspects of Southern history. In this case, home sweet home was a two-story antebellum structure that had clearly seen better days. Kaminski stared at the wide front porch, which was buckling at both ends and badly in need of repair, then turned her attention back to Gold. She seemed to be weighing her words. "Your goal," she finally said, "is to break up the ring. Do what you have to do, but be careful. I don't want anything bad to happen."

Gold stifled a small laugh. "Something bad has already happened. That's why I'm here." A long, uncomfortable silence ensued. Finally, he took a deep breath and stepped out of the car. "I'll call you tomorrow. Get home safe."

Kaminski leaned across the seat and squeezed his arm. "You do the same."

Gold found himself oddly touched by the gesture, but as soon as she pulled away, he turned his attention to the problem at hand. Focusing on the mission was essential, especially when large amounts of money were involved. From past experience, he knew that insurance claims were seldom simple, and often deceptively dangerous. The worst ones were known in the industry as "icebergs," which meant that they were bigger than they appeared to be, and a lot more treacherous – the bad part lurking just below the surface. If you ran into one of these bad boys, it could cost an investigator time and money – or even their life.

Surprisingly, there was nobody at the reception desk, so Gold took a seat and waited for somebody to show up. He didn't have to wait long. Two minutes later, a woman swept into the lobby, immaculately dressed in a chic business suit. She was amber-haired, and big-eyed, with a full figure and a wide mouth. She emanated old money, though it was *new* money that she had on her mind. "Ah, the bearer of good news," she drawled. "I'm Melanie Dupry. Welcome to Richmond."

Gold held out his card. "I'm Adam Gold with the Anchor Insurance Company. We spoke on the phone – about an hour ago?"

"Yes, of course. Any problem finding the place?"

"Your directions were perfect."

"Practice makes perfect. I speak to a great many tourists." She eyed him warily and accepted his card inspecting it for what Gold thought was a second or two too long. "How can I help you, sir?"

"I was wondering if you had a few minutes to talk about your claim."

She plastered a fake smile on her face. "Of course."

They went into her office, which was decorated with Confederate memorabilia and horse prints. Like its occupant, it was tastefully put together and neat as a pin. Gold sat in a large leather lounge chair, which seemed to engulf his entire body. He struggled to get comfortable, slightly embarrassed by the effort. "Nice chair," he muttered. "You could sleep on this cushion." He looked at the walls and smiled. "Horse lover?"

"Horse *owner*. I own a string of thoroughbreds." She pointed to a large print hanging directly behind her desk. "Do you recognize this mare? Her name was Seabreeze. She won a lot of races in her time. My brother and I own one of her colts – a two-year-old named Night Wind. He's got a pretty good shot at winning next year's Derby."

"Thanks for the tip."

"Thoroughbreds are a passion of mine." She flashed a quick grin. "What about you, Mr. Gold? What are you passionate about?"

"Insurance claims."

She pouted, her bottom lip fuller, her eyes narrowing. "All work and no play makes Jack a dull boy."

"If that's true, then I'm as dull as they come."

"I've heard that before."

Not having a clue where she was going with this, Gold gave her a half-smile and said, "I'm not familiar with your organization. What exactly do you ladies do?"

She showed Gold most of her teeth in a broad smile. "My goodness, you like to get right down to business."

"Time is money."

"So they say."

"Would you mind if I recorded our conversation?"

"Suit yourself. I've got nothing to hide."

"Gold produced a digital audio micro-recorder. "Ready when you are."

She swiveled around in her chair, making a small, squeaking sound, and stared out the window, leaving him hanging for a moment. Gold heard her mutter a mild obscenity under her breath, and he suspected it was directed at him. After heaving a theatrical sigh, she told him that the Sisters of the South was founded in 1885, the brainchild of two Virginians who were married to Confederate veterans. Like their better known rivals, the Daughters of the Confederacy, they were dedicated to collecting and preserving the "truthful history" of the War Between the States, and to protecting the places made historic by Confederate valor.

Their library, though modest in size, contained rare books, documents, diaries, letters, and personal records that were deemed to be of historic importance.

To be eligible for membership, a woman had to be at least 16 years of age, and she had to be a lineal or collateral blood descendant of someone who had served honorably in the Army, Navy, or Civil Service of the Confederate States of America.

No Confederate ancestor who had taken the much-maligned Oath of Allegiance before the end of the war was eligible for membership.

The Sisters of the South was a benevolent organization, but it didn't cotton to traitors.

In this day and age, any group that aligned itself with the Confederacy was bound to be controversial, but Melanie Dupry didn't give a damn about political correctness. In her view, the old South was part of her heritage – a heritage that was rich in honor and glory. She didn't expect a "Yankee" to understand, but cherishing and nurturing the past was part of her birthright, and she could no more help being a Sister of the South than she could help being an American.

After her speech, she turned her head this way and that, trying to figure out what it was Gold was thinking. She wondered if he was one of those arrogant Northerners that she detested. "I suppose you think I'm silly. A foolish woman living in the past, defending a lost cause. Maybe you even think I'm a racist." She had an iron grin on her face, not a look of amusement, or pleasure, but one of solid determination. "Frankly, my dear, I don't give a damn what people think. All I ask is that I be judged by my deeds. Just for the record, our group awards ten undergraduate scholarships per year. We also contribute to homeless shelters, homes for battered women and children, hospitals, and food banks."

Gold responded with the faintest trace of a smile. "Just for the record, I didn't come down here to refight the war. How you spend your time is your business. How my company spends its money is my business." He studied her eyes, hoping to read in them some sign she was getting the point. "Why don't we talk about your claim? Do you really believe that Stonewall Jackson's arm was stolen?"

"I most certainly do. Confederate artifacts are extremely valuable – especially in this part of the country. Why, just the other day, a Confederate battle flag, sewn by J.E.B. Stuart's wife, sold at auction for one million dollars." She smiled without a trace of humor. "Grave robbers may be sleazy, but they're not stupid. They know where the bodies are buried, and most of them know how to avoid getting caught. By the way, Confederate generals are not the only ones being targeted." She handed him a newspaper clipping, a two-paragraph article from the *Cleveland Plain Dealer*. Thieves had broken into the tomb of James A. Garfield, the twentieth President of the United States and the hero of the Battle of Chickamauga. "As you can see, these scoundrels don't discriminate."

"They only got a couple of spoons."

"They'll be back."

"You think so?"

"If at first you don't succeed…"

Gold lapsed into a brooding silence, recalling that Kaminski had said the same thing. If they were right, it was only a matter of time before the Anchor Insurance Company was hit with another claim. "Let's talk about your situation. When did you learn about the theft?"

"Two weeks ago."

"Did the grave robbers contact you?"

"No, I was contacted by a business associate." She rummaged through a desk drawer. "I swear, I'd lose my head if it wasn't attached. I wonder where I put that card." She made a show of deliberation.

"Well, in any case, I was contacted by a gentleman from Charleston. A reputable art dealer that I have known for many years."

"Does this reputable gentleman have a name?"

"Roger Fremont."

Gold made a note of it. "How did Mr. Fremont get wind of the crime?"

"Roger is a well-known ransom negotiator."

"You mean a fence?"

She made a sour face. "No, I mean an intermediary. A third party that will handle the negotiations in a discreet manner."

"Oh, I see." He made another note. "Does he do this out of the goodness of his heart?"

"There's usually a modest fee."

"How modest?"

"Five percent of the ransom."

"Twenty-five thousand dollars."

"In this case, yes."

"Who pays the fee?"

"The grave robbers."

"Who says there's no honor among thieves?"

She glared at Gold for several moments, then glanced down at her watch. "Do I detect a note of sarcasm in your voice?"

"A note? Try a symphony. Have you contacted the police?"

"Surely you jest."

"Do I look like I'm kidding?"

'She tried to keep herself from smiling. She didn't want him to think that she was being rude. Quickly she brought a hand up and rubbed her eyes with the back of it. "I don't meant to be ugly, but the police like to shoot first and ask questions later."

"What about the FBI?"

Dupry exhaled slowly and gave Gold a look that said she was losing her patience. "Why use a hammer when you only need a flyswatter?"

"Well, for one thing, the limb was buried on federal property. Secondly, the feds know how to handle kidnap and ransom cases. I would think you'd want their input."

"Their input would make some people nervous – and the last thing the situation needs is a bunch of nervous grave robbers."

Or some bad publicity, Gold thought. Sounding a little frustrated, he said, "Do we have a time limit?"

"No, but Roger – Mr. Fremont – thinks we should act quickly. He was hoping that you might have a check for me."

"That's not the way it works."

"What do you mean?"

"I investigate claims. Somebody else writes the checks."

"Based upon your recommendation?"

"Based upon the merit of the claim."

She leaned forward and spoke in a low, conspiratorial tone: "So where do we go from here, Mr. Gold?"

"I'd like to have a chat with Mr. Fremont. Do you think you can arrange a meeting?"

"When?"

"Tomorrow afternoon."

She rose and shuffled to a cabinet in the corner of her office. She copied information from a Rolodex card onto a notepad and brought it to Gold. "Here is Roger's phone number and address in Charleston. I'll call him and set up a meeting. Are you spending the night in Richmond?"

"Looks that way."

Her next comment surprised him. "Why spend it alone?"

"Excuse me?"

"I'd be happy to show you around."

"That's very kind of you, but I'm sure you've got better things to do."

"Haven't you heard of Southern hospitality?"

"I thought that was a myth."

She shook her head emphatically. Her tone was completely, almost passionately, determined. "You've got a lot to learn, Mr. Gold."

CHAPTER FOUR

There was more to Melanie Dupry than meet the eye, and her assertiveness reminded Gold never to judge a book by its cover. At first blush she seemed to be a genteel soul, but she was actually more of a steel magnolia, one of those Dixie chicks with a sweet disposition and a firm backbone. She insisted, absolutely insisted, that Gold spend the night at the Jefferson, Richmond's most revered hotel. In her view, it was the only place a true gentleman would stay, and if it was good enough for twelve U.S. Presidents, then it was good enough for Adam Gold.

"Elvis stayed here, too," she said proudly.

"Impressive."

"Twelve presidents and a king."

Gold felt the beginnings of a smile. He fought against it, but he lost. "I'm starting to feel inadequate."

"Well, you're standing in high cotton, that's for sure."

"Tough act to follow."

"Are you an Elvis fan?"

A frown flickered across Gold's face and was gone almost as quickly as it came. "Why do you ask?"

"I was wondering if you've been to Graceland."

"No, but I spent some time in Tupelo – Presley's birthplace."

"Did you enjoy your visit?"

"I'm not dying to go back."

The front lobby was Wednesday – evening calm. Across from the elevators, the receptionist sat behind a desk texting on a cell phone. When they approached her, she ended her text and gave them a warm, welcoming smile. She was well-groomed, well-spoken, and well-trained, and she sounded like an educated young lady. She spoke mainly to Gold, but shot glances at Dupry while reciting her well-rehearsed speech.

Gold tried to place her accent, eliminating possibilities as she spoke. Something Southern but not from Virginia.

"Have you stayed with us before?" she asked.

Gold smiled at her. "Before what?"

She acted like that was the funniest thing she'd ever heard, and covered her mouth while she leaned back and laughed. When she regained her composure, she said, "Are you a first-time guest?"

Against his better judgment, Gold asked, "How did you guess?"

"I detected a Northern accent."

"I'm from New York."

"Ah, the Big Apricot."

"Wrong fruit."

"Excuse me?"

"The Big Apple."

A smirk thinned her lips. "Welcome to Richmond."

"I'd like a quiet room. Nonsmoking. King-size bed."

"You're entitled to an upgrade." She endowed this last word with an excess of promise, and gave Gold a small, encouraging smile, accompanied by a gentle lift of her eyebrows. "A special reward for our first-time guests."

"Fancy that."

"We want your stay to be memorable."

"It already has been."

She swiped his credit card and said, "The Jefferson is a legendary hotel."

"So I've heard."

She seemed to be having trouble constraining herself, so without any encouragement, she began to recount the urban legends that were associated with the place. She began with ballet dancer Bill "Bojangles" Robinson, who had supposedly been discovered while working as a bellhop. After that, she pointed to the grand staircase in the lobby, insisting that the red-carpeted flight of stairs had been featured in the movie *Gone With The Wind*.

Finally, with her engines fully revved, she told them about Old Pompey, an alligator that had lived in a marble pool in the hotel's Palm Court for many years, surviving until 1948. Apparently Old Pompey was well-loved, and to this day, there were bronze reptile statues throughout the lobby.

When she finished her spiel, she said, "I don't know if you know anything about alligators, but they're fascinating creatures. They can reach 16 feet in length and weigh up to 1,000 pounds."

Gold's mind race back to a previous encounter with a couple of creeps named Butch and Lonnie. "Imagine that," he muttered. "I'd hate to run across one of those bad boys."

The receptionist saw something in Gold's eye that frightened her, so she changed the subject. "Any luggage?"

"Just one old bag," Dupry interjected. "But I know my way around." She reached for the room key and nudged Gold toward the bar. "Let's get a drink."

They found a quiet corner and ordered two glasses of bourbon – Blanton's – straight up, ice on the side. After the waiter left, Gold said, "*One old bag?*"

She laughed seductively, leaned forward, and whispered into his ear. "I just turned fifty."

"Fifty is the new forty."

"If you say so."

"You look great."

"Thank you."

"I'm serious. You don't look your age."

Her next comment surprised him. "I look better than I feel."

Gold frowned. "What's wrong?"

"My leg."

"Bad ankle?"

"Nope. I got kicked by a horse."

"Recently?"

"Couple of days ago."

Gold was letting his thoughts spill out as words. "I thought I noticed a limp. Have you seen a doctor?"

"I haven't had the time."

"You should make time."

"Easier said than done." She ran through a list of excuses, admitting that most of them were lame. One of these days she would have to start taking better care of herself. "I love horses, but they can be ornery and stubborn." She held out her left hand, displaying large teeth marks. "I got bit, too."

Gold studied her wound, frowning darkly. "The skin was almost punctured."

"Almost."

He shifted in his chair, his face expressionless, only his clenched fists giving a hint of what he was feeling and thinking. "Sounds like you've been around some dangerous animals."

"Do you know anything about horses?"

"As a matter of fact, I do." Once again, Gold's mind raced back to Mississippi, but this time to a more pleasant memory. Specifically, the night he met Buck Nelson – one of Elvis Presley's army buddies. Nelson, a farrier by trade, had shown him how to trim the hooves of a horse. Thinking back, he could still remember the horse nippers, the semi-circle of horn that was cut, and the fact that a horse carried most if its weight over its front legs. "Which is why the back hooves grow faster," he said with a smile.

"Very good, Mr. Gold." She waited until the drinks were served, then added, "Thoroughbreds are a special breed. They're high-strung and unpredictable."

He glanced at her injured hand. "Sounds like some people I know."

Dupry raised the glass to her lips, and she watched Gold carefully as he drank. "Are you referring to anyone in particular?"

"No, just a general observation."

"I thought you might be referring to me."

"We just met." Gold smiled at her. "I never judge a book by its cover."

"You know what I like to say? Never judge a person before you walk a mile in their shoes."

"I agree. That way when you judge them you're a mile away and you have their shoes."

She squirmed a little, reached up and pinched her ear as she sipped her drink. "Cute."

Gold didn't say anything. He just stared back, thinking it might be wise to drop the snappy patter and adopt a more folksy tone. The last thing he wanted her to do was clam up. "Do you live in Richmond?" he asked.

"Glen Allen."

"Where's that?"

"Ten miles north of here."

"What's your situation?"

"My *situation*?"

"Are you married?"

"Divorced. No children. Three horses." She raised her hand and rested her chin on her fist, studying Gold across the table – making a determination, he assumed, about how much she should tell him and what she should keep to herself. "Would you like to hear my life story? Is that what you want?"

"I'd settle for the good parts."

"There aren't too many of those." She finished her drink and ordered another round. "I was born and raised in Lexington, which is a nice place to live, but I had a lousy childhood. My parents died in a house fire, when I was in the fifth grade, and I went to live with my Aunt Helena and Uncle Lee. I liked my relatives, but they were very religious. Very strict, too. Jehovah's Witnesses. Need I say more?"

"No, I get the picture."

"After I graduated from high school, I went to Kentucky Wesleyan College, but I had to drop out during my senior year."

"Tuition problem?"

"Intuition problem. I suspected my boyfriend was cheating on me, found out I was right, and had a nervous breakdown." As much as she hated to admit it, she then proceeded to go from the fire to the frying pan. "After I recovered, I fell in love with a young man from Owensboro and got married, then I discovered that he was gay. Well, you know what they say. Some fools never learn." She laughed, but there was no joy in it. "I've come to the conclusion that most men aren't worth spit." She studied her nails, and the beginnings of a smile flirted with the edges of her lips. "When God created men, He promised women that good and honest men would be found in every corner of the world. And then He made the earth round."

Gold sat silently, weighing that remark. He pretty much knew the answer to his next question but decided to ask it anyway. "Were you miserable from day one?"

"No, but it was not a happy union. In fact, it was similar to the Union and the Confederacy."

"Nonstop battles?"

"Pretty much."

"How long did the war last?"

"Seven years, but there was nothing civil about it." The waiter returned with their drinks and a bowl of roasted peanuts. When he left, she said, "I did learn one thing. The ideal man doesn't complain, doesn't flirt, doesn't drink, doesn't smoke, doesn't gamble, and doesn't exist."

When Gold spoke next it was in a low, defeated tone. "You might be right," he said slowly. "My wife likes to say that men only have two faults: everything they say and everything they do."

"She sounds like a wise woman."

"That's what she tells me."

"How long have you been married?"

"Twenty-five years."

"Any children?"

"Two daughters. Both headstrong."

"Are you threatened by confident women?"

"No, but I have an opinion, too."

"When a woman wants a man's opinion….she gives it to him." She leaned closer, and Gold could smell her perfume and the liquor on her breath. "Are you happily married?"

Gold cocked an eyebrow. "Why do you ask?"

"Just curious."

"Most of the time."

"Honest answer."

"I'm an honest guy."

"I've heard that before." She grinned, then made a small dismissive gesture with her hand. "You're all the same."

Gold unleashed a long sigh, exhaling like a spent balloon. He was becoming uncomfortable with this conversation, and with the faint but distinct sense that she was intentionally baiting him. Maybe, he thought, it was time to explain the rules of the road. He leaned forward and spoke in a low, conspiratorial tone. "Just for the record, I never mix business with pleasure. Too confusing."

"For whom?"

"Everyone."

"Speak for yourself. I enjoy multitasking."

Gold felt as if he was losing control of the situation, and he didn't like it. "Maybe I should explain what I do for a living."

"Knock yourself out."

Gold gave her the abbreviated version, but it still took half an hour to explain that insurance investigators were basically claims workers, specialists who looked into questionable cases to uncover possible criminal or fraudulent activity. Like detectives, they combed through mountains of paperwork, conducted countless interviews, and performed surveillance. Some investigators handled simple fraud cases, which typically involved improperly filed paperwork or false identities. Experienced investigators, like Gold, handled instances of fraud by means of arson or theft, and in this capacity, they spent a great deal of time gathering and analyzing forensic evidence – from accidents and crime scenes.

Sounding a little bored, she said, "What a thrilling life you must lead."

Gold cleared his throat, a nervous habit signaling that he was about to say something disagreeable. "Do you understand what I'm trying to tell you, Miss Dupry?"

"I haven't a clue."

"Funny you should mention that word."

"Why is that funny?"

"Clues are what I look for." He smiled mischievously. "If we find enough of them, we can deny a claim, and sometimes people go to jail."

A shadow slid across her face. Something deep and dark registered, but to her credit, she managed to keep her voice calm and even. "I'll try to keep that in mind." She stood regally and tossed her hair. "If you're done with the theatrics, I'd like to go to dinner."

CHAPTER FIVE

The mind is a strange and mysterious wonder, and fed with enough alcohol, it is likely to reveal the good, the bad, and the ugly. In this particular instance, the booze allowed Dupry to vent her frustration with her fellow Virginians, who she scolded for their lack of interest in preserving their Southern heritage. She believed that the public should be up in arms about the recent spate of grave desecrations, but for some reason, nobody seemed to care.

Half-joking, and feeling no pain, she told Gold that he was partially to blame. After all, he was a Yankee, and as everyone knew, the indifference began during the Civil War, or as she called it, the War of Northern Aggression.

Gold gave her a resigned smile. "How did you come to that conclusion?"

"It's common knowledge."

"Uh-oh, you know what that means."

"Actually, I don't." She smiled faintly. "Why don't you educate me?"

"Common knowledge is more likely to be common than it is to be knowledge."

"My, what an astute observation."

"My momma didn't raise no fool."

"She didn't raise a history professor either." She signaled the waiter for some ice. "You've got a lot to learn, Mr. Gold."

Gold wondered if she were drunk. Her words seemed thick. Not slurred really, just labored. What did he expect after three shots of bourbon? "Please," he said gently, "enlighten me."

For a moment she appeared confused, unsure where to begin. Then, as if a veil had lifted, she began to ramble on about Hollywood Cemetery, a landmark in the western section of Richmond. Hollywood contained the graves of 18,000 Confederate soldiers, and it was also the final resting place of Presidents James Monroe and John Tyler, as well as Jefferson Davis and General J.E.B. Stuart, the commander of Lee's cavalry.

After the Battle of Gettysburg, the Union dead received proper burial, but the Confederate dead, 28,000 men, were thrown into shallow graves, tossed into pits, or left to rot on the battlefield. Many of the Confederate graves were poorly marked, unkempt, or vandalized by visitors, and many years would pass before the dead were reinterred in cemeteries such as Hollywood.

Gold listened politely, then said, "What's your point, professor?"

"Those who do not remember history are doomed to repeat it."

"Yeah, and those who do remember history are doomed to watch others repeat it."

She shot him a cold look. "Have you ever handled a claim like mine?"

"Nope."

"Swell."

"What are you worried about?"

"I'm just wondering if you're the right man for the job."

"Time will tell."

"We don't have a great deal of time."

"Don't worry, I'm a fast learner."

"Then you'd better start learning." She nudged her chair a little closer to him. "There are two types of ghouls – grave robbers and tomb raiders. One robs graves and the other steals artifacts from a tomb or crypt. Body snatchers are also a problem. Grave robbers and tomb raiders sell their goods on the black market, or though reputable art dealers like our friend in Charleston. Some of the loot winds up in a museum or school, but most of it goes to private collectors." She paused to take a sip of her drink. "Body snatchers usually will sell a corpse to a medical school, most often for the purpose of dissection or anatomy lectures."

Gold frowned, puzzled by her last statement. "I thought that was a 19th century practice."

"That's right, and back then they were called 'resurrectionists.' Corpses and cadavers can now be obtained legally, so body snatching is rare – at least in America." She took another sip of bourbon. "Unfortunately, the past saw many atrocities."

In her view, the worst atrocity occurred during the Civil War, but oddly enough, it had nothing to do with the Union or the Confederacy. In the aftermath of the Dakota War of 1862, 39 Dakota warriors were hung, and their bodies were buried in a riverside grave. Under cover of darkness, a group of doctors disinterred the Indians and divided the corpses among themselves. Incredibly, they were led by Doctor William Worrall Mayo, best known for establishing the private practice that later evolved into the Mayo Clinic. Dr. Mayo received the body of a warrior named "Cut Nose" and dissected it in the presence of other doctors. He then cleaned and erected the skeleton, keeping some of the bones in an iron kettle in his office.

Gold thought about that for a while, but chose not to comment. In truth, he didn't know what to say. In the end he swore under his breath and shook his head. "I suppose they could all be dangerous – grave robbers, tomb raiders, and body snatchers."

"Very dangerous."

"Any way to stop them?"

"No, but they can be slowed down."

"How?"

"By placing a Mortsafe around the coffin."

Gold frowned again. "What the hell is a Mortsafe?"

"A metal box and a framework of iron bars. Some folks call them 'zombie cages.' They were used in Scottish cemeteries, throughout the 1800s. They're reusable, provided they don't get destroyed by a Bobcat or backhoe."

"Those clowns use construction equipment?"

"Whenever they can. Saves a lot of time and trouble."

"True, but that makes it an expensive proposition."

"Expensive, but profitable – if you steal the right body."

Gold help up his hand, stopping her cold. "I've heard about Lincoln and Elvis."

Dupry stared at Gold for a few moments, thinking. "Have you heard about Charlie Chaplin?"

"No, I missed that one."

Lowering her voice, she told him that the "Little Tramp" had died on Christmas Day 1977 and was buried in a 300-pound wooden coffin in the village of Corsier, Switzerland. Three months later, two grave robbers stole his body and held it for ransom, demanding 400,000 Swiss francs for its safe return. "That would be about 400,000 dollars."

"Did they get the money?"

"Chaplin's widow refused to pay them."

"She *refused*?"

Dupry grinned. "She told the press that her husband would have thought it a ridiculous sum."

"What happened to the body?"

She went on to say that the robbers had persisted in calling Lady Oona Chaplin, demanding to be paid. In May, the police tapped the Chaplin's phone and were able to trace a call back to two men – auto mechanics from a nearby town. When the men were caught, they led police to Chaplin's remains, which had been buried in a cornfield 10 miles from the graveyard.

Gold waggled his eyebrows in poor imitation of Groucho Marx. "How eerie."

Dupry rolled her eyes at him. "They returned Chaplin in the same grave, but poured a load of concrete around the coffin. So you see, my boy, there's gold in them thar hills."

"If you don't get caught – which most of them do."

"Most, but not all."

Gold nodded. Another thing occurred t him. Why were there so many people willing to risk fine or imprisonment? What were the penalties for robbing a grave in Virginia? "I know you're not a lawyer, but you must have some idea."

She had more than an idea, she knew the law by heart and was able to recite it verbatim. "Disinterring or displacing part or all of any buried human remains is a Class 4 felony. Conviction is punishable by two to ten years in prison and up to $100,000 in fines." Her face, inches from his, was contorted with anger and, so it seemed, disgust with the creeps who robbed graves. "The law applies to all human burials, whether prehistoric, historic, or modern."

"So the folks who stole Jackson's arm could be looking at a long prison term."

"Undoubtedly."

"Which makes it even more dangerous."

"Getting cold feet?"

"Nah, I'm just getting warmed up. These people are bad actors, and they need to be put away." He slumped back in his chair, suddenly feeling weary. "I don't know what you get paid to maintain a grave, but whatever it is, it's not enough."

"Well, since you brought it up, gravesite care is funded by the DHR – the Department of Historic Resources. The annual appropriation is set at $5 per grave."

"The *annual* appropriation?"

"Large cemeteries receive less than that."

"Talk about having no respect for the dead."

"Believe it or not, that money is supposed to be used for the maintenance of cemeteries *and* graves." She shook her head. "Five dollars per grave, for erecting and caring for markers, memorials, and monuments. Five dollars per grave, for cutting the grass, trimming the trees, re-setting stones, and repairing fences. Simply outrageous."

Once again, Gold was at a loss for words. No wonder the poor woman was so stressed out. "You're a good soul, Miss Dupry."

"My friends call me Melanie."

"You're a good soul, Melanie."

She waved off the compliment. "Thank you, Mr. Gold."

"My friends call me Adam."

"Nice to make your acquaintance, Adam. I'm glad that we're going to be friends."

Gold glanced at her left hand and smiled. "You can never have too many friends."

"Amen."

He held her gaze, trying to show her that he meant it – trying to *feel* that he meant it – but he was more interested in her wound. To his immense relief, she looked away, giving him time to take a photograph of the bite mark. When she turned around, she saw the cell phone and frowned. "Sorry," he muttered, "I've been expecting a text."

She didn't respond and didn't indicate she even heard him. "Are you ready to order dinner?"

"Yeah, I'm starving. What do you recommend?"

"Something hearty. Tomorrow's going to be a long day."

Aren't they all? Gold thought. It sure seemed that way. He studied the menu. "Maybe I should order some horse meat."

"I beg your pardon?"

"To avenge your injuries."

Her expression darkened, and she said, "They're not that serious."

"Tell me something. How does an experienced rider get bitten and kicked?"

She lifted the menu and spoke from behind it. "By hand feeding apples and not paying attention. Generally speaking, a kick is designed to deliver a message. My horse was trying to tell me something. He might have felt threatened or frustrated, or been in pain. Maybe he wanted me to back off or let me know that he was the boss. Whatever it was, I wasn't listening, but I eventually got the message."

Gold smiled at her, but she didn't catch the smile – or the worried look in his eyes. "Sometimes it takes me a while to get the message, too."

CHAPTER SIX

South Carolina actually had two state mottoes, but the first one, *Dum Spiro Spero* ("While I breathe I hope"), was the one that Gold pondered as he rode across the Arthur Ravenel Jr. Bridge and into the city of Charleston. *The Holy City*, as Charleston was known, had a reputation for being one of America's most friendly cities, so Gold had no reason to think that he would get anything other than a warm reception from Roger Fremont. While he wasn't expecting to be welcomed with open arms, he was hoping that Fremont would keep an open mind and cooperate with the investigation. Truth was, nobody like to be interrogated, especially by a claims investigator. Hopefully, he wouldn't be one of those high-strung dealers who looked down their nose at the general public.

God forbid, Gold thought. He'd dealt with his share of snooty curators and uppity dealers, and he was in no mood for that sort of thing.

The taxi driver, an actual South Carolinian, offered the nickel tour, free of charge. He was very proud of his home town and took great delight in pointing out that Charleston was the first American city to export rice, the first city to build a theater, and the first city to open fire on those meddling Yankee abolitionists.

The shots were fired at Fort Sumter, which sat in Charleston Harbor, and was the number one tourist attraction in the city that had become the number one tourist destination in America.

Talk about irony.

In fact, this was a remarkable achievement, considering that the city had barely survived the Civil War, Reconstruction, an earthquake measuring 7.3 on the Richter scale, and Hurricane Hugo.

The hurricane alone had damaged three-quarters of the homes in Charleston's historic district.

The Blue Heron, Fremont's art and antiques shop, was located on King Street, which had its own remarkable past. Back in the day, before the chain stores arrived, the street belonged to the "Kings of King Street," a group of Jewish merchants comprising tailors, jewelers, and the owners of furniture and formal wear stores. Back then, the merchants spoke with Southern accents while using Yiddish slang, and during the Jewish holidays, King Street was a ghost town.

Despite its slave history, Charleston had always been a beacon of religious tolerance – and a city that was tolerant of alternative lifestyles. As Gold soon learned, Fremont preferred the term "alternate lifestyle," meaning that he would alternate between men and women. While he didn't flaunt his bisexuality, he did have a habit of kissing people on both cheeks, which Gold found rather amusing. Less amusing was his fake Charleston accent, which lengthened the mid-vowels and was designed to sound upper class.

"Welcome, to Chah-l-ston," Fremont drawled. "How was your flight?"

"Have you flown on US Airways?"

"Too gauche for me."

"Not even a pack of peanuts."

"Don't worry, there are plenty of nuts in Charleston."

Too easy, Gold thought. Instead of a quip, he offered his hand, focusing on the man and his merchandise. Both were interesting, in a Southern sort of way. Fremont was a short man, stocky – almost forty pounds overweight, Gold guessed – and prone to sweating, even in an overly cooled building. He was nattily attired, dressed in a blue Seersucker suit and with a pink bow tie at the throat of his button down shirt. He wore a lot of jewelry and a bit too much cologne.

The Blue Heron was housed in a century-old building, which was spacious and exquisitely appointed – high vaulted ceiling, white crown molding, oak floors, and lots of natural light from French doors that led out onto a plant-covered courtyard. The stock, if that was the correct term, consisted of art, antiques and artifacts.

Gold was like a kid in a candy store, not knowing where to look first. "What's the difference between an antique and an artifact?"

Fremont stopped in his tracks, staring at Gold in disbelief. "Don't you handle appraisals?"

"Investigations."

"My bad. I thought you were some sort of expert."

"No, just a lowly investigator."

"Well, the answer to your question is simple. An artifact is any object shaped by human hands, although the term is usually applied to objects which have archaeological or historical significance. An antique, on the other hand, is an artifact that has been assessed to have monetary value because of its age. In other words, all antiques are artifacts, but most artifacts are not antiques."

"Thanks for clearing that up."

Fremont led him inside a private office and offered him a drink. "Name your poison."

Gold cringed. "Too early for me."

"Well, you know what they say. It's five o'clock somewhere."

"Ain't that the truth."

Fremont got himself a glass with ice and filled it with bourbon, then crossed over to his roll top desk and sat down. "Melanie – Miss Dupry – urged me to give you my full cooperation, so how can I be of service, Mr. Gold?"

Gold placed his attaché case on his lap and discreetly switched on the recorder that was concealed inside. "You can start by filling in the blanks. I'm curious about these grave robbers. Who are they? Where are they from? Why did they contact you?"

Fremont glanced at Gold's case, then grinned. "Can we dispense with the cloak-and-dagger stuff?"

"Excuse me?"

"Must you record our conversation?"

Gold hesitated, then said, "It's standard procedure."

"Do you have a bad memory?"

"No, but it's easier this way."

"Why not take notes?"

"I write very slowly."

"You won't be able to use anything I say in a court of law."

"I don't intent to."

Fremont wasn't thrilled to concede the point, but he forged ahead, albeit grudgingly. "I'm dealing with a couple of bozos who call themselves Jesse and Frank James. I don't know their real names, nor do I want to. Jesse is the brains of the outfit, and from what I gather, he lives in Louisville. Frank supplies the muscle, and he's quite and intimidating fellow. He lives in Charleston, but spends a great deal of time on the Sea Islands, the barrier islands north of here."

Jesse and Frank James, Gold thought to himself. *How clever.* "Describe these desperadoes."

Fremont rubbed the back of his neck, the muscles tight with tension – tension brought on by thoughts of the James gang. "Jesse's a white dude, tall, thin, probably in his early fifties. He's got long, blonde hair and a thick moustache. He likes to pretend he's a cowboy, so he always wears a black Stetson, big ass belt buckle, and boots. He's got a mean disposition and acts like a schoolyard bully."

"What about Frank?"

"Big black guy. Built like a linebacker. Stands about six-foot-five. Solid muscle. Huge forearms and hands. Sharp tongue, but a dull mind. Not the type of brute that you want to piss off."

"He lives in Charleston?"

"I think so. He frequents a strip club called the Gender Bender. I go there, too. Mainly for the food."

"*The food?*"

"They have great sticky buns." He winked at Gold, then told him about his "alternate" lifestyle. "Are you shocked?"

"Not hardly."

"I'm surprised."

"I work in New York City."

"So?"

"Our sister cities are Sodom and Gomorrah."

Fremont shook his head and chuckled, the fat jiggling under his chin. "I like a man with a sense of humor."

"I like a man who lays his cards on the table. How do you know that Frank James spends a great deal of time on the Sea Islands?"

Fremont reached for his desk lighter and made a show of firing up a cigar, inspecting the smoldering tip, blowing smoke rings, and puffing away leisurely. Finally he looked directly at Gold and smiled. "I forgot to tell you something. Frank's a member of the Gullah community. You familiar with them?"

"Not in the least."

"I'm not surprised. They're spread across the Lowcountry, but they keep to themselves – in order to protect their cultural heritage. Most of them live on the Sea Islands, but a few live in Charleston and Beaufort." He took a swig of bourbon, then shook his head. "I'll tell you one thing. They're an interesting bunch."

"How so?"

If Fremont remembered correctly, the Gullah were the descendants of enslaved Africans, their name derived from Angola, the country where they likely originated. Some folks believed the name may have come from "Gola," an ethnic tribe that lived in present-day Sierra Leone . Whatever the case, most of the slaves that were brought into the Port of Charleston came from the west coast of Africa, where rice had been cultivated for 3,000 years. Enslaved Africans, from rice-growing regions, were highly prized because they possessed the skills and knowledge that were needed to construct tidal irrigation canals, dams, and earthworks.

They had also acquired some immunity from malaria and yellow fever, the tropical mosquito-borne diseases that had decimated the European settlers and white plantation owners.

In 1808, Great Britain and the United States outlawed the African slave trade, but slaves continued to be brought to the Lowcountry and Sea Islands, and over time, they developed their own unique Creole culture. When slavery was banned in 1865, many of the former slaves remained on the barrier islands, and due to their geographic isolation, they were able to retain their African heritage. Most of the Gullah still spoke the only African American Creole language in the United States, which contained elements of English and over 30 African dialects.

Incredibly, the barrier islands were accessible only by boat until the building of the first bridge in the 1950s.

"Those were the good old days," Fremont said bitterly. "In recent years the islands have gone to hell in a hand basket."

"Hurricanes?"

"Real estate development. Ever hear of Hilton Head? Most of the islands have been turned into playgrounds for the rich. I'm not opposed to capitalism, but you gotta draw the line somewhere."

"How many Gullah are there?" Gold asked.

"I'm not sure, but I think about a quarter of a million." He slouched back in his chair and looked at the ceiling and closed his eyes and shook his head ever so slightly, and sighed, peering down his pudgy nose at Gold. "They're a friendly, hospitable bunch, except for you-know-who."

"How many Sea Islands?"

"Over a hundred."

"So the odds of finding Frank James are slim."

"You got that right."

Gold stood up and circled the desk slowly. He finally reached for a copy of the *Yellow Pages*, opened it, and flipped through the pages until he found a listing for "Antique Buyers." Not unexpectedly, there were several columns of names. "Very interesting," he muttered, studying the page.

Fremont's chin lifted slightly. "What's that?"

"There must be a hundred listings related to 'Antique Buyers in Charleston.'"

Fremont glanced at the book and realized Gold was right: there were at least a hundred listings. He turned away. Nervously. He didn't like strangers invading his personal space. He'd felt that way ever since he was a kid, though nothing bad had ever really happened to him. Gold made interested sounds as he continued to scan the page, and that caused even more anxiety. "Are you looking for something?"

"I'm just wondering why the James boys chose you. I mean, there are so many dealers here. Am I missing something?"

"Maybe they liked my ad."

"Just level with me," Gold said softly, with a wide, friendly, "trust me" smile. "Have you been looking for love in all the wrong places?"

Fremont looked at him sharply, as if suddenly drawn out of a daze by the question "What the hell does that mean?"

"Letting it be known that you're a buyer who won't ask questions."

Fremont looked down at his fingers for a moment and then finally he looked him straight in the eye and said, "Don't be ridiculous. I'm as honest as the day is long."

Gold glanced at his wristwatch. "Day's half-over."

"Back off, Gold. I agreed to cooperate, not to be interrogated – or insulted."

"Forgive me. I've only had one cup of coffee. Why don't I buy you lunch?"

Fremont smiled, dispelling the tension. "Lunch would be nice."

"Mind if I pick the place?"

"What did you have in mind?"

"The Gender Bender Strip Club."

Fremont drew in a tiny breath, giving himself a moment to think. "You're a clever rascal. Devious, too."

Gold, not ruffled in the slightest, said, "Only the good die young."

CHAPTER SEVEN

Strip clubs were few and far between on the Charleston peninsula, and the ones that did exist were usually found in the northern part of the city, in the area that some folks called the "low rent district." If the truth be told, Charleston no longer had a low rent district, just a *lower* rent district. Gentrification, in the form of soaring rents and home prices, had quite literally changed the complexion of the city. Back in 1980, two thirds of the population was black, but by 2010, that had changed to two thirds white. It signaled a massive shift, especially for a city with only 128,000 residents.

"Quite a turnaround," Gold remarked.

"Progress is a bitch."

"Depends upon which side of the track you're standing."

"When poor folks see the light at the end of the tunnel, they jump out of the way. If not, they get run over by a train."

"Same way up north."

"Same way everywhere."

Gold studied the neighborhood they were driving through, surprised to see so many new houses standing beside so many old ones. He thought about "Frank James," wondering if he lived in this area, and if so, if he was still in town. A question occurred to him. "Have you seen the limb?"

"What limb?"

"General Jackson's arm."

"Of course I've seen it. Why do you think Miss Dupry filed a claim?"

"Why do you keep calling her Miss Dupry?"

"Excuse me?"

"I thought you two were old friends."

"Business associates."

"Did you give her the green light?"

"I gave her my professional opinion, and in my opinion, the item was authentic."

"What leads you to believe that?"

"I performed a cursory inspection, but there were signs of authenticity."

"What sort of signs?"

Fremont kept his left hand on the steering wheel, reached into his pocket with his right, and pulled out a shiny button. "I thought you might ask." He tossed the button to Gold. "They allowed me to keep a souvenir."

"Who's they?"

"The James boys."

"How thoughtful."

"What do you think?"

Gold frowned. "What am I looking at?"

"A Confederate button."

"Very cool."

"From Stonewall Jackson's uniform."

"Seriously?"

Fremont flashed a wicked smile. He went on to point out the distinguishing features of the relic, explaining that Gold was holding a Virginia State Seal Coat Button – a high convex, three-piece button that was approximately 22mm in size. The relic was in excellent condition, though slightly smudged with dirt, indicating that it had been excavated. The front showed the figures of Virtus standing over Tyranny, and the back was stamped with the words "SCOVILL MFG CO./WATERBURY Ct." The shank was still attached. "Notice the condition?"

"Good condition."

"Not good, excellent. No pushes, cracks, breaks, or repairs."

Gold was duly impressed. "Fascinating memento."

"How much do you think it's worth?"

"I have no idea."

"Regular buttons sell for two to three hundred. A button like this could fetch five thousand dollars – maybe more."

Gold's eyes widened perceptibly. "*Five thousand*?"

"Small change compared to the coat sleeve."

"You've got the coat sleeve?"

"No, but that's my price for handling the transaction."

"I thought the standard fee was five percent?"

"Five percent would be twenty-five thousand dollars. I'd rather have the coat sleeve. That may sound odd, but there's a method in my madness."

"I'm listening."

"A regular confederate uniform, in good condition, could easily sell for one hundred grand. Stonewall Jackson's uniform, or any part of it, might go for two or three times that price." A small, contented smile settled on his face. "That's my kind of return."

"Don't be surprised if you have to return the sleeve."

"They don't need the sleeve. Just the arm. If they give me a hard time, I'll threaten to contact the press. I know how these people think. They hate negative publicity."

Gold opened his mouth as if he were about to explode, then shut it. Tight. Finally, he said, "You've got it all figured out."

"If you want to be in the big leagues you have to play hardball."

Gold smiled inwardly, trying to recall how many times he'd heard someone say that. Usually it was an insured, playing games, trying to outsmart the company. For some reason, some people thought that acting tough was the same as being tough. But it wasn't. Not even close. A few of the smarter ones realized that it wasn't nice to fool Mother Nature – or a street-smart investigator – but others had to learn the hard way. As they drove along, Gold wondered which camp Fremont would fall into, hoping it wouldn't be the latter.

The Gender Bender was owned by a local legend named Pearlie Gates, a 300-pound black woman of Gullah descent. Miss Pearl, as she preferred to be called, ran a tight ship, but catered to a diverse cast of characters. Most of her customers were members of the LGBT community, but straight people went there, too, including a sizable number of Sea Island residents. If Miss Pearl liked you, she became a veritable chatterbox, blending English and Gullah in her conversation. If not, she clammed up or spoke only in her native tongue, which was difficult to understand. Fremont fell somewhere in between, which meant that it was up to Gold to melt her cold, cold heart.

With as much warmth as he could muster, Gold said, "Do I have the pleasure of addressing Miss Pearl, the pride of the Palmetto State?"

Miss Pearl frowned and cocked her head and gave Gold the once-over. "*The pride of the Palmetto State?*" She let out a howl of delight and slapped her thigh. "You a fawwu'd deeble ub'uh man, but I like a juntlemun who speaks his mind. Why don't you boys pull up a cheer and set awhile?" They sat at the bar, while she checked her makeup and hair before reaching for a bottle of whiskey. "I gin'nlly don't drink before noon, but this be a special occasion. We don't get many juntlemun visitors." She poured three shots, then lifted her glass high. "Here's to sweet-talk'um men."

"And gracious bartenders," Gold said.

Slipping off his shades, Fremont said, "How's business, Miss Pearl?"

"Could be better, that's fsutt'n. Hard to make a libbin' these days. Lousy patrons, late hours, and low profits. Bad combination." She looked at Gold. "I run this place by muhself."

Gold smiled sympathetically. "Hard to find help?"

"Hard to *keep* help. Nobody wants to work. Easier to suck the gov'ment teat. I'll tell you boys, I don't know what this country is comin' to. Most folks are so lazy they wouldn't work in a pie factory."

"There are plenty of people still willing to do an honest day's work," Gold said. "The trouble is they want a week's pay for it."

"Yes, suh, you suttinly right." She finished her drink and poured herself another round. "I sho'ly love whiskey. That's fsutt'n."

"Too much of anything is bad, but too much whiskey is barely enough."

"Did you just make that up?"

"Mark Twain."

She nodded, as if she understood. "What line of work are you in?"

Gold placed a business card on the counter. "I work for the Anchor Insurance Company."

She glanced at the card, then snorted. "I got more insurance than I need."

"I don't sell insurance. I buy information." He placed a fifty-dollar bill next to his card. "I'm looking for a guy who calls himself Frank James."

"Nubbah heard of him. What's he look like?"

Fremont described him, emphasizing his mean disposition and the fact that he was of Gullah descent. Gold noticed how she flinched when she heard the last part. "I've seen him in your club. He usually wears a Gamecock jersey and a Falcons gimme cap."

She fidgeted with her hands and seemed nervous. That was not altogether surprising – most people were when they were being questioned. "Several folks fit that 'scription."

"We're only interested in one person, "Gold said, placing another fifty on the bar. "What's his name, Miss Pearl?"

An undecipherable expression flitted across her face. "You didn't hear this from me."

"Understood."

"I don't know nothin' about Frank James. The person you're looking for is a no'count cullud man named Tyrone Teague. Puhaps you've heard of him. He played football for South Carolina, and played for the Falcons up in Atlanta. I heard he was a damn good linebacker. Got himself injured and had to quit the game. Took it hard. He came back to Charleston, began smokin' crack, and became a schemy tief."

Gold looked to Fremont for an explanation. "I didn't catch that last part."

Fremont smiled. "A tricky thief."

"'Zackly right," she said. "I nubbuh seen anyone fall so far, so fast. Tyrone used to kumbayah on weekends, but I ain't seen him in a while. I figured he was in jail. Maybe dead. Poor man lives by himself, keeps to himself, and ain't got no family." She hesitated a moment, thinking about the ramifications. "There's an old Gullah saying. Mus tek cyear a de root fa heal de tree."

Fremont interpreted. "You must take care of the roots in order to heal the tree."

Gold smiled faintly. "Where can I find this rotten tree?"

Her laughter was dark and mirthless. "You sure you want to do dat?"

"Yeah, I'm sure."

"Dat big dog, 'e bite'um."

"I've had my shots."

"Your funeral." She told him to drive down to Beaufort and take U.S. Highway 21 to St. Helena Island. "When you cross the bridge, head south, toward the marshland. Keep driving till you come to Lands End, which some folks call Fort Fremont." She glanced at Fremont and winked. "One of your relatives?"

Fremont smiled. "I don't think so."

She went on. "When you get to Lands End, just ask around, you'll find him. Only 8,000 folks on that island. Somebody's bound to know where he lives." She let the silence that followed hang for a moment. She was breathing hard, starting to perspire. Clenched into fists at her side, her hands were trembling. "If I was you, I wouldn't poke around at night. There's ghosts on St. Helena, and they mean business. You get off the grabble road and you might run into a haint. Dat happens, light out, or you'll lose your soul."

Gold chuckled a little under his breath. "You're saying there are ghosts out there?"

"Are you deaf? They're all over the place."

To prove her point, she told them about the Chapel of Ease, once known as the White Church, due to the fact it was constructed of oyster shells and lime. Heavily damaged by a forest fire in the 19th century, all that remained were the outer walls – and the burial vault of some prominent landowners. Union soldiers had stolen the door to the vault, so a bricklayer sealed up the entrance, but later that night the bricks were removed and neatly stacked beside the mausoleum. Proponents of the supernatural were convinced that angry spirits were to blame.

Further down the road stood the infamous "hanging tree," an ancient oak that was used to hang runaway slaves. After dark, a mysterious glow – known as the Lands End Light – would appear in the road. Miss Pearl had seen it herself, and it still gave her goosebumps. She described it as a single headlight, but as it came closer it grew larger, spreading across the road and producing a charge of static electricity.

So far, two people had lost their lives – not from the light itself, but in auto accidents while trying to chase down the source of the light.

Her tone was totally, almost passionately, determined. "Some folks say it's swamp gas, but I know better. My pappy told me the truth."

"This should be good," Gold muttered. "What did your pappy tell you?"

"The light is the soul of a Confederate soldier. The poor boy was out on patrol one evening, when all of a sudden, he was set upon by Union soldiers, one of whom sliced his head off with a sword!" She poured herself another drink. "Those Yankees tossed that boy's head in the bay, and now he roams the countryside looking for it!" Her throat was so tight, she couldn't speak for a moment. "I don't know about you, but I ain't got no 'tenshun of running into that damn rebel."

"You sure you won't join us?" Gold asked.

She shook her head emphatically. "No way, no how."

"Well, if I run into him, I'll give him your regards."

She stared at him for a moment, then turned on her heel, strode into her office, and slammed the door.

Fremont glared at him. "You've certainly got a way with women."

CHAPTER EIGHT

Roger Fremont wasn't a born coward, but somewhere along the line he'd developed a yellow streak that was a mile wide and 78 miles long – the exact distance between Charleston and St. Helena Island. While he was curious about Tyrone Teague, he had no intention of having a face-to-face confrontation with the man. In Fremont's view, that would be tantamount to committing suicide, and he intended to live a long and happy life.

"If you want to drive down to that Godforsaken island, be my guest. I'm staying in Charleston."

"Where's your sense of adventure?"

Freemont snorted. "Where's your common sense?"

"Huh?"

"The place is crawling with insects and alligators."

"Ah, wilderness."

"Have you ever seen a marshland mosquito? They're huge. Some of those suckers have their own landing strip."

Gold chuckled. "Ever hear of bug spray?"

"Ever hear of West Nile Virus?" He shook his head. "If the skeeters don't get you, the gators will. No, sir, I'm staying right here."

"I could use your help."

"You don't need me."

"You're the only one who can identify our friend."

"You've got a description. Use it. How hard can it be to locate a black linebacker with a limp?"

"I could use a second set of eyes."

Fremont gave him a small smile. "Sorry, Gold, you're on your own."

"You're making a big mistake."

"Send me a postcard."

They stopped for lunch at Jestine's Kitchen, a local favorite located on Meeting Street, in the heart of downtown Charleston. Though not fine dining, it was fine fare, and reasonably priced. After lunch, they went their separate ways, Fremont back to work, and Gold back to his room at the French Quarter Inn. He was tempted to take a short nap, but it was almost 2:00, so he touched based with his office and then hit the road.

The 90-minute ride was pleasant, most of it spent on Highway 17, a well paved road that meandered through the Lowcountry until it connected to U.S. 21 to Beaufort. Founded in 1711, Beaufort was the second oldest city in South Carolina, and was renowned for its scenic locale and antebellum architecture. Year after year the city was named as one of the best small Southern towns, and as Gold drove down Bay Street, it was easy to see why. In a word, Beaufort was charming. There were charming inns, charming restaurants, and charming shops. Lots of charm.

St. Helena Island was a different story. Across the Beaufort River, where 55 cotton plantations once stood, there were spreading oaks and

Spanish moss, and clapboard cottages surrounded by thick pine forest. The trees provided plenty of shade and an air of romance and mystery.

Gold made an ill-advised turn and soon found himself on a narrow dirt road flanked by weeds at the edge of a marsh. "Jesus," he muttered as his car hit a bump, then bottomed out with a thud before he could brake. "I must be on Tobacco Road."

Up ahead, where the road turned back to gravel, Gold spotted a Gullah farmer selling vegetables from the back of a pickup truck. He eased forward, then pulled off the road and got out of the car. "I think I'm lost," he said sheepishly. "I'm looking for Lands End."

The farmer scratched himself, then said, "I got collard greens and corn."

"I just need directions."

"'Gatuh meat, too."

"Maybe next time.

"Dat meat is fresh."

Gold blew air out through his nose in a long sigh. "Do you live around here?"

"'Jis down the road." He pointed to a dilapidated shrimp shack leaning against a Magnolia tree. "I was born in da'dey shack. Fibbywerry fifth, nineteen hundred and thirty-five."

Gold did a quick calculation and raised an eyebrow. "You look great. Fit as a fiddle."

"I follow Chryce. B'long to the Baptis' Chu'ch. I don't drink, smoke, gamble, or chase dem women." He smiled, revealing two rows of crooked teeth. "No sense chasin' what you can't catch."

"Amen, brother."

"Did you drive over from Beefu't or Chass'stun?"

"Charleston."

"Been there once. No eentruss in goin' back."

"To each their own."

"Huccome you here in St. Helena?"

"I'm looking for someone." He hesitated, wondering if it was worth a shot. *Why not?* he thought. *What have I got to lose?* "Do you know a man named Tyron Teague?"

"I know *'bout* him. He used to be a football player. Big son of a gun. He got himself hurt and had to quit the game." He let Gold chew on that for a moment, then added, "He don't spend much time on the island."

"Do you know where he lives?"

"No, I sho'ly don't." He hesitated, looking Gold over. Then he said haltingly, "You should go tuh dat Penn Center. They got records datin' back to slabery times." He explained, or tried to explain, that the Penn Center was one of the country's first schools for freed slaves. After the school closed, in 1948, Penn became the first site to preserve and protect the heritage of the Gullah community. "You should go 'cause dey gonna know where dat boy lib."

Gold gave it some thought, then said, "How do I find this place?"

"Turn 'round and go back the way you come. Stay on the main road and turn right at MLK Drive."

"Thank you, sir."

"You're welcome."

Gold handed him a ten-dollar bill. "Take care."

The farmer stared at the bill, then frowned. "What's dis for?"

"A token of my appreciation."

"You want some wegitubbles?"

"No, I got what I need."

"What'd you get?"

"Food for thought."

Gold turned the car around, waved goodbye, and drove off. When he glanced in the rearview mirror, he noticed that the farmer was still staring at the money, still frowning. He chuckled, wondering what the old man what thinking.

Although finding the center was relatively easy, locating the person in charge took a while. Midweek in mid-August meant a handful of visitors and a skeleton staff. Finally, after fifteen minutes, Gold bumped into a pleasant woman who identified herself as Sungila Taylor, a museum docent. She was a striking woman – tall and lithe, with skin as smooth as buffed bronze. Her bone structure was flawless, her eyes charcoal black. Her hair was braided in dreadlocks, decorated with colorful beads. They chatted amiably for a few minutes, and then she offered to give Gold a private tour. Before he could reply, she took him by the arm and led him into the museum.

As they strolled past the various displays, she told him that the center was originally established as a school, designed to "test the capabilities of the Negro for freedom and self-support" during the Civil War.

Founded in 1862 by two Northern missionaries, it was one of the first schools to provide a formal education for formerly enslaved West Africans.

After the school closed, in 1948, the Penn Center dedicated itself to preserving and protecting the heritage of the Gullah community. In the 1960s, it promoted the Civil Rights Movement, serving as the only location in South Carolina where interracial groups could meet and mingle.

The center contained a small rural cottage, and it was here that Martin Luther King, Jr. drafted his "I have a dream" speech.

Gold was intrigued by the Gullah culture, and enamored with his guide, but the afternoon sun was starting to wane and there was work to be done. The work of locating Tyrone Teague. Steering her back to the problem at hand, he asked if she was a football fan.

She cocked her head to the side. "Not particularly. Why do you ask?"

"I was just wondering if there were any professional players of Gullah descent."

"Your guess would be as good as mine."

Gold rubbed his chin, pretending to give it some thought. "I seem to remember one guy. A linebacker named Tyrone Teague. I think he played for the Falcons." He stood in the doorway, fanning himself with a folded magazine, watching her closely. "Name ring a bell?"

She tugged at an ear, placed her glasses on her perfect nose, and cleared her throat. "Yes, I've met Mr. Teague, but I had no idea that he was a professional football player. I thought he was just an overgrown foul-mouthed child and a violent bully."

Gold stared at her, chewing on his lower lip for a moment, then finally said, "Sounds like you've crossed swords."

"No, just paths, but that was enough for me. Mr. Teague is one of the reasons that our violent crime rate is three times higher than the rest of the state."

"*Three times higher?*"

"Our property crime rate is higher, too."

"Huh, how do you like that."

"I don't like it one bit. Thanks to a few bad apples, our rates are also higher than the national average."

Gold pressed her for specifics. She searched her memory and then elaborated. St. Helena Island, with a population of only 9,000, had a crime rate higher than the national average in almost every major category, including violent crime, murder, forcible rape, and robbery.

"Jesus," Gold said. "I never would have guessed."

"I blame Teague – and his miscreant friends. I wish they would leave and never come back."

"Maybe I can help you out."

"Excuse me?"

"Where can I find Mr. Teague?"

She cocked her head to one side and eyed Gold closely. She had followed her natural instincts and befriended this stranger, but now he was asking about a known felon. *What the hell is going on here? Who is this nosy outsider?* "I don't think that I caught your name," she said warily.

"My name is Adam Gold. I'm one of the good guys."

"You a cop?"

"Insurance investigator."

"*Insurance?*"

"You look surprised."

"I am surprised. You sound like a Yankee."

"I work for the Anchor Insurance Company." He gave her a card. "As you can see, I've come a long way."

"What do you want with Teague?"

"Would you believe an autograph?"

"No, I wouldn't."

"I didn't think so."

"Most folks try to avoid him. You want to find the man. Why?"

Not wanting to reveal too much, Gold said, "I'm working on a claim. It's a long story, but Teague's involved and I need to speak to him. I'd be grateful if you could point me in the right direction."

"Before I start pointing, there's something you should know. Teague isn't your run-of-the-mill criminal. The man is despicable ghoul, a damn grave robber."

Gold sighed. "That's a serious accusation."

"Why do you think he moved here, for the salt air? Ten to twenty million Africans were transported as slaves, and many of them wound up on the Sea Islands. St. Helena is covered with shallow graves, and some of them contain valuable artifacts." Sadly, most of the dead were young. Very young. She told him that the mortality rate among black children on the South Carolina coastal rice plantations was astonishingly high – nearly 90% of all children died before they reached the age of 16 years. "We know that they were slaves because they were uniformly buried east-west, with the head to the west – facing Africa."

"Are the cemeteries protected?" Gold asked.

"There are no cemeteries. No formal ones. Slaves were buried on marginal property – land that was unsuitable for planting. Graves were scattered, often without headstones, head-boards, or even sticks."

Gold seemed puzzled. "How does Teague find them?"

"Some were marked with shells, and some of those are still above ground."

"*Shells?*"

"Bleached sea-shells. The practice has been traced back to the BaKongo belief that sea shells enclosed the soul. There are poems and prayers about the practice." She recited one: "The sea brought us, the sea shall take us back. So the shells upon our graves stand for water, the means of glory and the land of demise."

"The land of demise," Gold muttered. "Good title for a book."

"Or an obituary. Do you still want to find Teague?"

"More than ever."

She looked nervously at the nearest window, which framed a portion of clear blue sky, where seagulls periodically swooped down for shrimp. Exhaling sharply, she turned and gave Gold a long, hard look. "I hope you know what you're doing."

Gold gave her a reassuring smile. "I've been doing this a long time."

She felt a tightening in her throat. She brushed her long, braided hair with her hand. She could feel the sweat bead on her forehead. "There's a bar. Three miles from here. The Black Swan. If Teague's on the island, that's where you'll find him."

"I assume he's a regular."

"A regular menace. If I were you, I'd be very careful."

"I'm always careful, Miss Taylor. By the way, how do I make a donation?"

"I'll tell you how." She stared hard at him. "Get rid of Teague."

CHAPTER NINE

Back in the thirties, the Black Crab would have been called a juke joint, the term "juke" believed to be derived from the Gullah word joog, meaning rowdy or disorderly. In its present state of disrepair, it amounted to little more than a dilapidated shack with a liquor license. In the beginning these places catered to plantation workers and sharecroppers, but nowadays they functioned as a haven for the drunk, the lazy, and the unemployed. Most of the patrons were black, although the bartender was a white guy. A big white guy. Somebody ordering a beer referred to him as "Bull," which was fitting. Bull was a great moose of a man, with wide shoulders and shaggy brown hair that fell over his ears and curled around the base of his thick neck. He had a mean, pockmarked face and cold gray eyes that shielded all traces of emotion. For one fleeting moment, Gold toyed with the notion of asking him if it was still "happy hour," but he decided against it. "Afternoon," he finally said. "Shot of whiskey and a cold beer."

The bartender eyed him for a moment, making a professional evaluation that the newcomer posed no potential threat to his booming business. "Any preference?"

"A glass and a bottle."

Bull spoke, as if to himself. "Comedian."

Gold looked in the mirror behind the bar, hoping to see someone who fit Teague's description. The room was dark, hot, smoky, and inhabited mostly by men dressed in jeans and t-shirts. There were two women at the end of the bar, but they looked like they had been ridden hard and put up wet. "Nice place you have here."

Bull instantly stopped pouring. "You lookin' for trouble, mister?"

"No, I'm looking for Tyrone Teague." Gold placed a fifty-dollar bill on the bar. "Know where I can find him?"

Bull immediately changed his demeanor and showed a keen interest as he pointed to a dimly lit booth. "Tyrone's over yonder." He swooped up the fifty, and grinned. "Be polite. He's in a piss-poor mood."

"Losing lotto ticket?"

"Somebody put a hex on him."

"A *hex*?"

"One of those Gullah curses."

Gold smiled. "And here I thought I was having a bad day."

"I think it was the scrawny witch that lives on the salt pond. She's mean as a snake. I heard she turned a city feller into a frog!"

"Leapin' lizards. Why'd she do that?"

"The ol' boy got mad about something and called her a toothless nigger."

"Bad move."

"He had no cause to be ugly."

Gold nearly choked on his first sip of the whiskey. He sputtered and wiped his chin with his sleeve while Bull looked on with concern. Finally, he said, "Smooth."

"You all right?"

Gold waved his concern away. "What is this stuff?"

"Homemade hootch. Do you like it?"

"If I were you, I wouldn't quit my day job." Gold winked at Bull to show he was teasing. Then he grabbed his beer and strode across the dance floor, approaching Teague cautiously, as if he were a wild animal. The man was built the way you'd expect an ex-football player to be built; he was a large, bulky man, overweight and rumpled, his football jersey stained and wrinkled, his pants sagging under a beer belly. Gold sat across from him and played with his beer glass. Finally, he said, "Tyrone Teague?"

Teague lit a cigarette and tapped the ash into Gold's glass. "Who wants to know?"

"Take a wild guess."

"Fuck off, mister."

"My name's John Doe."

Teague stared at his cigarette. "Who gives a shit."

"My last name is spelled d-o-u-g-h. As in money."

Teague stared at him blankly, his mind in a fog. "What are you babbling about?"

"I'd like to put some money in your pocket."

"What did you have in mind?"

"Artifacts."

Teague raised his eyebrows in surprise, then grinned. "How did you get my name?"

"A little jailbird. You interested?"

"I might be. What are you looking for?"

"West African jewelry. Amulets, bracelets, beaded necklaces. Whatever you can dig up. I'm also interested in decorative art – the kind you find on graves."

"I don't mess with jewelry – too hard to find. Besides, those are my ancestors you're asking me to rob."

"Yeah, I heard that you had Gullah ancestors."

"You heard right." Teague, interestingly, did not speak with a Gullah accent, or use any of their words. "I don't pilfer from my own people. Bad juju."

Gold went silent while he considered this. "Funny," he said at last. "You don't strike me as the superstitious type."

"Why don't you leave before I strike you with my fist."

"Did I catch you in a bad mood?"

"I'm always in a bad mood."

Gold looked up and met his eyes, trying to figure out if Teague was playing games with him. He guessed that was the case. He wasn't a bad actor really, Gold thought. He displayed just the right mix of anger and disdain. "Well," he finally said," I guess I'll take my business elsewhere."

"I guess you will."

Gold smiled to himself. The first thing these small-time gangsters did was hide behind some sort of code. In reality, they'd sell their own mothers for the right price. But what was the right price? Only one way to find out. "Hot in here."

Teague released a quick, short burst of laughter. "If you can't stand the heat, stay out of the Carolinas."

"Funny."

"I thought so."

Gold broke his gaze and looked past him, as if there were something fascinating over his shoulder. "I don't think that window unit is working." He began to fan himself with a thick wad of cash. "Well, I guess I should head back to Charleston."

Teague smiled, showing most of his smoke-stained teeth. "What's your rush?"

"I thought you said…"

"I said I don't pilfer from my own people. I didn't say anything about white folks."

"I don't understand."

Teague found himself grinning manically, and helpless to do anything about it. The money was making him salivate. "I could lead you to some graves. Let you dig around in the dark and keep whatever you find. If you get lucky, you could fill your pockets with bling-bling. How's that sound, buckruh?

"Buckruh?"

"It's Gullah. Means white man."

"There's a coincidence. I actually have a buckruh list." He tossed a brochure on the table. "I picked this up at the Penn Center. If you look inside, you'll find a list of graveside items that were used to break the chain of death. I'd like to get my hands on those items."

Breaking the "chain of death" referred to the Gullah belief that breaking dishes and earthenware released the spirit and prevented other family members from following in death. Most of the broken items were containers – pitchers, cups, bowls, tureens, and medicine bottles – which kept their shape when broken.

Teague started to smile, but stopped when he realized how long this was going to take. "I hope you're not afraid of the dark."

"Nah, I was a Boy Scout."

A wicked smile flashed across Tyrone's face. "Brave guy, eh?"

"Now and then."

"Ever walk through a graveyard at night?"

"Not recently."

"You're in for a treat."

Gold didn't like the sound of that, but it was too late to turn back now. "Where are we going?"

Teague informed him that the evening would begin at his house, where they would drink some beer, grab some dinner, and wait until nightfall. After dark, they would drive to Orange Grove Plantation, a privately owned property on Wallace Creek, a branch of the Beaufort River. The plantation had once been owned by an indigo planter named Peter Perry. Indigo, of the genus *indigofera*, was a shrub that grew in warm climates, and thrived in the Lowcountry. Its leaves were once an important source of indigo dye, which became the second most important cash crop in the region after rice.

In 1800, Perry built a house, and purchased 46 slaves to cultivate 473 acres of land. Over the years, the original buildings vanished, and all that remained was a tabby hearth from a kitchen outbuilding – and a short tabby wall, which enclosed the plantation cemetery.

"The white folks are buried in the cemetery," Teague said. "The slaves were buried elsewhere, mostly in the underbrush. I've found five or six graves, but there are dozens more. They're not easy to find, but they're out there. All it takes is a strong back, and a strong heart. You think you're up for it, buckruh?"

"Stop calling me that."

"What do you want me to call you?"

"John Doe will do."

"You think you're up for it, Johnny?"

"Did you say the property was privately owned?"

"Yeah, but you don't have to worry. The owner is never around."

"What about cops?"

"Not a problem. There's no police station on the island."

"Perfect."

"No hospitals, either."

"Let's hope we don't need one."

"You've got to be careful. Watch where you step. Did you bring snake boots?"

Gold stiffened. "There are snakes on the island?"

"A few."

"What kind of snakes?"

Teague took his time, enjoying the look of fear on Gold's face. Maybe this would be a fun night after all. He leaned back and stared at Gold without blinking, deep in thought. "What kind of snakes?" He gave it some more thought, then said, "Rattlesnakes, copperheads, and cottonmouths. Coral snakes, too. Yes, sir, we got 'em all, and they're all bad news. We got some bad spiders, too. The black widow and the brown recluse. Some folks would rather get bit by a snake than a spider. Not me, but I'll tell you one thing. Spider bites are awfully painful." He rolled up his sleeve and displayed a long, ugly scar near his elbow. "Check this out."

Gold stared at the scar, repulsed by the ugliness of the damn thing. "Jesus, that must have hurt."

"Damn straight."

"Black widow?"

"Yep."

"Hard to believe that a spider could do so much damage."

"Who said anything about a spider?" Teague was laughing, a sneering, bullying laughter, just the kind you'd expect from a slimeball who robbed graves. "Hell hath no fury like a woman scorned!"

Gold turned around to face the window. Through the shutters he could just make out the parking lot. Some of the regulars were starting to leave, heading home for dinner, or God knows where. No such luck for him. He would be spending his evening with a grave-robbing comedian. Trapped in a cage of his own making.

CHAPTER TEN

By the time they left the Black Crab it was dusk, and the distinctive music of the Lowcountry was beginning to crank up. Some of the sounds were familiar: bullfrogs, cicadas, katydids, and birds. Some were less familiar, and difficult to identify; the bellowing, growling, hissing and squawking. Much to his dismay, Gold was starting to realize that St. Helena Island was one big wildlife area, filled with all manner of creatures and critters.

In fact, the island contained a dazzling array of terrain types: forest, wetlands, salt marshes, dune fields, and shrub thickets. Taken together, it formed a nearly perfect environment for wildlife, and there was plenty of it, including deer, raccoons, bobcats, birds, snakes, and alligators.

Teague was kind enough to mention that the largest alligator ever caught weighed over 1,000 pounds and was almost 16 feet long. Fortunately, it was caught in Alabama, not South Carolina. Still, the reptiles on St. Helena were just as mean, just as dangerous, and as far as Gold was concerned, way too close for comfort.

Even so, Gold had to admit that the island possessed a mysterious charm, an aura that was both captivating and intimidating. It also possessed a distinctive smell, the pungent, slightly salty smell of pluff mud – the dark marsh soil that remained in place after the tide receded.

The spooky atmosphere was further enhanced by the ruins of the rice plantations, most of them barely visible in the tall grass. The eerie silhouettes were usually surrounded by live oak trees, their gnarled limbs shrouded in gray clumps of Spanish moss. Route 21, Gold thought, had to be one of the spookiest roads in the nation, and certainly the most daunting in South Carolina.

Teague's humble abode wasn't much better. For some reason, he'd chosen to live in a fishing shack, perched on the edge of a saltwater estuary. Despite the remote location, the shack had running water and electricity, which was miraculous considering the neighborhood. In the front yard, which was mostly sand, crab traps were piled high, almost obscuring a Carolina Skiff that was resting on a rusty trailer.

"What's with the traps?" Gold asked.

"I'm a crabber," Teague answered. "I got out on weekends. Weather permitting. I don't much care for the work, but it's a good way to supplement my income."

"Man does not live on the dead alone."

"Huh?"

"Never mind." Gold swatted a mosquito. "I used to do some crabbing. When I was a kid. My friends and I would bait a hook with a chicken neck and lower the line off of a pier. Most of the crabs we caught were too small to eat." He took a closer look at the traps, being careful not to cut his hand on the rusty wire. "What kind of bait do you use?"

"Chicken necks and razor clams."

"Some things never change."

"So they say."

"What do you catch, blue crabs?"

Teague was dying for another beer, but he took a minute to explain how things stood. The blue crab was the only crab that had any commercial or recreational importance in South Carolina. The crab's scientific name, *Callinectes sapidus*, translated to "savory beautiful swimmer," and that said it all. Throughout the Lowcountry, gourmets preferred the blue crab's sweet meat over all other locally caught seafood.

Large males, often called Jimmies, had brilliant blue claws and legs. Mature females, or "sooks," had bright orange tips on their claws. Both males and females had large, powerful claws that were used for food gathering, defense, digging, and sexual displays.

And both genders could inflict severe injury if handled improperly.

Teague picked up a dead crab and held it close to Gold's face, smiling mischievously. "You don't want to run into a cast of crabs. Once they get hold, they don't let go." He held up his left hand and stuck out the pinky, the tip of which was missing "I speak from personal experience."

"Damn, you sure get bit a lot."

"I guess it's because I'm so sweet."

"Or just unlucky."

"You think I've had bad luck? Did you hear about the guy who walked into a whorehouse and asked to fuck a ten-dollar hooker? The cheap bastard came back two weeks later, complaining that he had crabs. The hooker says, what'd you expect for ten bucks? Lobster?"

Gold rolled his eyes. "Cute."

Teague nearly bust a gut laughing, but there was nothing pleasant about the sound of his laughter. "Come on, John Boy, I'll buy you a beer."

As they walked toward the shack, Gold noticed something peculiar. All of the windows and doors had a blue trim hastily painted around them. *What the hell?* he wondered. Before they stepped inside, he asked Teague for an explanation, but the man seemed reluctant to talk about it. 'Did you run out of blue paint?"

"Some folks call that indigo blue," Teague said. "I call it haint blue, because it keeps the Boo Hag away."

"The *Boo Hag?*"

Teague became nervous and waved him inside, quickly closing the door behind him. "Sun's going down," he whispered. "You don't want to be caught outside without a garlic wreath."

Dear God, Gold thought. *Now what?* For a moment he thought that Teague might be joking, but then he saw the look on his face. The man looked like he'd just seen a ghost. "I don't mean to pry, but do you have a vampire problem?"

"No, we've got a Boo Hag problem. If you're smart, you'll wear a wreath tonight."

"Wait a minute. Let me get this straight. You want me to wear a garlic wreath?"

"Only if you want to keep your soul."

Gold felt a giant headache coming on. He squeezed his eyes shut, then opened them. "All right, Teague. I'll bite. What the hell is a Boo Hag?"

Teague fetched two beers, a bottle of Jim Beam, and a couple of moderately clean glasses. He told Gold to help himself, get comfortable, and prepare to learn about the dark side of the Lowcountry. In a deathly somber tone he explained that the Gullah people believed that human beings had a soul and a spirit. Good souls went to heaven, but the spirit stayed behind to watch over the deceased's family. Bad souls went to hell, and their evil spirit became a Boo Hag – a skinless, bright red creature with bulging blue veins. These creatures stole energy from the living while they slept. They did this by sitting on a person's chest, "riding" the unfortunate victim until dawn. If someone felt tired or listless the Boo Hag was probably to blame, and keeping the evil spirit at bay was no easy task.

"The creatures are clever," Teague said. "They can get into a house through an open window or a crack in the wall. I don't know if it's true, but I've heard that they can even squeeze through a keyhole."

Gold contemplated this while pouring himself a double whiskey. Under normal circumstances, he would have passed on the alcohol, but right now he needed a stiff drink. "How does one prevent a visit?"

"Well, there's no surefire method, but you can improve your chances by painting around the doors and windows. Only indigo blue will work. You can also spread salt around the house. That will do the trick."

"What if you have high blood pressure?"

"Huh?"

"Never mind. What else can you do?"

"Straw brooms are handy. You see, a Boo Hag is a curious and compulsive thing and it has to count every strand before it starts riding someone. If you keep a few brooms out, you'll keep it busy until dawn. Once the sun comes out, they must return to the underworld." He wedged a chew of tobacco under his lip and offered the plug to Gold, who shook his head. "I hope I'm not making you feel uncomfortable."

"Don't be silly."

"Some folks just don't dig the dead."

"You certainly do."

"Yeah, that's for sure. I do a lot of digging."

"How did you fall into that line of work?"

Teague knew that sooner or later he'd be asked that question, but it still annoyed him that he had to explain himself. He didn't enjoy talking about the past, especially with a complete stranger. The abridged version would have to do.

Like most gifted athletes, Teague had focused only on sports, never imagining that he might sustain a career-ending injury. When that day came, his world turned upside down, and he had to scramble to make a living. He soon discovered that the world had little use for a washed up football player. After five years of failure, he left Atlanta, returned to Charleston, and tried to turn things around. When nothing panned out, he stopped playing by the rules and went for the quick buck – the type of money that made the underworld go round.

"I've done alright," he said proudly. "I made enough to buy some land, a boat, and start a business. I'm not rolling in dough, but I'm comfortable."

"Ever feel any guilt?"

"About what?"

"Robbing graves."

Teague shifted on the couch, leaning forward with eyes narrowed. "I'm just a guide. You're the one that wants the souvenirs." He gulped down his whiskey and stumbled into the kitchen, muttering under his breath. "Are you hungry?" He didn't wait for an answer. "I'm starving. I've got some stew." He lifted the lid of a pot and sniffed the content. "Made it myself. If I were you, I'd eat something. It's gonna be a long night." He turned up the heat, then grabbed a couple of bowls. "Every try Frogmore stew?"

"Nope."

"You're in for a treat."

"I'll bet. What's in it?"

"Sausage, shrimp, corn, and potatoes. Plus my secret ingredient."

"Sounds good."

"Tastes good, too." When the stew came to a boil, he ladled out two portions. He gestured for Gold to take a seat, then brought the bowls to the table. "You want to say Grace or something?"

"No, I'm good."

"Dig in, John Boy."

The first bite when down smoothly, but then the Tabasco sauce came out and things got a little dicey. Still, it was pretty darn good, similar to a Cajun boil, but without the crawfish. They finished the first bowl and went for seconds, and when they were done, Gold let out a loud belch. Teague belched, too.

"Frogmore stew," Gold said. "Mighty tasty."

"I'm glad you liked it."

"What was your secret ingredient?"

Teague grinned. "More frog."

"Excuse me?"

"The green stuff wasn't asparagus."

"Frog legs?"

"No, I use the whole critter."

Gold winced. "The whole frog?"

"Gives the stew more flavor. Body, too."

"Funny."

"Want some more?"

Gold shook his head. "If the truth be toad, I'm full."

"The truth be *toad*?" Teague slapped his thigh and burst out laughing. "I like your sense of humor. I'll bet it's gotten you out of a few scrapes." He filled their glasses with more whiskey. "Do you know the difference between a frog and a toad?"

"No, I can't say that I do."

Teague knew the difference, and with a full belly he was only too happy to elaborate, which he did, for about thirty minutes. The bottom line, as far as Gold could tell, was that frogs lived in moist climates and had feet that were adapted for leaping and swimming, whereas toads preferred dry climates and had short legs that were used to walk instead of hop.

When biology class ended, Teague staggered over to the couch and announced that he was going to take a short nap. He fell asleep as soon as his head hit the pillow Gold stared at him in disbelief, amazed that a person could fall asleep so quickly. Maybe he was onto something. Like the man had said, it was going to be a long night.

A very long night.

CHAPTER ELEVEN

An hour and a half later, Teague woke up, feeling refreshed and raring to go. He grabbed a flashlight and a .30-30 lever-action Winchester and peeked outside. "No sign of a Boo Hag," he whispered. "Let's make a run for the boat."

"*The boat?*"

"We can't take the truck"

"Why not?"

"Private property. There's a locked gate."

"Swell."

"No big deal. We'll glide up the creek and sneak through the back."

"In the dark?"

"There's a full moon tonight."

"I don't know about this."

Teague felt the impulse to curse and resisted it. "If you want to call it off, that's fine with me."

Gold was tempted to do just that, but of course, that wasn't part of the plan. The idea was to entrap Teague, threaten to have him arrested, and then force him to turn on his partner. If Gold backed out now, there would be no way to find "Jesse James," the so-called brains of the outfit. "Are you sober enough to drive?"

Teague let out another one of his humorless laughs. "Hell, I know these waters like the back of my hand."

Famous last words, Gold thought. He fished a mini-Maglite flashlight out of his pocket and swept it along in front of him as he stepped outside. "Let's get started."

"Now you're talking, buddy-boy."

Gold nodded doubtfully, still trying to come to terms with the idea. "God, I hope you know what you're doing."

"You don't have to worry about that."

"I hope not."

Teague lifted his flashlight and raised a single finger to his lips to indicate "Sssshhh." After checking the yard, he quietly closed the door and locked it with a key. "Keep your voice down. You don't want to wake up the dead."

"Heaven forbid."

"Shit! I forgot to bring the garlic."

"Well, we're off to a good start."

"Too late now. We don't want to miss the incoming tide."

Weariness clouded Gold's face, and without another word Teague attached the boat trailer, climbed in the truck and backed the skiff down a gravel ramp. They climbed aboard, stowed their gear, and slid away from the shore, where they were instantly engulfed by a light mist.

The poor visibility made Gold nervous, and he wondered out loud if they should turn on the running lights.

Teague looked at him as if he were dumber than ditchwater. "I ain't got no lights, and even if I did, I wouldn't turn them on. We don't want to attract any attention - or a bunch of damn bugs."

"Yeah, I didn't think about that."

The night was oppressively hot, the air temperature close to ninety, and all was motionless. Within minutes, the mist became fog. Under these foggy conditions, the visibility was further reduced, and now they could only see a hundred yards in front of them. The fog was annoying, but not half as bad as the damn insects. The estuary and surrounding marshes were a breeding ground for mosquitoes and nosseums, and worst of all, horseflies. Adult horseflies only lived for a few days, but during that time, 20 of them could drain almost a third of a pint of blood in as little as 6 hours.

"How much further?" Gold asked.

"Depends on the traps."

"What traps?"

"The crab traps. I might have to add some bait."

"*Now?*"

"State law. No baitless traps. Big fine if you don't obey the rules." He handed Gold a bucket. "It won't take long if we work together. I'll pull up the traps, and you throw in the bait. Two necks per trap."

Gold could barely see the chicken necks, but he sure could smell them. They'd been "marinating" for several days and smelled putrid. The odor made him gag, but it had no effect on Teague. None whatsoever. "You got any gloves?"

Teague smiled. "Your hands cold?"

"No, I just don't feel like touching these slimy things."

"Sorry, mate. No gloves."

"How many traps do you have?"

"Twelve."

"I'm sorry I asked. Are you sure this can't wait until morning?"

Teague looked into Gold's tortured eyes for a long moment. Then he stopped smiling and spoke in a more forceful and commanding voice. "You need to pay attention to what you're doing. If you fall overboard, you're in big trouble."

"How deep is this water?"

"Four feet."

"You call that trouble?"

Teague grabbed a sweat towel and wiped his brow. "You've got a lot to learn. Do you remember that ugly scar on my elbow? I didn't get that from a black widow. I got it out here, when I was careless and fell into the water. When I went over the side. I landed on a Southern stingray. You familiar with those things?"

"I know what they are, but I've never encountered one."

"Lucky man. That's one encounter you would never forget. No, sir, that's a scar that just won't heal." He began to rub his elbow absent-mindedly, almost as if he were still in pain. "There is nothing, and I mean nothing, more painful than the sting of a ray."

Naturally, he felt obliged to describe the pain in excruciating detail. He also felt obliged to mention that several species of stingrays were found in the waters off South Carolina's coast. In fact, there were seven species that frequented the shallow and estuarine areas, including the Southern stingray, roughtail stingray, smooth butterfly ray, spotted eagle ray, bullnose ray, cownose ray, and Atlantic ray. Each one of them had a hard, spear-like tail that it used as a defense mechanism. Each tail had a sharp, serrated barb on the end, and those barbs contained a toxic substance, or venom, that was injected into the victim. Death from a stingray sting was a rare occurrence, but was still possible if the barb penetrated the chest or abdomen.

In any case, the victim usually wished they were dead.

The symptoms included fever, chills, nausea, vomiting, tremors, paralysis, seizure, and decreased blood pressure.

Gold let this sink in before asking about first aid.

Teague shrugged. "Not much a person can do. Hot water can help – temporarily."

"Where do you get hot water?"

"I got mine from the water flow value on my outboard motor."

"Smart thinking."

"If I was smart, I wouldn't have fallen overboard in the first place. He thought back, then shook his head in disgust. "I should have stayed still or done the 'stingray shuffle.' When you shuffle your feet, you kick up mud and sand, and that scares off the ray."

"I'll have to remember that."

"Yeah, that might be wise. There are thousands of rays out here. They give birth in September, and when they start pupping, they get real aggressive."

Finding the traps was easy, but pulling them up and checking the bait took some effort. The task was made even more difficult by the stifling heat. The bugs were enough to drive a person crazy, and maybe – just maybe – a person had to be a little crazy to do this type of work.

A sane person would never be out on a boat, in the middle of the night, tossing chicken necks into a crab trap.

They were just about done when Teague announced that the motor sounded "funny." There was probably something wrapped around the propeller, most likely hydrilla or a discarded fishing line. He decided that it would be best to beach the skiff on a mud flat and pull up the motor before any damage was done.

Gold was instructed to stand on the bow and toss the anchor when they got close to the mud flat. That part went smoothly, but then he was told to climb out and make sure that the anchor flukes were secure. Leaving the boat, with fog all around them, did not seem logical, but he did as he was told. When he reached the anchor, he pulled out his flashlight and shone the beam on the flukes. They seemed to be in deep enough, but before he could take a closer look, he was struck from behind.

He never saw what hit him. Suddenly his jaw snapped shut, something flared behind his eyes – and he was out. For how long he couldn't tell. A few minutes. Half an hour. An hour. He had no way of knowing, but when he came to, he was lying face down in the mud. It took a few seconds for his eyes to adjust to the dark, but when they did, he realized that he was all alone. Teague was gone. So was the boat. The air trembled with the on-again, off-again rasp of cicadas and, in the distance, the mournful cry of an owl. And there was something else.

The water level in the estuary was dependent on the twice-daily influence of the high and low tides. When Gold looked around, he noticed that the water level was beginning to rise, and before long the mudflat would be completely submerged. He had to move to higher ground, but there was none.

The Lowcountry mudflats were a harsh habitat, sparsely covered with spartina grass and little else.

In a few minutes, he would be covered with six feet of salty, silty tidal wash. He had to act quickly, but what could he do? When he stood up, he spotted a small log that had been snagged on the mudflat. He stumbled over and worked it free of the mud, and then held on for dear life as the water continued to rise.

The full moon illuminated the bottom of the estuary, and when Gold looked down he saw hundreds of stingrays gliding beneath him. They were quite graceful, and looked harmless enough, but he knew that he would be in a world of trouble if he touched one.

The log was providing enough buoyancy to float above the rays, but it was partially waterlogged and difficult to maneuver. An hour went by, maybe two – it was difficult to tell, before the water was deep enough to push the log toward land. Swearing under his breath, Gold began to kick and paddle, determined to reach the shore. The mission was accomplished just before dawn, but he still had to wade through the mud, which immediately swallowed his shoes. After floundering a few steps, he finally reached dry land, and not a moment too soon.

A wave of dizziness and exhaustion buckled his knees, and he tumbled into the tall grass. Lying in the grass with his eyes closed, he drifted in and out of sleep, increasingly conscious of the sunlight on his face. He didn't want to get up. He wanted to stay where he was and rest. But no. He had to get up. He had to keep moving.

He stood up slowly, stretching muscles made doubly tired by hours of paddling and kicking. There was no wind, no sound, nothing to mask the heat and humidity. When he checked the time, he discovered that his stainless steel Rolex was gone. Either Teague had stolen the watch or it had slipped off during the night. He guessed that it was nine o'clock, maybe later.

Carefully, he made his way to the road and headed toward the Black Crab. If he could reach the bar, he would be all right. He'd call the police, have Teague arrested, and then seek medical help.

All he had to do was reach the bar.

The good news, Gold thought, was that he didn't have far to walk.

He had to keep moving.

Don't stop. Don't look back.

Jesus, it was hot out. Even the insects were lying low.

Suddenly, out of the corner of his eye, Gold say a car barreling down a dirt road, perpendicular to where he was standing. The driver seemed to be in a hurry, and the vehicle was closing quickly.

Gold's mind raced. What were his options? By his calculation, he had precisely none. All he could do was stand there and wait. Then, out of nowhere, he remembered the gun that Kaminski had given him back in Virginia.

When he reached for the Smith & Wesson, he discovered it was gone.

That bastard Teague, he thought to himself.

Time to face the music.

Hopefully, it wouldn't be his swan song.

CHAPTER TWELVE

Gold had occasionally wondered when his luck would run out, where he would be at the time, and how the end might come. He'd guessed he'd be shot or stabbed, or conked on the head one too many times. He never imagined that he'd be run over by a car.

Life was full of surprises.

He blinked several times and braced himself for trouble.

But the car came to a screeching halt a few feet from where he was standing. The wheels kicked up a cloud of dust, making it difficult to see, but when the dust cleared, he got another surprise. The driver was a woman. She remained in the vehicle, mouth ajar, staring at him.

Gold could scarcely believe his eyes – or his luck. It was Sungira Taylor, the docent from the Penn Center. He smiled, then grew instantly apologetic once he saw the expression of fear on her face. "I seem to have lost my way."

"My God," she exclaimed, running toward him. "What happened?"

Gold's lips moved slowly, as if he were laboring over every word. "Boating mishap. I, uh, fell overboard."

"Are you hurt?"

"No, but I've had a long swim. I need to ….rest."

She felt his forehead. "You're burning up."

"Hot out."

Little worry lines invaded her polished image, creasing outward from her mouth in rays of tension. "This is not good. You're sick. You need to get off your feet." She looked as his bare feet, then frowned. "Where are your shoes?"

"Lost them in the mud."

"Good Lord, you've had a rough morning."

"The evening was worse."

She kept trying to discern from Gold what had happened and what was the nature of his injury, all to no avail. The patient was simply too weak to talk. "Very well," she said at last. "You're coming with me."

"Coming where?"

"To my house. You need some water and you need to rest."

Gold nodded enthusiastically, coming to grips with the fact that he was starting to feel dizzy. Without hesitation, he took her arm and slowly made his way to her car. Sinking into the passenger seat, he breathed a sigh of relief. All things considered, this was a good development. A welcome respite from the heat of the day.

Yes, sir, life was full of surprises.

As they drove off, Gold continued to count his blessings, but by the time they reached her house, he was sweating profusely and shaking like a leaf. The color had drained from his face, leaving it a pale, expressionless mask. Sungila quickly ushered him inside, reaching the couch just before he collapsed.

Gold drifted in and out of consciousness for the rest of the day and most of the night. When he woke up it was still dark, and he listened to the night around him, the sounds of cicadas and bullfrogs mingling with the raspy sound of his own breathing. He could feel the dryness in his throat and the dampness of the sheet beneath him, but he just couldn't stay awake long enough to figure out where he was or how he got there.

The next time he opened his eyes it was midafternoon and the summer sun was high and bright. His first reaction was to try and sit up, but when he raised his head, sharp pains shot through his chest, forcing him to remain still. He lay on his back staring up at the ceiling, his brain racing to piece together the puzzle. *Where the hell am I? How did I get on a couch? Where are my damn clothes?* It took a while, but eventually the fog in his brain began to clear, and then it hit him. Ignoring the stabbing pain in his chest and the throbbing welt on the back of his head, he called out Sungila's name.

She came running out of the kitchen, and a new sense of urgency kicked in when she saw that he was still trembling. "Stay where you are," she ordered. "You're not out of the woods just yet."

"What's going on?" he asked. "I feel like crap."

"You're sick."

"What's wrong with me?"

She found a hand mirror and held it up to his face. "You see that rash on your neck?"

"Damn, are those mosquito bites?"

"No." She reached out and felt his swollen lymph glands. "I'm afraid you've got West Nile Virus."

"Son of a bitch, Gold muttered. "Are you sure about that?"

"Positive."

Gold tried to remain calm and focused on concealing the fear that was clawing at his gut. "What's the prognosis?"

"You'll live. The disease is only deadly when the virus enters the brain. Inflammation of the brain is called encephalitis. Inflammation of the brain and spinal cord is called meningitis. You don't have either, and if you follow my orders, the virus will be out of your system in twenty-four hours."

"Your *orders?*"

"I intend to cure you, Mr. Gold."

"Are you a doctor?"

"No, but I possess medical skills."

"What is that supposed to mean?"

She gave him a couple of sips of broth, then calmly explained that she was a practitioner of Hoodoo medicine, the West African form of herbal healing that treated illnesses using roots, herbs, barks, and teas. From the look on his face, she could tell that he was not overly impressed with her credentials. "I also dabble in black magic, but there's not much call for that sort of thing these days."

Gold stared at her, dumbfounded. He was almost afraid to ask what she meant by *black magic*, but his curiosity got the better of him. "Are you referring to hexes and spells?"

"Yep."

"Well, I can see where business might be off – now that we're in the twenty-first century."

She didn't rise to the bait of the insult, but she did go on to finish her thought. 'I don't fool with black magic because it's too messy. Conjurers use animal parts, feathers, blood, and bones. I like to keep a clean house, so I stick with root medicine."

Conjurers? Animal parts? Blood and bones? I'll never get out of here alive, Gold thought to himself. *The woman is a complete whack job.* Another thought occurred to him. "What was in that broth?"

"Boiled willow bark."

"I was hoping you'd say beef or chicken."

"Willow bark is a wonderful substance, similar to aspirin. The bark of a willow tree can reduce headache pain, muscle pain, menstrual cramps, rheumatoid arthritis, and gout."

"Is it safe to consume?"

"As long as you don't go overboard."

"Huh?"

"The active ingredient in willow bark is Salicin, which is the chemical that killed Beethoven. Of course, Beethoven ingested a huge amount of the stuff before he died."

"Well, there goes my music career."

"You'll be fine."

"Maybe we should drive over to Beaufort."

"In your condition?" She shook her head. "Too risky."

"I'm willing to take the chance."

"I'm not."

"I hate to be a burden."

"Don't worry, I've never lost a patient."

"Let me guess. I'm your first patient."

"Second."

"Terrific."

She told him not to worry, that they had access to the best pharmacy in the world. Unfortunately, it wasn't Walgreens, CVS, Walmart, or Rite Aid. In her view, the best pharmacy in the world was St. Helena Island, which contained over 100 medicinal plants. The list included sweet gum, myrtle, and blackberry for diarrhea and dysentery; swamp grass for poultices; sassafras tea for colds; galax for high blood pressure; nightshade to reduce fevers; and ironweed to improve sexual potency.

Gold yawned. "I guess that covers just about everything."

"Just about."

"I do have one question, though."

"Yes?"

"Where are my clothes?"

"Hanging on a line."

"You washed my clothes?"

"They were covered with mud." She stayed quiet a moment, then said, "What's wrong? Do you feel violated?"

"No, of course not, but …"

"I have four brothers. Trust me, you don't have anything that I haven't seen before."

Another yawn. "I'll take that as a compliment."

"You may take it any way you wish."

"I'm starting to feel sleepy again."

"The willow bark has certain side effects."

"Like premature death?"

"No, like drowsiness."

"I can barely keep my eyes open."

"Well, don't fall asleep yet. I need to apply a poultice."

Oh God, Gold thought. *Now what?*

Working quickly, she ran into the kitchen, mixed some ingredients together in a bowl, then returned with the bowl and a hand towel. She dipped the towel in the odd-smelling concoction and wrung out the excess fluid. "I'm going to press this to your chest. You might feel a stinging sensation."

"Whoa, there," Gold said, raising a hand. "What the hell is that stuff?"

"*Rosmarinus officinallis.*"

"English, please."

"Wild rosemary." She smiled, seemingly amused by his discomfort. "Never heard of it?"

"I think I dated her in high school."

"If so, you might remember that she can open body pores and sweat out illness."

"Yeah, that was her."

She pulled down the sheet that was covering his body and slapped the poultice on his chest. He winced, but swallowed the curse word that was on the tip of his tongue. Deep down, she felt sorry for him, but she remained cool, calm, and collected. "You'll feel better when the herbs soak in."

"I hope so."

"I said it might sting."

"Bees sting, that hurt like hell."

"It wasn't the poultice. You bruised your ribs." She gently touched a black and blue area on his left side, but even her light touch made him wince. "You might have cracked a rib, but we won't know without an X-ray."

"They probably have an X-ray machine in Beaufort."

"I'm sure they do."

"I'll pay for the gas and tolls."

"Ye of little faith."

"Nothing personal. I'm not a fan of that old black magic."

"I told you before, I practice Hoodoo, not Voodoo."

"Same difference."

"Not quite." She reminded him that while both had roots in African culture, Hoodoo was a type of folk magic, Voodoo an established religion. "They're as different as night and day."

The difference was lost on Gold, although it was actually quite profound. Hoodoo was developed to allow people to use supernatural forces in order to improve their daily lives. These forces were used to improve health, luck, love lives, and social lives. It could also be used to harm, curse, or seek revenge, but those were the areas that she avoided.

Voodoo, on the other hand, was a highly structured religion, the word itself derived from the Haitian Creole word *Ayizo*, meaning "mysterious forces that govern the world." In addition to worshipping a god called Bondye, Voodoo included offerings, ceremonies, dance and music events, and spirit possession.

Sungila could have gone on and on, and probably would have, but Gold was fading quickly. As briefly as she could, she told him what to expect, then she urged him to relax and let the willow bark work its magic.

Gold started to object.

She shrugged a *whatever* shrug.

A moment later, he closed his eyes and fell asleep.

She sat back and blew a stray strand of hair out of her face. "Sweet dreams," she said. "You can thank me later."

CHAPTER THIRTEEN

Sungila sat across the room from Gold, observing him the way an artist might stare at a blank canvas. She noticed that he wasn't wearing a wedding ring, and she wondered what that meant. More specifically, she wondered if he was single or married, or somewhere in-between. She'd find out soon enough – once they began to talk – but for now she was left to speculate. There were times when her gut feelings verged on extrasensory, but this wasn't one of them. For some reason, her instincts told her that he was a free agent, but she knew this might be wishful thinking. If she wasn't careful, she thought, she could make a fool of herself over this handsome man with the wicked sense of humor.

Sungila grinned slightly. *You are so full of crap*, she thought to herself. *You know all the good men are taken.*

When Gold began to stir, she scooted closer to the couch. A minute later, he woke up, blinking rapidly until his eyes adjusted to the light. With a little help from Sungira, he sat upright, then turned sideways and looked at her questioningly. "How long was I out?"

"Six hours."

They regarded each other for some time without speaking; then Gold shook his head. "You should bottle that stuff."

"The willow bark?"

"The rosemary, too. I went out like a light."

"Yes, I noticed. How do you feel?"

"I feel…fine."

She leaned forward and felt his forehead. "Your fever's gone."

"You're a hell of a nurse. I'm sorry I gave you a hard time."

Sungila bestowed on him her sweetest smile. "You're forgiven. Are you hungry?"

"No, but I could use some water."

She fetched a glass of water, then returned to her chair, wrapping her arms around her legs, pulling them tight against her chest. She tipped her head to one side like a bird, studying him. She was wearing a pair of gray sweats and a small T-shirt that barely covered her belly button. Out of the blue, she said, "Who's Fremont?"

Gold frowned. "Why do you ask?"

"You were talking in your sleep."

"I guess I had a bad dream."

"I guess so. You threatened to kill him."

"I'm not surprised."

"One of Teague's friends?"

"Friend or partner, I'm not sure which."

"Tell me about him."

"You don't want to hear about that clown."

"Sure, I do." She gave him another smile. "It's part of the healing process."

Gold wasn't exactly sure where to start, but with a little prompting he relayed the whole story, starting with Stonewall Jackson and ending with his ill-fated boat trip with Tyrone Teague. He spoke for an hour, but she didn't move a muscle the entire time. She just sat there, still as a statue, taking it all in.

When Sungila realized she was sitting there with her mouth open she shut it and tried to think of something intelligent to say. "They want two million dollars? For a severed limb?"

"Yep."

"They've got a lot of nerve."

"We call it chutzpah."

"I smell a rat."

"I smell a pack of rats." He gave a little snort, half annoyance, half-amusement. "Let me tell you something about these lowlifes. They view themselves as criminal masterminds, but they don't have a brain between them. They think that insurance companies are made of money, and that we'd be glad to pay a ransom to cut our losses. Nothing could be further from the truth. Most of the time we go to the mat, and in this case, we have two million reasons to fight back."

Sungila raked long fingers through her dark hair. "You seem to think that Fremont is part of the gang."

"Well, it's starting to look that way." Gold closed his eyes for a moment to organize his thoughts. Then he reminded her that Fremont was the one who told him about Frank and Jesse James. He'd also mentioned the Gender Bender, which led him to Pearlie Gates, and then to St. Helena Island. "Oh, what a tangled web we weave…"

Sungila chewed pensively on her lip. "What does Fremont look like?"

Gold described him in detail – right down to his colorful bow tie and fancy French cuffs. "He lives in Charleston."

"We've met."

Gold blinked several times and said, "Are you sure it was Fremont?"

"Yes, but he introduced himself as Robert Freeman."

"When did you meet him?"

"Last summer – at the Penn Center. He asked me about some Gullah artifacts."

"What did he want to buy?"

"He wasn't buying, he was selling. I remember talking to him. He was very persistent. I told him to go to hell. He had no right to be selling Gullah artifacts." She displayed a shy little grin. "He was really pissed off, but I didn't care. I told him and his chauffeur to get off our property and never come back."

"He had a chauffeur?"

"Tyrone Teague."

Gold stared at her, thunderstruck. "Well, well, well," he said at last. "How do you like that. Teague's a regular jack of all trades." He shook his head in disbelief. "Did he get pissed off, too?"

"Oh, yeah. He called me a house nigger and told me to expect a late night visit." After a time she said carefully. "I got even."

"How?"

"I put a hex on him."

Gold was thinking. "I thought black magic wasn't your thing."

"In his case I made an exception."

A thought occurred to him. "I heard about the hex – from the bartender at the Black Crab. He, uh, referred to you as a scrawny witch."

"Beauty is in the eye of the beholder."

"If it's any consolation, Teague is worried sick. I don't know who he fears more, you or the Boo Hag."

She snorted derisively. "Hopefully one of us will finish him off."

Gold leaned closer, as if someone might be listening. He said softly, "From your lips to God's ears." He was tempted to ask her if she lived alone and then thought better of it. "Do you lock your doors at night?"

Sungila's dark eyes widened as if she found the question slightly impertinent. Then it dawned on her that he was just concerned about her safety. "You don't have to worry about me. I never sleep alone."

Gold scratched his head, wondering what that meant. He studied her for a long moment, then decided that it was none of his business. "Better safe than sorry."

"I sleep with a 12-guage shotgun."

"Oh, I thought you meant…"

"I'm single."

Now Gold was really puzzled – and determined to learn more about her. He smiled pleasantly at her, then said, "Tell me about yourself."

Her eyebrows lowered suspiciously. "What do you want to know?"

"Whatever you want to tell me."

"I wouldn't know where to begin."

"Start with your name. Sungila sounds like it might be African."

"Central African. My ancestors were Bantu." Her ancestors had, in fact, earned the dubious honor of supplying most of the slaves that were brought to the Sea Islands. Back then, Gullah slaves were given two names – a *proper* name that was used by white folks, and a *basket* name, used by family and friends.

"Names were of great importance, and they changed throughout life."

"Why did they change their names?"

"To mark a new stage of life. The Gullah call it name shifting, and it is still quite common in our community." She could see that he was puzzled, so she reminded him that Frederick Douglass, the great orator and statesman, had started out as Frederick Bailey. Sojourner Truth, the famous abolitionist, was originally named Isabella Baumfree. She went on to tell him that the custom continued during the twentieth century, most notably in the jazz world, where black musicians frequently adopted colorful nicknames. Among the most famous were Ferdinand La Menthe, who became Jelly Roll Morton, Louis Armstrong who became Satchmo, and Charles Parker, who became Yardbird.

"What about you?" Gold asked. "Do you have a nickname?"

"No, I stuck with Sungila."

"Well, it's a lovely name."

"Thank you." She gave him a slow, sideways glance laced with amusement. "Would you like to know what it means?"

"I'm all ears."

"Sungila means to *save, help or deliver*."

Gold stared at her, seemingly deep in thought. Then he said, "It fits you perfectly." He touched her arm. "Thank you for saving my life."

Figuring that it was now or never, she retrieved her cell phone and placed it on his lap. Quietly, matter-of-factly, she asked, "Do you need to call someone?"

Gold had almost forgotten about the two women in his life – his boss and his wife. They were probably wondering where the hell he was, and why he hadn't touched base. In a perfect world, he thought, he wouldn't have to worry about people worrying about him. In a perfect world he could do his own thing, and not give others worry lines and gray hair. "I suppose E.T. should call home."

"Home meaning wife?"

"Home meaning wife and boss."

Sungila's heart sank. "Make your calls. I'll make dinner."

Thirty minutes later, worn out from talking, Gold got off the phone and took a quick shower. While dressing, he replayed the conversations in his head, amused that both women had asked the same questions and made the same remarks. In essence, they were thrilled that he was alive and well, but royally pissed that he hadn't called sooner. Neither one of them wanted to hear any excuses, regardless of their validity.

Weird how the line between his wife and boss was starting to blur, but he figured it was an occupational hazard – one that he would have to strive to avoid.

When Gold walked into the kitchen, Sungila eyed him with mild astonishment. "You look like a new man."

"I feel like one," Gold said. "I appreciate your hospitality."

"Kindness is a Gullah tradition. Besides, we claims people have to stick together."

Gold stared at her, mouth agape. "You worked in claims?"

"Five long years."

"Are you pulling my leg?"

"Atlanta Life Insurance Company. We mainly sold life insurance, but we had our share of fraud."

"I'm not familiar with Atlanta Life."

"We only did business in the South, and most of our customers were African-American." She was quick to assure him that his was no fly-by-night operation.

The company was founded by Alonzo Herndon, a former slave and sharecropper, who became Atlanta's first black millionaire. In 1905, Herndon purchased the Atlanta Benevolent and Protective Association for $140, and five years later, that became the Atlanta Life Insurance Company. In the beginning, the carrier offered simple life and health policies, paying a small benefit upon death. Herndon's business model was based upon the Gullah benevolent societies on the Sea Islands. "Our societies paid for medical bills and burials. At first they were secret societies, but as things changed, they became public" With a faint smile, she added, "Our burial customs are rather unique."

Gold nodded. "I know about the grave decorations."

"From Teague?"

Gold colored slightly, surprised by the question. He instinctively scanned the room, as if someone might overhear him. "I took a brochure from the Penn Center. They listed the items that your people leave. I thought that was pretty cool."

"Did it mention the burial service?"

"I don't think so."

Sungila, standing at the stove, stirring a large pot, described the Gullah way of dealing with death. When a person died, somebody from the benevolent society would be sent out to wash the body with soap and water. Men performed this task for men, and women prepared the bodies of women. After the body was wiped clean, coffee was placed underneath the arms, legs, and open cavities. Coffee was then rubbed over the body, which was displayed for two or three days before being wrapped in a white sheet and placed in a casket.

In Sungila's family, they followed Bantu tradition and held an all-night funeral observance. Mourners were expected – and encouraged – to sing, pray, and preach the gospel. The more noise, the better. Shrieking and shouting were used to scare off the spirits of hell, who were always lurking around, waiting to grab possession of another soul.

There are places in the world where funerals are conducted with more pomp and circumstance. But St. Helena Island wasn't one of them.

Gold sat back and looked out the window at the evening sky. For almost a minute, he didn't speak. His mind was focused elsewhere, on the pleasant aroma that was driving him crazy. "What's for dinner?"

"Something healthy."

"Uh-oh. Here we go again."

She dismissed that comment with a characteristic curl of the lip. "As a matter of fact," she said, filling two bowls, "I made you something special. An authentic Gullah dish."

Gold braced himself. "What would that be?"

"Frogmore stew."

There was a beat before Gold cleared his throat and said, "We need to talk…"

CHAPTER FOURTEEN

Early the next morning they drove to the Black Crab, hoping to find Gold's car in the parking lot. Luckily, it was still there, but it was covered with big, white splats of bird poop. When Gold saw the condition of the vehicle, his heart sank. He stared at the mess in silence, and when he glanced over he caught Sungila secretly smiling.

'What's so funny?" he asked.

"Nothing."

"My car looks like a Rorschach test."

"Seagulls," she said. "The bane of my existence."

"Did you bring your shotgun?"

"Nope."

"Too bad."

She eyed him impishly. "If I were you, I'd stop at a car wash."

"You think?"

"There are three in Beaufort."

"I don't have time to stop."

"What's the rush?"

"I need to get back to Charleston. I want to have a chat with Roger Fremont."

Sungila looked uncomfortable. The skin around her eyes creased and she looked at Gold and then out across the parking lot. "Do you think that's wise? I mean, you just got out of a sick bed."

"Which means that I'm not sick anymore."

"You could use another day of rest."

Gold put an arm around her, clumsily, trying to reassure her that he was up to snuff, but she wouldn't be comforted. "You worry too much."

"One of my endearing qualities."

"One of many." He kissed her on the forehead. "I'll give you a call before I leave Charleston."

"Promise?"

"You have my word."

She kissed him on the check. "That's good enough for me."

Gingerly, Gold opened the car door and climbed inside. Clumsy as usual in the realm of the emotions, he tried to think of something sweet to say, but the words escaped him. All that occurred to him was *Thank you*, even though it seemed inadequate. "I know you won't accept any money, so I'll be sending a donation to the Penn Center."

"Thanks. We could use the money."

"Keep your eyes open. Teague could still be on the island."

"I've thought about that. If we cross paths, he'll be sorry." She opened her purse, revealing a Pink Lady handgun. "I won't hesitate to shoot."

"You carry a pistol?"

"Only all the time."

"Why?"

"I can't fit a cop in my purse."

Gold chuckled, genuinely amused. He leaned closer, as if someone might be listening. "Aim for his crotch. You'll be doing the world a big favor."

Pulling back from the car a few inches, Sungila looked into his eyes for a long moment. Then she smiled and pinched Gold's cheek, and said, "Be careful."

"Don't worry about me. I intend to live forever, or die trying."

"Sounds like a plan."

With some difficulty, Gold fastened his seat belt, then slowly drove off, watching Sungila in the rearview mirror. He thought about her for the next hour, wondering, as most men might, what she would be like in bed. He imagined it would be a night to remember.

Thinking about her made Gold smile, but as soon as he reached Charleston his thoughts turned to Fremont, and how to handle the situation at hand. Gold was tempted to walk into his office and beat the crap out of him, but that would be counterproductive. Besides, investigators were supposed to outwit the bad guys, not beat them to a pulp. The best way to deal with Fremont was to find his Achilles heel – and then start squeezing.

And that's exactly what Gold intended to do.

Squeeze until it hurt.

After parking on King Street, Gold took a moment to study the entrance – and exits – of the Blue Heron. The store was located in one of the prettier buildings on the street, although the front was starting to show signs of wear. He noticed that the logo, a bird in flight, and the frames of the twelve-pane windows were painted indigo blue. He wondered if this was done to ward off evil spirits or was simply a coincidence. The paint job reminded him of his night on the water, and the more he thought about Teague, the angrier he became.

After counting to ten, he made his move, but the first thing he discovered was that the front door was locked. He peered inside, surprised that there were no customers in the store, and no sign of the owner. A card in the window read *Out to lunch*. This was strange, since it was ten o'clock in the morning. Rather than knocking, he made his way down the narrow alley that led to the backyard. The garden was deserted, but the French doors were propped open, so he walked inside and found Fremont yakking on the telephone.

Fremont had his back to Gold, but when he heard footsteps, he whirled around, startled, and caught his breath. He slowly put the phone down, his mind literally catapulting forward to one devastating scenario after another. His chin began to quiver, then his entire face collapsed. "What are you doing here?"

Gold stared hard at him and spoke slowly. "Surprised to see me?"

Fremont forced himself to take a deep breath, and then another. The blood had drained from his face, and for a moment, he looked like he was going to faint. "Where have you been?"

"I decided to take a vacation."

"On St. Helena Island?"

"Why not? It's a lovely place. Have you ever been there?"

"Once or twice."

Gold scrutinized him a bit longer and then shuffled over to a credenza and picked up a Confederate sword. He studied the engraving on the blade, then said, "I went crabbing, but I didn't catch a damn thing."

"I'm sorry to hear that."

"Lousy guide."

"Maybe you'll have better luck next time."

"There won't be a next time. My crabbing days are over."

He ran a finger along the blade, a smile playing across his lips. "If you lie to me again, your days might be over, too."

Fremont glanced at his watch without really looking at the time. "I don't know what you're talking about."

"God, I hate when people say that, because they always do. I guess it's the first thing that comes to mind. A knee jerk reaction. Who knows? If I was in your predicament I might say the same thing." He walked across the room and stood before a display case that contained three porcelain bowls. He tapped one of them with the tip of the sword. "These are beautiful."

"Be careful with that sword."

"Am I making you nervous?"

"Yes, you are."

Gold reached for one of the bowls and held it up to the light at the window, turning it this way and that. "Exquisite detail. Ming dynasty?"

"Yuan."

"How much?"

"Ten thousand."

"Each one?"

"They're quite rare."

"Must be nice to own three."

"They're not mine. I took them on consignment."

"Jesus, I hope they're insured."

"Trying to drum up business?"

Gold hated it, this game of cat and mouse, but he supposed it had to be done. Still, there was a time limit to his patience. "Why'd you set me up, Roger?"

"You think I set you up?"

"I know you did. Your friend Teague was waiting for me, and I walked right into his trap. Turns out it was sort of a crab trap."

"Look, I don't know what happened between you and Teague, but I had nothing to do with it."

"Nothing?"

"Not a damn thing."

Fremont's face was impassive. Gold knew that look. It was the look of a liar, caught. He'd seen it a hundred times before, but it still repulsed him. Very well, he thought. Time to squeeze. "I was hoping we could do this the easy way, but if you want to play games, let's start with *catch*." He tossed the bowl to Fremont, but it slid through his hands and shattered on his desk. "Oops."

"You son of a bitch!" Fremont yelled. "Have you lost your fucking mind?"

"That and my patience," Gold said calmly.

"Jesus Christ, you didn't have to break the damn bowl!

Gold seemed unmoved by Fremont's outrage, and there was even a sparkle of mischief in his eyes. "I didn't break it, you dropped it. Big difference." He reached for another bowl. "Would you like to try it again?"

Fremont's face went white. "If you throw that bowl, I swear to God, I'll call the police!"

"Well, that should be interesting."

"I mean it, Gold!"

"No, you don't. You'd have to tell them that you and your friends are thieves. The authorities won't take kindly to the fact that you've been stealing Gullah artifacts and robbing Civil War graves. Hell, those are hanging offenses in this part of the country."

Fremont muttered something to himself, then buried his head in his hands. "Why are you doing this to me? Why?"

Gold scratched himself under the chin, not even acknowledging the question. "I'll ask you one more time. Why did you set me up?" He waited for an answer. He knew that not everyone was motivated solely by money. There were other currencies. Fame, jealousy, power, rage, and revenge, to name a few. One of them had taken hold of Fremont. But which one was it? "If I had to guess, I'd say you did it for the money. Am I right?"

Without looking up, Fremont said, "Please don't break another bowl."

"Answer me, Roger."

Fremont gnawed his lower lip.

Gold's patience was wearing thin. "Last chance," he said. "Was it the money?"

Fremont looked at him, squirming with uneasiness. "They promised me twenty-five grand."

"Ah, the five percent commission."

"Business is slow. I needed the money."

"But I was standing in your way."

"I wasn't expecting an investigation."

"So why not get rid of the investigator? Is that what you thought?"

"Teague was supposed to scare you off. Make you think twice about staying down here. Nobody was supposed to get hurt."

"No, no…" Gold thought for a second. "Good heavens, no. Just fun and games."

"Teague's a violent man. He went overboard."

"Actually, I was the one who went overboard, and therein lies the problem. Somebody has to pay the piper. I don't know where to find Jesse and Frank, so that means you're the fall guy." He pressed the tip of the sword under Fremont's chin. "Would you mind standing?"

Fremont eyed him coolly. "Why?"

"Citizen's arrest."

"You're joking."

"I'm afraid not."

"Wait a minute. Let's not do anything rash. Maybe we can make a deal."

"A deal?"

"Keep the bowl. It's one of a kind."

"So are you."

"Consider it a gift."

"I'm thinking bribe."

"Think whatever you want, just don't turn me in." The poor man looked panic-stricken. "What do you say? Do we have a deal?"

"No, but we're getting close. I don't need a bowl, but I do need a name and address."

"Whose name and address?"

"Jesse James."

Fremont stared at him, unbelieving. "Jesus fucking Christ. Are you trying to get me killed? Do you know what that sick bastard would do to me if I give you that information?" Feeling sick to his stomach, he sat forward on the edge of his chair, clasping his desk with trembling hands. "If you thought Teague was scary..."

Before he could finish his sentence, Teague walked through the back door, chuckling to himself. He slammed the door behind him, making the windows rattle in their frames. He gave Fremont a murderous look, then said, "Finish your sentence, faggot."

Fremont began to shake with fear. His face turned bright red. He started to speak, but the words stuck in his throat.

Teague made no effort to disguise the fact that he was enjoying himself. "What's wrong, sweetie Cat got your tongue?"

Gold looked contemptuously at him. "Back off, Teague."

Teague turned toward Gold, glared at him, and then grinned wolfishly. "I'll deal with you in a moment."

"You'll deal with me now."

"You got something to say to me?"

"I'm bringing you in, Frank. Dead or alive. You decide."

Teague cocked his head to the side. "Just how much saltwater did you swallow?"

"Let me put it another way. You're under arrest, moron."

Fremont's mouth opened and shut several times before anything intelligible came out. "Must we call names?" He was clutching the arms of his chair as if it were moving. "Let's be civil and discuss this like gentlemen."

"Shut the fuck up!" Teague shouted. He ran his tongue along his bottom row of teeth. "You know something, buckruh? I should've shot you when I had the chance."

"Yeah, you should have," Gold said. "You won't get another chance."

"Don't be so sure."

Gold eyed Teague for a moment longer, then looked at Fremont. "Teague's a coward. He likes to hit people from behind. No wonder he couldn't make it in the NFL."

"You got a big fucking mouth," Teague snarled.

"Better than a yellow streak."

Teague went on scowling at him for perhaps twenty seconds, then he snorted a little laugh.

Fremont braced himself for trouble.

Seeing the animal-like rage on Teague's face, Gold instantly knew this was it. The man was about to kill him. Of that he had absolutely no doubt.

Fremont scarcely had time to push himself out of the way before all hell broke loose.

Teague suddenly sprang wildly at Gold, his hands up and going for his neck. Gold was ready and reacted aggressively, raising the sword to stop him. But Teague didn't stop. He charged forward, as if he were after a quarterback. Driven by the momentum of Teague's weight, Gold then flew backward, three maybe four feet, and they slammed into a wall. The blow drove all the air out of Gold; he thought it had broken him in half.

Teague was in much worse shape. He'd hit the floor rolling and slammed into Fremont's desk, knocking the Chinese bowl and other decorative – and breakable – items onto the hardwood floor. When he pushed onto his knees and tried to stand, he realized that the sword had penetrated his chest and broken in half. He stared at his blood-soaked shirt in disbelief, too dizzy to get up. Stripping off his shirt and throwing it across the room, he pressed a fist over the wound, trying to stop the bleeding. "Jesus! Jesus! Jesus!" he kept whispering over and over. "Help me! I'm dying!"

Gold racked his brain, debating how he could help, but before he had a chance to act, Teague fell to the floor in a crumpled heap.

A moment of stunned silence passed.

Gold breathed quietly for a minute, marshaling his thoughts.

Fremont stood, his expression one of horror. He felt his heart thumping, the blood darkening his face. He wondered if he should say what he was thinking – that they were both in deep shit. *Damn*, he thought. *Damn! Damn! Damn!*

Gold stepped forward and checked for a pulse. Nothing. "He's dead."

Fremont closed his eyes for a moment, as if trying to shut it all out. "Are you sure?"

"Yeah, I'm sure."

"Oh my God, this is bad."

"Worse than bad."

Fremont sank back into his chair. He rubbed hs face with both hands. "What are we going to do?"

"Depends on your mood."

"My mood?"

"You've got two choices. One, you can turn yourself in, face a lengthy trial, lose your business, and spend the next ten years in prison. Two, you can report a robbery, claim self defense, become and hero, and go on with your life. The choice is yours."

Fremont's voice cracked with sudden anger. "I didn't kill him!"

"Neither did I. Technically speaking, he killed himself."

"Why do I have to step forward?"

"Your place of business. A man has a right to protect his livelihood."

"Jesus, how did I get into this situation?"

"You left the back door open."

Fremont felt the impulse to run away – to bolt, right then – but where could he go? In the end, the law – or Gold – would catch up to him. Sooner or later, he'd have to face the music, so why not face it now, while he still had a chance to stay out of jail? He gave it some thought, then said, "What about the police? Do you think they'll believe my story?"

"No, of course not. But they will believe me. I'll be your eyewitness."

Fremont managed a trembling smile. "You'll vouch for me?"

"What are friends for?"

"You're a good man, Gold."

"*Ex unitate vires.*"

"Huh?"

"It's Latin. From unity, strength."

Fremont felt like hugging Gold, but then remembered where he was and what had happened. Instead, he offered to give him the last remaining Chinese bowl, describing it as a token of his appreciation. "Don't worry about the cost. I'll turn in a claim."

Gold snorted a gruff little chuckle, half-amused, half-indignant. "Keep the bowl. All I want is that name and address, and if I don't get it, you and I are gonna become pen pals."

Fremont scrunched his face in concentration for a second. "Pen pals?"

"You heard me."

"I don't understand."

Gold put his face in front of Fremont's and said in a slow, distinct tone, "Get your act together, Roger. If I don't find Jesse James, you go to the pen." He raised a halting palm when Fremont opened his mouth to speak. "Don't talk. Write."

CHAPTER FIFTEEN

Chief Solomon Carter, the head of the Charleston Police Department, led a force of 450 officers and 120 civilians, making it the largest police department in the state. College educated, he'd risen through the ranks quickly, starting as a probationary officer and working his way up to chief in less than twenty years. Now forty, he was a short man, stocky, muscular, with piercing blue eyes highlighted by dark circles earned over the course of two decades dealing with the worst element of Charleston society.

Nowadays, he enjoyed a round or two of golf, and when forced by duty to interrupt his game, he was not a happy camper. Unfortunately, the untimely death of Tyrone Teague required his immediate attention, so he grudgingly packed up his clubs and drove back to the station.

When he entered the interrogation room, Fremont and Gold were waiting for him, and if looks could kill, they would've both been dead men. His hair – what was left of it – was plastered to his head from the heat and humidity. *What does it matter anyway?* he thought, and he took his right hand and slid it across the top of his head to rid it of the excess moisture. "Do either of you gentlemen play golf?" he asked abruptly. Before they could reply, he added, "I love to play golf. As a matter of fact, that's what I was doing before you ruined my day." He smiled at them tightly. "I also like to read. Do you gentlemen like to read?" Once again, the question was rhetorical. "In my line of work, I come across a lot of fiction. For instance, I just read a very entertaining police report. Weak premise, but entertaining." He boosted himself up onto a desk, then poured himself a cup of coffee from a thermos jug, and sipped from it. "Would you like to tell me what really happened to Tyron Teague?"

Fremont remained silent. But his eyes said quite a bit.

Gold took a few moments before answering. "Are you the good cop or the bad cop?"

Carter glared at him for a heartbeat, then said, "I beg your pardon?"

"I know the routine," Gold said. "Are you the good cop or the bad cop?"

Carter played with his bow tie and gave Gold one of his patented scowls. "I'm neither, son. I'm the pissed off cop." He leaned forward, just a little. "Do you know why I'm pissed off?"

"Somebody grab the last donut?"

Carter shook his head in a slow, disappointing manner. "Smart aleck, huh?"

"If I was smart, I wouldn't be here."

"You must be Mr. Gold."

"That's right."

"The Yankee investigator."

"Insurance investigator."

"Who do you work for?"

"Mainly Uncle Sam, but now and then I handle a claim for the Anchor Insurance Company."

"Never heard of them."

"Then they've probably never heard of you."

"Where are they located?"

"New York City."

"Figures."

"Excuse me?"

"You've got the manner of a city slicker."

That comment caused Gold's left eyebrow to rise a half-inch. He placed a business card on the table. "Feel free to verify my employment."

"All in good time. First I'd like to know what you're doing in Charleston."

"Didn't know I needed a reason to visit."

"Answer the question."

"Just passing through."

"Don't be so sure. If you don't corporate, you might be here a while." He rose and started pacing. "You working on a claim?"

"More or less."

"Tell me about the more part."

"There's not much to tell. Mr. Fremont is one of our policy holders. He turned in a claim, so they sent me to investigate."

"Must be a sizable claim."

"I'm afraid so."

"Do you investigate every claim?"

"No, just certain ones."

"Why this one?"

"Big numbers."

"What are we talking about?"

Gold didn't look up. He spoke quietly and gave nothing away by his body language. "Two antique bowls. Yuan Dynasty. Very expensive. Completely destroyed."

The chief thought about it for a second and with a tired sigh said, "The report mentioned something about porcelain chards."

"Those chards cost a pretty penny. Then thousand each."

"How did they break?"

"Vandalism."

With a no-nonsense tone, Carter asked, "Did somebody break into the store?"

"Looks that way."

"Teague?"

"No, I don't think so. Probably kids. Nothing was taken."

Carter looked at Fremont. "When did this crime occur?"

"Two days ago. After hours."

"No alarm?"

"Malfunction."

"Bad timing."

Fremont removed his small, silver-rimmed glasses and began to clean the lenses with his tie. "The little bastards kicked in the back door and went berserk. I hope they rot in hell."

Carter nodded slowly, and then he asked the million dollar question. "Did you report the crime?"

"No, I didn't. I was too upset."

"But not too upset to file a claim."

"I wasn't thinking straight. Twenty thousand dollars is a lot of money."

"All the more reason to contact the police."

"What can I say? I made a mistake." He gave a slight shrug and added, "Live and learn."

Carter stared at him icily, and Fremont could feel his resentment, his bottled-up anger at the whole situation. Abruptly, he turned away and looked at Gold. "You gentlemen have an answer for everything. If

I didn't know better, I'd think you rehearsed your testimony." He stuck his nose up next to Gold's and said in a low, mean growl, "Never try to bullshit a bullshitter, son."

Gold stared at him, forcing his face to remain blank. "What are you implying?"

"I think that Teague broke those bowls. I don't know why, maybe he was trying to shake down a merchant. You show up, try to intercede, and things spin out of control. Sound plausible?"

"I'm not the hero type."

"Do you think I was born yesterday?"

"What was yesterday, Wednesday?"

Carter ignored Gold's flippancy. "Didn't you tell the responding officer that Mr. Fremont was holding the sword that killed Teague?"

"Yes, I believe that was part of my statement."

"That's exactly what you said."

"I'll take your word for it."

Carter laughed a nasty patronizing laugh. "Damn, that would make old Roger a bonafide hero. I can see the headlines now: Local merchant kills armed intruder. Good triumphs over evil! Courage saves the day!"

"I hope they spell our names correctly."

"I hate to rain on your parade, but you overlooked one minor detail. Your fingerprints were found on the handle of the sword. How do you explain that, Mr. Gold?"

"Well, let's see. Maybe that was because I was the one who pulled the blade out of Teague's chest. By the way, what sort of prints did you find?"

"Excuse me?'

"Latent, patent, or impressed?"

Carter shook his head and spoke with a weary tone. "All I know is that two sets of prints were found."

"Probably latent or patent."

"What's the different?" Fremont asked.

Gold looked at the chief. "May I?"

Carter looked back at him with contempt. "Be my guest, Mr. Hoover."

Unperturbed, Gold continued. "Latent prints are normally invisible to the naked eye. They're made by someone touching an object and leaving behind body secretions like oils and sweat. Patent prints are easy to see, and are made when a person touches a surface with a bloody or greasy finger."

Carter's assessment of Gold was improving by the minute, but he wasn't about to show it. "Hot damn," Carter said. "We've got a Junior G-Man in our midst! Why don't you tell your buddy where we send our prints?"

Gold, maintaining his calm demeanor, guessed that the prints were sent to IAFIS – the Integrated Automated Fingerprint Identification System. The system had been created in 1999, and relied on computer technology, eliminating the slow-moving crime labs that were previously used. Nowadays a request was handled in a matter of hours, which was reasonably impressive, considering the scope of the examination. A detailed report could identify a number of characteristics, including friction ridges, which were formed prior to birth, and the top and bottom layers, known as the stratum corneum and the stratum mucosum.

Since no two people in the world had identical prints, the reports were invaluable to law enforcement.

"What about identical twins?" Fremont asked. "Don't they have the same fingerprints?"

Chief Carter almost choked on his coffee. "Where the hell do you think you are, the police academy?"

Gold ignored the outburst, forging ahead. "I once handled a polyovulation claim. If I remember right, identical twins have identical DNA, but different fingerprints.

"Fascinating," Fremont said.

Carter's hand shot up, commanding silence. He was losing his patience with Gold. His ruddy complexion was turning even redder. If the truth be told, the chief was used to intimidating his guests. So much so that when people didn't shiver and quake, he became highly agitated, scaring them half to death. At least that's the way it usually worked. But every once in a while he ran up against someone who was capable of shrugging off his threats, conjecture, and pure bluster.

Maybe it was time to focus on the weaker link.

Carter glared at Fremont and said, "You look a little green around the gills."

Sweating, breathing hard, Fremont stared at the chief for the longest moment, then said, "Are we under arrest?"

"Wouldn't be the first time, would it, son?"

"No, sir."

"No indeed. You've been a bad boy. Your rap sheet shows two arrests for lewd and lascivious conduct. Prostitution and indecent exposure. My my, what do you think about that. Two felonies." He crossed his arms, and gave him a flat look. "You're not exactly a pillar of the community."

"I try to stay out of trouble."

"Trying and doing are two different things. Well, we're a tolerant bunch. We don't like to judge our fellow citizens." His face went blank for an instant before a broken smile flittered back. "Judge not, lest ye be judged."

Despite his nervousness, Fremont folded his arms stubbornly across his chest and said, "Nobody's perfect."

Carter let out a halfhearted chuckle. "That," he said, "is an understatement." He pulled a chair around the table and sat directly in front of Fremont. "I'd say you're about half-honest. Am I getting close?"

Fremont scratched at the corner of his mouth, a smile playing around his lips. "Too close."

Carter kept his cool. He slowly extended his thick index finger and pointed it at Fremont. "If you lie to me, I'll squash you like a bug. I don't believe you killed Tyrone Teague. Not for a moment. You're not the violent type." He glanced at Gold. "I think it was your partner in crime here. Am I right?"

"You read the report."

"Do I look like I just fell off the back of a turnip truck?"

Fremont scrunched his face in concentration for a second. "I'd rather not comment on your physical appearance."

Carter fixed him with a wary look. "You know something you're not telling me?"

"I know a lot of things I wouldn't tell you, but nothing about Teague's death."

"I don't believe you."

"That's your prerogative."

Carter lifted his shoulders in a small shrug. "Suit yourself. I hope you like this place." He gestured around them. "I've got a feeling you'll be seeing more of it." Fremont was undoubtedly lying, but lying for his own – probably very good – reasons. In any case, there was no use in beating a dead horse. They'd reached an impasse, and there was nothing that Carter could do or say that was going to change that. Still, he wasn't happy that the contest was ending in a draw. "I want you to remember something. Obstruction of justice is a serious crime."

Fremont and Gold's eyes locked in some kind of mutual understanding across the small space between them. It didn't last long, though. Both of them, realizing that they were about to walk free, restrained their enthusiasm. "So," Gold said, "are we free to go?"

Carter leaned back in his chair, his arms crossed, impatience etched on his face. "Yeah, you're free to go."

Gold theatrically used his finger to clean out his ear. "I'm sorry, chief. I thought I just heard you thank us for dropping by."

In his darker moments, which were much more frequent of late, Carter sometimes found himself wondering why he stayed on the force, what he'd done to deserve such abuse. Swallowing the profanity that was on his tongue, he thanked both of them for their time.

Gold smiled a little, sighed, and put a hand on Fremont's shoulder to nudge him along. "Nice meeting you chief."

Carter snorted. "Don't be a stranger."

CHAPTER SIXTEEN

The Anchor Insurance Company bristled with nervous energy. Gold could feel it the moment he walked into the lobby on Thursday morning, his first day back. Labor Day Weekend, the last three-day holiday of the summer, was just around the corner, and his colleagues were in a frenzy. The goal was to leave with a clean desk and a clear mind, so nobody bothered to greet him or inquire into his absence.

Upstairs, on the fifty-fifth floor, Irene Kaminski, the president of the company, was finishing a long distance call. She was speaking in English and German, and from what Gold could gather, she was trying to make a point about loss reserves. When she saw him standing in the doorway, her eyes widened slightly, but other than that her face registered no response. She waved him inside and mouthed, *Sit down.*

"So the numbers look good," Kaminski said, her eyes probing Gold's face. "Our reserves are where they need to be. *Ja, das ist akzeptables.* I'll call you next week. *Danke. Auf Wiederhoren.*" She hung up, then gave a small, defeated laugh. "Bean counters. They're all the same." She maintained her robust smile, but a touch of suspicion appeared in her eyes. She shook Gold's hand. "Welcome back. I'm glad to see you're still in one piece."

"I prefer it that way."

"You look beat."

Gold had slept poorly the night before, so fitfully that he had the impression he hadn't slept at all. He remembered lying awake in bed, watching the clock's numbers blink and change in the dark. At daybreak, he finally fell asleep, but by then it was time to get ready for work. "Did you miss me?"

"You've got some explaining to do."

"What else is new?"

Kaminski tried to maintain composure but could not. The red veins in her neck began to stick out, and she glared at him. "You're starting to give me gray hair."

Gold looked up, puzzled. He wasn't sure if Kaminski was serious. "Something wrong?"

"Yes, something's wrong. Something's always wrong. You just can't seem to stay out of trouble." She waved a manila folder in front of his face. "I read the autopsy report."

"Anybody I know?"

"Tyrone Teague."

"How'd you get that?"

"Ask and you shall receive." She paused for effect, then said, "You forgot to mention the swordplay."

"I didn't have time. I was trying to catch a flight."

"What happened?"

"I got a window seat."

She rolled her eyes toward the ceiling. "I don't care about your flight. Tell me about the trouble."

"There's not much to tell. Teague charged me when I was holding a sword. The next thing I know, the blade's in his chest and he's on the floor. He bled to death right in front of us."

"*Us* meaning you and Fremont?"

"Right."

"Terrible way to go."

"There are few good ways."

"So they say."

Kaminski's reaction to Teague's death seemed oddly detached. "What did the medical examiner have to say?"

The autopsy revealed that the sword blade had severed one of his coronary arteries before entering the left ventricle, the strongest chamber of the heart – the chamber that pumped oxygen-rich blood to the rest of the body.

Gold put on a sad smile. "I'm sorry it had to end that way. Teague was a bastard, but he didn't deserve to die."

"You didn't deserve what you got either. I've got news for you, mister. You're lucky to be alive."

"Yeah, I know."

"How'd you come to cross paths with that character?"

Gold filled her in on all that had occurred since his arrival in Charleston, including his meetings with Roger Fremont, Pearlie Gates, Teague, and Sungila Taylor. When he got to Sungila, he went on and on, singing her praises as if she were the best thing since sliced bread. Halfway through is dissertation he realized that he was going overboard with the compliments. He dropped his gaze, embarrassed. "In any case, she saved my life."

"She sounds like a remarkable woman."

"One of a kind."

"Attractive?"

"Somewhat."

"I thought so."

"Huh?"

"Love is blind."

"What's that supposed to mean?"

Kaminski was on her feet, leaning forward over his fists on the desk. "How did Teague know that you were back in Charleston?"

"I don't think he did know. He seemed surprised to see me."

"He just happened to be in the area?"

"He spends a lot of time in the city."

"Uh-huh."

Gold cleared his throat and did his professional best not to look annoyed. "What's your point?"

"You might be missing the big picture. Didn't I just hear you tell me that your pretty little nurse despised Teague?"

"Nobody liked him."

"But she also feared him."

"So?"

"What if she tipped him off?"

"Wait a minute. Are you saying that she told him where to find me?"

"It's a possibility."

Gold appeared to find her remark amusing. "Why would she do that?"

"Maybe she wanted you to do the dirty work. You know, get rid of Teague." She leaned forward across the desk, and her eyes got even bigger. "Think about it. She knew where you were going and when you'd be there. All she had to do was make one phone call."

Gold felt a surge of anger. "You're barking up the wrong tree."

"Maybe. Maybe not. I guess it doesn't matter. We should be grateful that Teague is out of the picture."

"You got that right."

She tossed the autopsy report on her desk. "Never look a gift horse in the mouth, isn't that what they say?"

Gold stared at her, surprised to find her face a mask, her gaze muted and dull. *What the hell just happened? What was that all about?* It suddenly occurred to him that she'd crossed the line emotionally, and now she was pulling back, regaining her composure. He waited a moment, then said, "Yeah, that's what they say."

"By the way, why was Teague using an alias?"

"He was trying to be clever."

"I don't understand."

Gold told her about the James Gang, but she still seemed puzzled. Choosing the name of an outlaw didn't make much sense to her. In truth, it didn't make much sense to Gold either. "Teague wasn't much of an outlaw, but his partner in crime might be a different story."

"What do you know about him?"

"Just his name and address."

"Well, that's a start."

"Fremont was kind enough to provide the information."

"How did you get him to talk?"

"I made him one of those offers you can't refuse."

Kaminski frowned. "I'm not sure what that means and something tells me I don't want to know." *Let he who is without sin cast the first stone.* She always liked that parable, and for some reason, it seemed appropriate. "So, tell me, who's playing the role of Jesse James?"

Gold dug his notebook out of a shirt pocket. "Jubal Morgan. Lexington, Kentucky."

"Lexington?"

"Bluegrass country."

"Yes, I know. Have you been there?"

"No, but I hear it's a lovely place."

"Send me a postcard."

Gold sighed. "When do you want me to leave?"

"Next week." She made a note of Morgan's name and address. "The sooner the better."

"What the rush?"

"Miss Scarlett is driving me crazy."

"Who?"

"Melanie Dupry. She calls every day, checking on the status of her claim. I explained the process to her, but she thinks we're stalling."

"Aren't we?"

"No, we're not. We're conducting a preliminary investigation, which is standard procedure. Do I have to remind you how this works?"

No, please don't, Gold thought. Wisely, he swallowed his words. "Would you like me to give her a call?"

"No, but I'd like to hear about your interview. Was she cooperative? Did she answer your questions?"

Gold glanced down for a moment, shifting his gaze away from her, lifting his attaché case and placing it on her desk. "Would you like to listen to the interview?"

Kaminski made a skeptical face. "You recorded it?"

"Every word."

"Did she know that she was being recorded?"

"I told her up front, and she gave me her blessing."

"She did? That's odd."

"Why do you say that?"

"Most insureds would be intimidated – or offended."

"She said she had nothing to hide."

"If I had a nickel for every time I heard that…"

"I know," Gold said. "You'd be a rich woman."

"A very rich woman."

"You're starting to sound like a claims investigator."

"Methinks the lady doth protest too little."

"Too little?"

"I get suspicious when an insured is so cooperative. Nine times out of ten, that's a bad sign."

"Whatever." He dug a digital audio recorder out of his case and checked the power, then turned it on and played the tape. They listened without comment, each lost in thought. When the tape ended, Gold said, "What do you think?"

"I don't know what to think."

"You look worried."

"There's a lot of money at stake."

"Did you hear something in her tone? Something you'd like to share?"

"No, but I've got a bad feeling about this woman. I don't like the way she presents herself – like she's some sort of debutante." After some deliberation, she added, "Maybe I'm being a little hard on her. She might have been irritable because of her mediation."

"What medication?"

"She mentioned something about Vicodin."

"Why is she on painkillers?"

"Broken arm."

Gold tilted his head and looked vaguely skeptical. "She broke her arm?"

"Compound fracture."

"Jesus, what happened?"

"She fell off a horse."

Gold's face was expressionless, but inside a sinking feeling had taken the bottom out of his stomach. Okay, this was getting weird. First she gets kicked in the leg, then she gets bitten on the hand, and now she's got a broken arm. How could anyone be so unlucky? The woman was riding for pleasure, not playing competitive polo. Something was wrong with this picture. What troubled him most was not the severity of her injuries, but the frequency of them – and the queer, unshakable feeling that they were caused by something other than horses.

Kaminski saw something in Gold's eye that troubled her. "Are you all right?"

Gold exhaled deeply. He looked drained. "Yeah, I'm fine."

"You look tired."

"I could use a long weekend."

"You're in luck. Labor Day is just around the corner." She walked around the desk, touching his shoulder in mute sympathy as she passed behind him. "Why don't you knock off early and get a head start?"

"I wanted to run a background check on Morgan."

"I can handle that. You run along and enjoy the weekend."

Gold raised his index finger and touched the side of his cheek, as if in deliberation. "Are you sure you don't mind?"

"Hey, that's why they pay me the big bucks."

"All right, I'll see you Tuesday morning."

"Any big plans?"

Gold took his time answering. "Believe it or not, I need to see a man about a horse."

CHAPTER SEVENTEEN

The next morning, Gold lingered in his study until ten o'clock before making his grand entrance in search of breakfast. The kitchen was empty, but somebody, presumably his wife, had made coffee and set out a platter of bagels, lox, and cream cheese. The food was a thoughtful gesture, intended for the man of the house. Gold scarcely had time to pour himself a cup of coffee before a familiar voice behind him said, "How much sleep do you need?"

Gold looked over his shoulder, smiling at the sight of his lifelong friend, Kevin McVey, now a security expert at the Department of Energy. "I wasn't sleeping. I was paying bills. When did you get here?"

McVey glanced at his watch. "Thirty minutes ago. Patty let me in, and I'm supposed to remind you to pick up some beer."

"See what happens when you marry an Irish girl."

"Watch it, Gold."

Gold held up his hands in mock innocence. "You got me wrong. I'm glad she likes beer. It's a hell of a lot cheaper than wine."

McVey came over to the table to shake Gold's hand. "You don't deserve such a good woman. Look at this spread. I never see anything like this at my house."

"Who asked you to live alone?"

"My ex-wife."

"Did she tell you not to remarry?"

"You think it's easy meeting women?"

"I don't seem to have any problems."

"That's because you pose no threat. You flirt with them, but you're like the dog that chases the car. The moment the car stops, you turn tail and run."

Gold rolled his eyes, wondering if he was just baiting him now. "I can be as threatening as the next guy. Remember Sally Ridge? And Sarah Kidd? I kissed both of them."

"Actually, they kissed you, and from what I recall, that's all they did." He sat and poured himself a cup of coffee. "Am I right, lover boy?"

Gold didn't answer. Instead, he pulled out a chair and sat, bringing his feet up on the chair across from him so he could lean forward, elbows on the table, chin resting on clenched fists. After what seemed like a long time, he said quietly, "I was hoping that you and Irene might get together."

"She's a wonderful woman, but…"

"Too set in her ways?"

"Something like that."

Not a big believer in sugarcoating, Gold said, "She's been on her own too long."

"I know the feeling." McVey regarded him with a smile. "We had a good time while it lasted."

"Well, that's something."

"You're lucky to have a boss like her."

"Yeah, she's a hell of lot better than you-know-who."

McVey frowned. "Let's not go down that road again."

They reminisced about good times, talked about the New York Yankees and the team's chances of winning another pennant. They also bemoaned the closing of Nathan's Famous, and agreed that losing the Oceanside location was a harbinger of doom. Through his second bite of bagel, Gold mumbled, "I love their hot dogs."

"Best damn French fries on the planet."

"Sixty years on Long Beach Road."

"Fifty-nine, but who's counting?"

"Damn shame."

"The country is going to hell in a handbasket."

Gold took a long sip of coffee from his mug trying to think of how to turn the conversation in another direction. He put his mug down, leaned back, and said, "Thanks for coming over."

"A friend in need..."

"How long have you been in town?"

"Two weeks."

"Long time."

"My parents are happy about it. I haven't seen them in a while."

"You could use a vacation."

"I'm not on vacation."

"You're not?"

"Try administrative leave."

Gold frowned. "What does that mean?"

"It means that my employer is investigating an allegation of misconduct, and that I'm on temporary leave, with pay and benefits intact."

"Jesus, Kevin, what happened?"

McVey stared at him in helpless frustration. Dammit, he had to tell Gold the truth. If he tried to be cute, his old friend's bullshit detector would go off. Sounding a little defeated, he said, "I stepped on somebody's toes."

"Somebody important?"

"The director of Interpol."

"*The head honcho?*"

"I don't mess around."

"Apparently not. Who's the director of Interpol?"

"A high-strung woman named Muriel Barbancourt."

"French?"

"Thoroughly."

"Well, that explains your predicament."

"Not quite."

Gold smiled with uncertainty and a trace of sadness. "What'd you do to piss her off?"

McVey drew a breath and let it out slowly. "I left France."

"A lot of people leave France."

"I was told to remain in the country."

Gold recoiled slightly. "What are you talking about?"

In spite of his natural wariness, McVey eased back in the chair and told Gold the truth – not the whole truth, but enough to explain his suspension. A high-ranking official from a well-respected organization had asked him not to leave Viviers, but her request had been ignored. In the aftermath, an inspector from Scotland Yard had been shot and killed, a criminal investigation had fallen apart, and a valuable tapestry had been lost. The French police – and Interpol – were livid, and in order to cover their own butts, they blamed American interference.

McVey reminded him that after the incident in Avignon, they drove down to Marseille, ditched their motorcycle, and went their separate ways. "I was anxious to get back to the states, but I should have stayed behind."

"Hold on one second," Gold said, getting his mind around the situation. "Why were you asked to remain in Viviers?"

McVey looked pained. "Long story."

Long story? Gold thought. Sounded like a polite way of telling him to mind his own business. He didn't want to push, but he was dying of curiosity. "Does this have anything to do with your trip to Corsica?"

McVey sat up, rigidly. His eyes flashed with annoyance. "No," he said solemnly, cutting him off. "But even it if did, I wouldn't tell you about it. You know that's against the rules."

A look of mock irritation crossed Gold's face. "I don't believe this crap. I tell you everything."

McVey almost smiled. "Then tell me why you wanted to see me."

"Okay," Gold said, under his breath. "I can take a hint." Scowling, he sat back and crossed his arms. "I need to pick your brain."

"What's up?"

"How many summers did you work at Belmont Race Track?"

"Three or four." He smiled with recollection. "That was a long time ago."

"What did you do there?"

"I worked as a stable hand. I cleaned out stables, fed the horses, and did some grooming. After a while, I was allowed to apply creams, ointments, and fly spray. I also did some hoof picking." He did a little drumroll on the table. "Are you looking for a part-time job?"

Gold disregarded McVey's question ad stared directly into his eyes. "Did you ever get bit?"

"By a horse?"

"No, by a jockey."

It took a moment for the sarcasm to register, and McVey chuckled. "Uh-oh, I sense trouble." He gave the question some thought, then said, "Yeah, I got nipped once or twice. Comes with the territory. Why do you ask?"

"Where were you bitten?"

"On the hand."

"Perfect."

"Huh?"

Gold pulled out his cell phone and showed McVey the photograph of Melanie Dupry's hand. "Does that look like a horse bite to you?"

McVey was no veterinarian, but it did not require a medical degree to tell that the marks were too small to be equine. He sat back, kneading his fists into his thighs. "I'm no expert, but those look human to me."

"I thought the same thing. Unfortunately, I have to be sure. Any ideas?"

"Show the photo to a forensic dentist."

"Do you know one?"

"Yeah, I know one. Sid Rubenstein. NYPD. We worked together when I was on the bomb squad. In my humble opinion, he's the best in the business."

"Do you think we could see him today?"

"*We?*"

"Got anything better to do?"

"I thought I might relax and enjoy the weekend."

Gold dismissed the idea with a wave of his hand. "You don't know how to relax."

"I could learn."

"You can't teach an old dog new tricks."

To Gold's surprise McVey laughed, hard and long. He had to wipe his eyes before attempting an answer. Something had tickled his funny bone. Finally, when he regained his composure, he said, "You crack me up."

"What's so funny?"

"You sound like my ex-wife."

"I do?"

"She used to say the same thing – about old dogs."

"Sorry about that."

"No problem. I told her that old dogs know plenty of tricks. That's how they manage to live so long."

"You might be right."

McVey poured himself another cup of coffee from a silver carafe. He didn't want to push too hard, but he was curious about the photograph. His instincts told him it had something to do with a claim, but there was only one way to find out if that was the case. He let the silence between them hang for a moment, then said, "Never a dull moment in your line of work." He searched for some encouragement in Gold's face, found none, and continued anyway. "Would you mind telling me what this is about?"

"I hate to burden you with my problems."

"I've got broad shoulders. Besides, I may have to explain things to your next of kin."

"Very funny."

"Who's joking?"

Gold shot him a dirty look, but went on to give him a blow-by-blow account of the preceding week. In typical fashion, McVey listened intently, taking it all in as his mind raced in a hundred different directions. After twenty minutes, they were both worn out, so Gold gave it a rest. "Why don't you call your friend and set up a meeting?"

"Would you mind if I finished my breakfast?"

"Take a bagel for the road."

"What's your hurry?"

"No hurry, I'm just ready to go. Do I seem anxious?"

McVey cursed, and ran a hand through his thick, prematurely gray hair before answering the question. "Don't take this the wrong way, but you're chomping at the bit."

CHAPTER EIGHTEEN

Forensic dentistry.

Now there is a strange occupation, Gold thought. The idea of examining a dead person's teeth made him gag, but it was an integral part of the criminal justice system, and often the only forensic science that could determine age, race, occupation, and socioeconomic status of unidentified human remains.

The identification process was crucial to criminal investigations, but it also played an important role in the application of civil law. The primary goals of forensic dentistry, or forensic odontology, included the proper handling, examination, and evaluation of dental evidence, which could later be used in a court of law. "Evidence" included teeth, bite marks, radiographs, photographs, and DNA.

Between bites, McVey explained the difficulty involved in becoming a forensic dentist. First, a person had to earn a Bachelor's degree from an accredited college or university. Undergraduate studies would ideally include pre-dental courses, such as pathology, anatomy, and physiology. After obtaining a degree in pre-dental studies, candidates were required to attend dental school, usually for an additional four years. Upon graduation, they had to pass a licensing exam, and after that, they were encouraged to work with a coroner's office or medical examiner. Finally, after a few years of hands-on experience, they had to obtain membership with their local governing forensic dentistry association.

Even jumping through all the hoops did not guarantee employment.

"Positions are few and far between," McVey said. "If you land a job with the NYPD, you've got it made."

"Job security?"

"And big bucks."

"How big?" Gold asked.

"Somewhere between $150,000 and $200,000 per year."

"Sweet."

"Sweeter than you think. Most dentists work as consultants, which means that they also have a private practice."

"So what's that worth, another hundred grand?"

"Depends on the practice. Some guys pull down half a mil a year."

"Damn, there's gold in them thar fillings."

"You can say that again."

Gold merged onto the Southern State Parkway, heading west, toward the borough of Brooklyn. They were on their way to Michael's, a legendary Italian restaurant in Marine Park. Dr. Rubenstein, who preferred to be called *El Sid*, had agreed to meet with them for the price of lunch. Between courses, he would be glad to answer their questions, and if the Chianti kept flowing, he would stay all afternoon. They were amused by the good doctor's terms and conditions, and they had to admit that he knew his dining spots.

"I've been to Michael's," Gold said. "Excellent pasta."

"The best in Brooklyn."

"El Sid a gourmet?"

"More of a gourmand."

"What's the difference?"

"A gourmet is a person who enjoys and appreciates fine food. A gourmand implies a tendency towards gluttony. Both however, are connoisseurs."

"*Merci*, Monsieur McVey."

"*Mon plaisir.*"

Gold sighed. "One trip to France and the guy thinks he's Jacques Pépin."

McVey threw his head back and grinned, obviously enjoying himself. "Take Exit 11N, Flatbush Avenue North. When you get to Avenue U, turn left, then turn right onto Gerritsen Avenue, and then left onto Avenue R. You got all that?"

"I don't speak French, but I understand English pretty well."

Situated on the corner of Avenue R and Nostrand Avenue, Michael's was an unimposing family-owned-and-operated restaurant, established in 1964, and considered one of the best Italian kitchen's in New York. The menu focused on traditional dishes and delectable pasta creations, both served in a comfortable, if dated, dining room.

El Sid was waiting for them at the bar, sipping a Campari and soda and nibbling on a bowl of pignoli nuts. McVey handled the introductions, and after a few minutes of small talk, they adjourned to a corner table. The restaurant was half-empty, but they still kept their voices down, which took some doing. Rubenstein was an extrovert, a man with a ready smile who enjoyed telling jokes, and he had a contagious laugh. He was on the short side, a bit overweight, but not beyond redemption. He wore glasses with tortoise shell frames that kept sliding down his nose, which required that he repeatedly push them back up with his thumb. When he finished his aperitif, he said, "Did you guys hear about the Indian guru who refused Novocain? He wanted to transcend dental medication!"

Gold laughed politely.

"Thanks for coming," McVey said. "Sorry about the short notice." He ordered a nice bottle of Chianti and asked for three glasses. "I owe you one, Sid."

Rubenstein nodded. "How are things at the Department of Energy?"

"Electrifying."

"Cute."

"You still putting the bite on taxpayers?"

"It's a dirty job, but somebody has to do it."

"Right."

Rubenstein told another joke, this one much longer, and by the time he delivered the punch line, the wine was on the table. The waiter poured three glasses and left, allowing them to make a quick toast before they got down to business. Eyeing them over the rim of his glass, the dentist could barely contain himself. "I was surprised to hear from you, Kevin. We haven't spoken in a while. Why did you want to see me?"

"I want to show you something," McVey said. He glanced sideways at Gold. "Show our friend Exhibit A."

Gold took out his iPhone and scrolled down to the photo he'd taken in Richmond – the shot of Melanie Dupry's hand. "What do you think, doc?"

Rubenstein glanced at the photograph. "Somebody got bit on the hand."

"Tell me something I don't know."

"Like what?"

"Does this look like a horse bite to you?"

Rubenstein adjusted his eyeglasses and took a closer look. "Definitely not."

"Are you sure?"

In response, Rubenstein ran a hand through his hair, then paused, unhurried, and took a long sip of wine. He studied Gold coolly, assessing him in one long take that seemed to last for minutes and that left Gold clueless as to what he concluded. "Allow me to explain." He told them that he'd originally intended to become a veterinarian, and had attended Cornell University, taking a number of courses related to equine care. Back then, injuries from horses resulted in roughly 100,000 emergency room visits per year. Only three to four percent of those injuries were due to bites. "In other words, getting bit by a horse is not a common occurrence. If it was common, there would be a lot of sick people. Humans can get a number of diseases from horse bites, some of them quite serious." The list included rabies, tetanus, rhodococcus equi, staphylococcus, and a host of viral infections. "I, er, hope I'm not ruining your appetite."

Gold managed a weak smile. "Of course not."

"Don't worry about us," McVey said. "We ate a late breakfast."

Rubenstein frowned. "You're not eating?"

"No, but you're our guest, so order what you want."

"If you say so." He ordered baked clams and then continued the equine seminar, telling them that at five years of age, a horse will have between 36 and 44 teeth. Most of the teeth will be four to five inches in length. Like humans, horses incurred some dental problems, mainly due to wear. Other problems included abscessed, loose, infected, or cracked teeth. "I'm not a vet, but I know a horse bite when I see one. What we have here is an entirely different type of animal – the most dangerous creature on earth – *homo sapiens*!"

So there you have it, Gold thought. Another complication. Something else to worry about.

"I figured as much," McVey said. "I've been bitten by a horse. I don't remember marks like those."

Rubenstein frowned again. "When were you bitten?"

"During my misspent youth. I had a summer job at the Belmont Race Track."

"Doing what?"

"Stable hand."

"You never told me about that."

"You never told me about Cornell."

"Excuse me," Gold said. "Let's get back to the bite marks. How do you know they're human?"

Rubenstein bristled, but kept his cool. He tore off a chunk of bread and politely asked Gold to pass the olive oil. "What did you say you do for a living?"

"Insurance."

"Salesman?"

"Investigator."

"Are you good at your job?"

Gold cleared his throat and glanced at McVey, who made a motion with his hand as if to say, "Answer the man." He thought it was an odd question, but he answered it just the same. "Yeah, I'm pretty good."

"Well, so am I." He put his hands on his hips and stuck out his chin. "In fact, I'm one of the best. Ask McVey and he'll tell you the same thing. I've handled a thousand cases, and I know a human bite when I see one. Hey, did you guys hear the joke about the walrus and the tooth fairy?"

They braced themselves for another bad joke, and that's exactly what they got. And this one was longer than the last one. While

Rubenstein droned on, the waiter hovered in the background, seen but not heard, fussing with a tablecloth, reorganizing the salt and pepper shakers, refolding the already immaculately folded linen napkins. Low conversation filled the restaurant. Servers glided back and forth between the kitchen and the dining room bearing huge plates of pasta. Finally, after five long minutes, the clams arrived and the comedy routine ended.

Silence ensued, and it was golden, but it didn't last long.

After the last clam went down, Rubenstein ordered a veal chop. He was about to tell another joke when Gold steered him back to the teeth marks. "I'm just curious. How can you be certain that they were made by a human being?"

Rubenstein sat back in his chair – one leg crossed over the other – a tan designer shoe dangling from his foot. His relaxation was so complete you could almost reach out and touch it. "Elementary my dear boy. Horses are herbivores. They eat grass, leaves, and all types of plants. They have different teeth than we do. Specifically more molars because they need flat teeth to grind branches, grasses, and seeds. Humans are omnivores, which means that we eat both plants and animals. Because we eat meat, we have sharp teeth, incisors and canines. Incisors cut and tear food. Canines do the same. Our teeth are unique, and they leave distinct impressions, depending on the pressure applied by the biter." He took a sip of wine, then added, "There are three types of impressions. Clear, obvious, and noticeable. Significant pressure, medium pressure, and violent pressure. Your photograph leaves a lot to be desired, but I'd classify it as an obvious impression."

Gold was tempted to tell him that *he* was making a good impression, but he was afraid it would lead to another long joke. "Can you tell if the biter was male or female?"

"If you look close, you'll see that the bite has caused an avulsion and contusion. The removal of skin and a bruise. In my opinion, that suggests that the victim was bitten by a male, but that's only a guess." He leaned farther back and leveled his gaze at Gold, waiting for the impact of his words to kick in. He didn't have to draw the picture any more clearly. "In general, men have larger tooth crowns and heavier third molars and canines. Still, it's very difficult to determine if someone is male or female based solely upon teeth marks. I just have a hunch that somebody lost their temper and became violent."

Gold smiled nervously and, not knowing how to respond, said, "You might be right. Our victim has incurred a number of injuries. Three, to be exact. I'm starting to wonder about the company she keeps."

Rubenstein's demeanor seemed to change. He became more somber. "Are you suggesting an abusive relationship?"

Gold nodded, but just barely. The thought made him cringe, but it was certainly a possibility. A third of all injuries to women requiring emergency room treatment were a direct result of abuse by a male partner. As they all knew, domestic violence against women had become one of America's most critical health issues. Every year, between two and four million American women were assaulted by their male partners, and sadly, over two thousand were killed.

Nobody felt like talking – or even thinking – about a creep who was biting women, but since the evidence was in front of them, they had to address one other issue. A skin break, like the one in the photograph, increased the risk of infection, and in Rubenstein's view, it made it necessary for the victim to get a tetanus booster.

"Do you know the victim?" Rubenstein asked.

Gold nodded again. "She's one of our insureds."

"You should tell her to get a shot."

"Do you really think that's necessary?"

"I certainly do. Infection can occur even in properly treated bites." Some of the signs were obvious, and some were not. He mentioned the most common, which were pain and tenderness, redness, swelling, fever and pus drainage. "Did you notice any of these?"

"No."

"Well, that's good news."

"I suppose so."

"I think she dodged a bullet."

"I hope so."

"She might not get so lucky next time."

From past experience, Gold knew that "a next time" was likely. The recidivism rate of domestic abuse was somewhere between fifty and eighty percent, depending on a number of factors. What he didn't know, but would soon discover, was just how bad Melanie Dupry's situation had become.

CHAPTER NINETEEN

Gold left Michael's Restaurant in a fog, sorting out the sordid details provided by the great El Sid. Watching the dentist devour a veal chop had been a real treat, reminiscent of the velociraptors scene in *Jurassic Park*. Lots of biting, chewing, and gnawing on bone. Not a pretty sight. On reflection, Gold realized that he'd been thinking about Melanie Dupry the whole time. He kept envisioning the nasty bite on her hand, and he found it hard to believe that a woman like her would put up with such abuse. She seemed so confident and strong. Was it all just an act?

McVey leaned over and tapped him on shoulder. "You're going the wrong way."

"Huh?"

"You turned west."

"We're not going back to Long Island."

"Where are we going?"

"Manhattan."

"Why are we going to the city?"

"I need to speak to someone."

"Haven't you had enough conversation for one day?"

"I'm a glutton for punishment."

"Two gluttons in one afternoon. What are the odds?"

"Do you have something better to do?"

"I could be spending time with my parents."

Gold dismissed McVey's answer with a wave of his hand. "You could be watching *Dancing With The Stars*."

McVey smiled. "Who we going to see?"

"Sammy Wong. Victor Wong's niece."

"*Niece?*"

"Her real name is Samantha. She works for the MIB."

"Men In Black?

Gold sighed. "Medical Information Bureau."

"What's that?"

Speaking slowly and choosing his words carefully, Gold described the MIB as a cooperative data exchange, created by the insurance industry to provide underwriting details about an applicant's medical history. Upon request, medical reports were given to insurance companies, in order to help them assess risk of life and health insurance coverage. A typical MIB report was limited to brief descriptions of specific medical conditions that might impact an applicant's health or longevity. The database only contained information on individuals who had previously applied for heath, life, disability, critical illness, and long-term care insurance.

Because of its penchant for secrecy – and its use of secret code – the MIB was the subject of much speculation. In actuality, the cooperative was created to provide fraud protection to insurers, and individuals could obtain a free copy of their consumer file at any time.

McVey had a pretty good idea why they were making a detour, but there was no sense guessing about the mission. "Whose file do you want to see?"

"Melanie Dupry."

"I thought so."

"I know what you're thinking."

"You do?"

"You're thinking that this has something to do with that damsel in distress nonsense."

"Well, now that you mention it…"

Gold cut him off, trying to explain that his actions were about more than playing the knight in shining armor. Sure, he wanted to help a battered woman, but he also had a hunch that by helping her he would be helping his employer. There was a remote possibility that her claim and her abuse were somehow related, and if that were the case, it made perfect sense to pursue the matter.

McVey had a better idea. Instead of running around like a chicken with its head off, Gold should take advantage of their friendship. "Why don't I lend you a hand?"

"You've done enough."

"Two heads are better than one."

Gold was silent for a moment, considering the offer. He had to admit that it would be nice to have someone watching his back. "What do you know about grave robbers?"

"Not much, but I know something about graves."

"No doubt you've filled a few."

McVey grinned. "I'm not referring to my distinguished military career. When I was on the bomb squad, the NYPD had some special maps. We knew the location of every cemetery in the city, and we knew where all the bodies were buried. Some were in places you wouldn't expect."

"I'm listening."

McVey knew that he was "talking out of school," but since it was Gold, he didn't care. The two of them had shared many secrets in the past, and by comparison, this one was small potatoes. "What do you think Bryant Park, Central Park, and Washington Square Park all have in common?"

"Are you serious?"

"Deadly serious."

"They were all cemeteries?"

"Every one of them."

"Jesus, I never knew that."

McVey told him that New York City began forbidding burials south of Canal Street in 1832. In 1851, burials below 86th Street were outlawed. Washington Square Park had once served as the city's potter's field, and to this day, it contained the graves of some 20,000 people – most of them victims of a yellow-fever plague.

Prisoners from a nearby prison, who were hanged from the park's trees, were also buried there.

"My goodness," Gold said. "You certainly know your cemeteries."

"Do I get the job?"

"The position is yours."

"Let's hope it remains vertical."

"Huh?"

"My position."

The home office of the MIB was located in Massachusetts, but they also had a branch office in Greenwich Village – three blocks north of Washington Square Park. Samantha Wong, known to her friends as Sammy, was the office manager and the only person who had carte blanche authority to access the database. In order to gain her cooperation, Gold had to convince her that he wasn't on a fishing expedition, and that he had no intention of sharing the information. Accordingly, he went out of his way to assure her that he was acting as a Good Samaritan and would never betray her trust.

"I'm sorry," Gold said. "I know I'm putting you in an awkward situation, but this might come down to a matter of life or death."

"That serious?" she asked.

"I'm afraid so."

Sammy Wong had known Gold for a long time – ever since her college days – and she knew he was a man of his word. A man who could be trusted. Still, it was not easy to hand him the keys to the kingdom. There were over 15 million files in her database, and in her mind, that represented 15 million possible lawsuits.

Oddly enough, it was McVey, a complete stranger, who nudged her over the line. He took out his identification and placed it in front of her. "You'd be doing both of us a big favor."

"You're a federal agent?" she asked.

"Security specialist. Department of Energy."

"I'd feel better about doing this if the request came from you."

"Consider it done."

An official-sounding request was all that she needed to spring into action. They looked on in amazement as she flew through a series of steps and gained access to the database. When she turned the computer toward them, they saw that the screen was filled with 3-digit numbers.

"Abracadabra," she said with a smile. "The Rosetta Stone of underwriting."

Gold leaned forward, staring at the screen. "Are those the secret codes?"

"Most of them."

"How many are there?"

"Two hundred and thirty."

"What do they represent?" McVey asked.

"Mainly medical conditions," Wong said. She told them that the codes that appear most frequently were the ones that indicated high blood pressure, asthma, diabetes, and depression. Other codes, seen less often, indicated smoking and participation in high-risk sports. After some gentle prodding, she admitted that there were some "special codes" that signified criminal activity, drug use, and sexual deviation. Almost as an afterthought, she added, "We do not collect, maintain, or store any medical records. There are no examination reports, attending physician statements, lab test results, x-rays, or underwriting files. Our members simply receive medical and avocation codes, which may or may not have some underwriting significance."

"How do we get started?" Gold asked.

"All I need is a name."

"Melanie Dupry."

She typed in the name, followed a few links, and waited for the computer to work its magic. In less than thirty seconds they had a full profile. "Who is this woman?"

"One of our insureds."

"Too bad."

Gold frowned. "Why do you say that?"

"She's been a naughty girl."

"How so?"

She enlarged four of the codes, allowing them to see the numbers clearly. The first code indicated that she was involved in some sort of high-risk sport. "Unfortunately, there are not footnotes, so I can't tell you what type of sport."

"I can tell you," Gold said. "Horseback riding."

"Equine activity." She gave it some thought, then said, "Yes, that would certainly qualify as high-risk."

"She's been injured a number of times."

"Well, that might explain the second code." She hesitated, choosing her words carefully. "Sustained drug use."

"*Sustained drug use?*"

"Over a decade."

"What sort of drugs?"

"Pain medication." She pointed to an asterisk. "The sub-codes show prescriptions for Vicodin, OxyContin, Neurontin, and Motrin. I don't know exactly what's wrong with her, but she seems to be in constant pain."

Gold glanced at McVey and said, under his breath, "I know the feeling."

"Do you know the nature of her injuries?" McVey asked.

"A few of them. Bruised leg, horse bite, and broken arm."

"Unlucky gal."

"Very unlucky."

"Too unlucky," Gold said.

"Uncle Victor likes to say that people make their own luck."

"Your uncle likes to say a lot of things."

She managed a weak smile in return, a smile that abruptly vanished when she turned back to the screen. "The last two codes are the most troubling. The first one indicates sexual deviation. I have to admit, it's not very common."

Gold gave her a dubious look. "What the hell is that?"

"The MIB defines sexual deviation as behavior that is not morally, biologically, or legally sanctioned by society."

Sounding a little frustrated, Gold said, "That covers a lot of ground."

"Including masochism," McVey said.

"*Masochism?*"

"Pleasure in being abused or dominated. A taste for suffering."

Gold managed a hollow laugh, even as the sense of despair he felt grew stronger. "I'm familiar with the term."

"Something to consider."

Wong cut in, pushing her chair between them. "I'm not suggesting that she's masochistic, but there's a reason for the code. Maybe she's into something else. Do you know anything about her private life?"

"Not a lot, but I know that she was married to a man who was gay. They got divorced after he came out. Could that explain the code?"

"I don't think so."

"What about the last code?" McVey said. "What's the deal with that?"

The question, though inevitable, caught her off guard, and from the look on her face, it was obvious that she was reluctant to give them more bad news. "Keep in mind," she said at last, "some of these codes might be old and no longer applicable."

"We'll keep that in mind," Gold said. "What's the story?"

"911 is another one of our special codes."

"What does it indicate?"

She looked away and said, "Criminal activity."

CHATPER TWENTY

There's an old saying in the insurance industry: An executive is one who hires others to do what he – or she – is hired to do. While truer words were never spoken, Irene Kaminski was an exception to the rule, one of those rare leaders who didn't mind getting down and dirty. Delegating authority was not her strong suit, and in order to keep up her energy level, she ate healthy and exercised regularly. Her exercise regime included jogging, weight training, and Taekwondo.

In Korean, *tae* means "to strike or break with the foot"; *kwon* means "to strike or break with the fist"; and *do* means "way of life." Ergo, Kaminski's way of life included the ability to strike or break things with her foot and fist – a skill whose implications were not lost on her colleagues and subordinates.

A smart person, like Gold, never kept the boss waiting. Wise move, considering that the boss had recently earned a second degree black belt and was now a *gyosannim* – instructor – at the Red Dragon Martial Arts Studio on Fulton Street.

Promotion from one rank, or *dan*, to the next could take years, especially for a female. Much to her credit, Kaminski had broken through the glass ceiling – and a whole lot of boards – in rapid fashion. She was said to possess *In-Nae*, perseverance and patience. In fact, those two traits were always on display, inside the *dojang* and out in the real world.

When she saw Gold, she bowed, then waved him inside the classroom. "Good morning. How was your weekend?"

"Not long enough. And yours?"

"Productive."

"There's a surprise."

She began to pace back and forth, full of energy. "Guess what I did?"

"Broke some boards?"

"Made some calls."

"Sounds exciting."

She couldn't contain herself. "I contacted the Kentucky State Police. Spoke to a Colonel Smith in Frankfort. I got quite an earful regarding Jubal Morgan." She pulled him off to the side and lowered her voice. "He's currently under investigation for a number of crimes."

"What sort of crimes?"

"Arson, insurance fraud, racketeering, and animal cruelty – all related to thoroughbred horses."

Again with the horses? Gold thought. The sport of kings was beginning to look a lot less noble – and a lot more shady – than he'd ever imagined. This new revelation reminded him of the past cases he'd read about, insurance fraud claims in which expensive horses, most of them show jumpers, were insured against death, accident, or disease, and then killed to collect the insurance money. Well, he thought, if a person could stoop to robbing a grave, he was capable of almost anything.

"Did you tell the police about our claim?" Gold asked.

"Yes, and I sent them a copy of our file."

"Good. Maybe they can help us nail this son of a bitch."

"Maybe we can help them, too."

Gold cocked an eyebrow. "What did you have in mind?"

"An undercover assignment. I want you to fly out to Lexington and pose as a horse buyer. You can go to an auction and mingle with the racing elite. While you're there, you'll be introduced to Morgan by an undercover officer from the Kentucky State Police. Befriend Morgan and offer to so some business together. Maybe he'll get greedy and try to sell you a Civil War artifact."

Gold smiled. "I like the way you think. But how do we get him to the auction?"

"Easy. All you have to do is go to the right one."

Before he could ask what she meant, she told him about the September yearling sale at Keeneland, located in the heart of Kentucky's famed Bluegrass region. For twelve days each September, horse racing's elite gathered in Lexington to bid on yearling Thoroughbreds – a young horse of either sex that was between one and two years old. As the world's leading Thoroughbred auction house, Keeneland had sold more champions and stakes winners than any other company in history, and they also operated a race track, hosting some of the most important races in America.

The yearling sale attracted the attention of buyers, sellers, trainers, and agents – and it was bound to attract the attention of a bottom feeder like Morgan.

Colonel Smith had assured her that Morgan – and a slew of other miscreants – would be lurking around the auction, hoping to turn a fast buck. There were certainly a lot of bucks to turn. The results of the previous September sale were mind-boggling: In the twelve days of the event, over 2,000 horses were sold, generating about 200 million dollars – or roughly 17 million dollars per day.

Gold allowed doubt to creep into his voice. "Seventeen million per day?"

"You heard right."

"No wonder they call it the sport of kings. Only a person who owns a country could afford a Thoroughbred."

"So it seems."

Gold laughed unpleasantly. "We've got one other problem."

"What's that?"

"I know very little about race horses."

"You could learn."

"I've got a better idea. Why don't we hire a consultant?"

"A consultant?"

"Somebody to show me the ropes."

"Who did you have in mind?"

"A guy who plays the ponies."

"Victor Wong?"

"Victor's on vacation. I was thinking of Kevin McVey."

"McVey?"

"He used to work at a race track. He still likes to place a wager now and then. I could pick his brain and learn a thing or two about the sport." He leant closer, as if someone might be listening. "It wouldn't hurt to have a federal agent by my side."

She gave it some thought, surprised to learn that McVey was a gambler. She'd never seen that side of him. Then again, there were many sides she hadn't seen. "Do you think he'd be willing to help us?"

"If we made it worth his while."

"What about his other job?"

"He's a free agent. Comes and goes as he pleases." Gold paused for a moment, then said, "You know those cloak and dagger types. They like to moonlight."

Kaminski wasn't sure why, but she began to blush. "All right," she whispered. "Give him a call. Set something up. I'll leave your tickets with my secretary."

"Might be wise to fly first class."

"Excuse me?"

"Horse buyers don't fly coach."

She jabbed him with a finger. "Don't push your luck."

"Just saying."

"By the way, you need to rearm yourself."

"You want me to bring a gun?"

"Jubal Morgan is a dangerous man. A lot more dangerous than I thought. According to Colonel Smith, he's been in trouble with the law his entire life." She held his gaze for a moment, then licked her lips nervously. "He also spent some time in a psychiatric hospital."

"Uh-oh, the plot thickens."

"The poor lad had a troubled childhood."

"How troubled?"

"He was diagnosed with an impulse-control disorder. He had a compulsion to set fires."

Gold, clearly shaken, took a deep breath. "He was a child pyromaniac?"

"The worst kind. Some children start fires just to find out what will happen. Others start fires because of a pathological reason. Apparently Morgan was physically and verbally abused by his parents. He set fires to relieve tension."

"Jesus, he sounds like Anthony Cardone."

"Who's that?"

"Just some creep I used to know. He, uh, died before you took over."

She stepped a little closer. "Colonel Smith can't prove it, but he thinks that Morgan set the fire that killed his parents."

"They were killed in a house fire?"

"They died in their sleep. Smoke inhalation. Morgan and his sister survived. They were separated and sent to live with relatives."

"I guess he didn't live happily ever after."

"Not by a long shot. He's currently under investigation for arson, but not for burning down a house. They think he set fire to a stable."

"A *stable?*"

"Seven thoroughbreds were burned alive, including a stakes winner."

"Jesus, that's awful."

"Awfully sick, if you ask me."

"The fire is probably connected to insurance fraud."

"You guessed it."

"Those bastards never learn."

"They think they can get away with murder."

Gold reminded her that sometimes they did get away with murder – for a while. He was referring to the infamous horse murder scandal, crimes that took place between 1970 and 1990, when close to 100 horses were killed to collect the insurance money. The scandal was one of the most gruesome stories in racing, and the biggest insurance scam in the history of equestrian sports. All told, 55 people were indicted and convicted of insurance fraud, mail and wire fraud, obstruction of justice, extortion, racketeering, and animal cruelty.

In addition, the candy heiress Helen Brach disappeared and was presumed to have been murdered by the perpetrators of these crimes.

When Kaminski was reminded of that, she grew even more somber. "Maybe you should bring two guns."

"I'll be careful."

"I've heard that before."

"Why so worried?"

"I've dealt with equine fraud. I know how dangerous those criminals can be. They're greedy, ruthless, and unspeakably cruel." Years before, she told him, she'd insured a stud farm in Slovenia. The farm raised Lipizzan stallions, the famous show horses associated with the Spanish riding School in Vienna, Austria. The Lipizzan breed had survived World War I and World War II, but in 1983 a viral epidemic threatened a large breeding stock. In Piber, Austria, forty horses and eight percent of the expected foal crop were lost before the epidemic was brought under control. During those dark days, an unscrupulous breeder in Slovenia killed several stallions, claiming that they had died from the virus. A subsequent investigation uncovered the ugly truth – the horses had been electrocuted. "I was the claims examiner who discovered the truth."

After a moment of silence, Gold found his voice. "The horses were electrocuted?"

"Killed for the insurance money."

"Damn, that's cold."

"Barbaric would be a better word."

"I thought those bastards used drugs."

Kaminski stiffened, her voice grave, her eyes seeming to moisten. "Allow me to explain." She told him that some horse murderers used intravenous injection, typically a very high dose of pentobarbital or sodium thiopental. The problem with this method was the time and money it took, and the risk of leaving a paper trail. Electrocution was much easier, less costly, and difficult to detect. "Our insured simply sliced an extension cord down the middle into two strands of wire. Then he attached a pair of alligator clips to the bare end of each wire. One clip was fastened to the stallion's ear, the other to its rectum." Her eyes reddened, and she wiped at them angrily. "All he had to do then was plug the cord into a wall socket and step aside. Somewhere between 220 and 240 volts shot through the horse, carrying enough current to stop the heart."

Distressed by her pain, Gold pulled her close to him, but even as he did so he felt awkward. He could feel her breasts against his chest, firm and full, and her soft waist, and the heat of her body. "Think of it this way. Now it's payback time."

She leaned sideways to reach for a bottle of water, and her cleavage opened wide. Gold's eyes crawled right in. He couldn't help it, and she didn't seem to mind. "What do they say about payback?"

"They say it's a bitch."

"Speaking of...I got another call from Miss Scarlett."

"Melanie Dupry?"

"She left two messages."

Figuring that the time was right, Gold told her about his meetings with Sid Rubenstein and Samantha Wong. He held nothing back, including his own opinion of the situation. Her reaction surprised him. Instead of commending him, she pulled back and frowned. "Idle hands are the devil's workshop."

"Something wrong?"

"Just puzzled."

"About what?"

"Why are you so concerned about Miss Dupry's welfare?"

"Her welfare and ours might be connected."

"How so?"

"I'm not sure, but I think she's hiding something."

"Another hunch?"

"What can I say? Women have intuition and men get hunches."

Kaminski sighed. "Let's hope she doesn't turn your head."

"Not a chance.""

"I've heard that before, too."

Gold winked at her. "Haven't you heard that gentlemen prefer blondes?"

CHAPTER TWENTY-ONE

Gold had a lot to learn about Thoroughbred horses, but as usual, he was pressed for time. McVey suggested that they spend an afternoon at Belmont Park, the perfect venue for a crash course on racing. Belmont had first opened in 1905, and was located in Elmont, New York, on the western edge of Long Island. The facility featured Thoroughbred racing throughout May and June, and into late July. In September and October, it hosted the Fall Championship, which attracted thousands of spectators and was almost as popular as its most famous event – The Belmont Stakes.

First held in 1866, the Belmont was known as the third leg of the Triple Crown, the most prestigious accomplishment in Thoroughbred racing. Horses that were good enough to win the Kentucky Derby and the Preakness Stakes usually entered the Belmont Stakes, but there were no guarantees of winning. Only eleven horses had won the Triple Crown since 1919.

McVey thought it would be a good idea to sit in the Garden Terrace Dining Room, a lively restaurant on the fourth floor of the Clubhouse.

The restaurant offered an excellent view of the entire racetrack, and two essential amenities – air conditioning and cold beer.

A ten-dollar tip got them a window table, and a tip about the fifth race. "Silver Ridge," whispered the maître d'. "The going is good and he'll finish in the money."

When the man walked away, Gold said, "What was that?"

"A tout."

"Maybe we should place a bet."

McVey smiled. "You've got a lot to learn."

"He must know what he's talking about."

"Yeah, that's why he's working here. Ready for school?"

Gold heaved a great sigh. "How long is this going to take?"

"Depends on your outlook."

"My outlook."

"How long to do want to stay alive?"

"What's that supposed to mean?"

There was no trace of levity in him when he leaned in and said "You're about to walk into the lion's den. If I were you, I'd prepare myself. The more you know, the better your chances."

Gold settled back in the padded leather seat, and smiled a bit sheepishly. "Carry on, professor."

McVey purchased a copy of the *Daily Racing Form* and told him that they had about an hour before post time – the first race of the afternoon. During that time, he would try to pick a few winners and explain the basics of horse racing. He began by stating that there was a scholarly side to handicapping. Bettors with a mathematical bent chose their picks by the numbers, studying speed figures and track variants. Others relied on genetics, focusing on pedigrees and breeding. Some even studied video reruns, trying to spot a troubled horse or one that was underrated.

"In other words," McVey said, "it's not just about luck."

"There's a method to the madness."

"Exactly. You have to be able to recognize early speed, quitters, and closers."

"How hard could that be?"

Another smile. "The first race is a maiden race for three-year-old colts. The distance is six furlongs, or three-quarters of a mile."

"Just a moment," Gold said. "How can a colt run in a maiden race? I thought colts were young male horses."

"The word 'maiden' has nothing to do with the sex of a horse. It simply means that none of the horses running have ever won a race before."

"Must be tough to pick a winner."

"Hence the term 'gambling'."

Gold ordered two beers. "Are we gonna place a bet?"

"Nope."

"Why not?"

"I don't see a horse that I like."

"All ten are bad?"

"No, but there's no clear favorite."

"What about Kingdom Come?"

McVey shook his head. "He likes to spit the bit."

"We can't have that."

"No sense wasting money."

"What's wrong with Barbara's Boy?"

"He's a shipper. He travels from track to track. Tires easily."

"He's standing in a horse trailer. How tired can he be?"

"Merry Wing is a fair runner, but the jockey's bug boy."

"What the hell is that?"

"An apprentice."

"Always something."

After wetting his throat, McVey explained – or tried to explain – the pari-mutuel betting system and the meaning and purpose of a claiming race. He wasn't sure how much Gold understood, but he plowed ahead, into the wonderous world of wagering terms. He defined Win, Place and Show, then offered a simple explanation of the Daily Double, an Exacta, and a Trifecta. "Any questions?"

"Just one. Shouldn't we focus on horses, rather than betting?"

"The two go hand in hand." He placed a pair of binoculars on the table. "Racing has its own vocabulary, and if you want to stay in one piece, I suggest you learn the language."

The language of the track included a number of colorful terms, as well as some words that sounded similar but had entirely different meanings. The most obvious were frontstretch, backstretch, and homestretch.

Gold was amused by the jargon. "That's a lot of stretching."

"You'd better learn the difference."

"Yes, sir."

"When you get to Lexington, you're bound to hear some talk about conformation. Are you familiar with that term?"

"Isn't that a Catholic ritual?"

"You're thinking of confirmation."

"I figured it was a long shot."

McVey shook his head. "I thought you played CYO baseball."

"I did."

"Didn't you learn anything?"

"Yeah, I learned not to curse in front of a priest."

McVey chugged his beer, then belched in his fist. "You're driving me to drink."

"You don't need a chauffeur."

"You want another beer?"

"Not yet."

From the corner of his eye McVey could see the waiter studying him uncertainly. He signaled for another round, then returned to the subject at hand. "Conformation is the word that's used to describe how a horse is built physically. The art of picking a horse out at auction has everything to do with determining which physical characteristics will have an impact on the horse's ability to race. What' I'm trying to say is that a legitimate buyer will know what to look for. If you want to come across as real, you need to know what to look for, too."

"Should I take notes?"

"No, but try to concentrate."

McVey told him that the "average" Thoroughbred stood 16 hands tall and weighed 1,000 pounds. A hand was four inches, and horses were measured up to their withers. Conformation began with balance, correct proportions in the neck, back, and hip. The head came second, and a smart buyer looked for eyes that were big and intelligent. Ideally, the nostrils would also be big and the ears alert, pointing, and moving in all directions.

"Should I check the mouth?" Gold asked.

"Do you want to lose a finger?"

"Just thought I'd ask."

"When you get to the auction, take your time and study the horses carefully. Don't be afraid to ask questions, and most importantly, don't forget to take a side view of the animal. Keen-eyed buyers always take a side view. Pretend that you have a mental checklist, and study the feet, ankles, knees, legs, shoulders, and neck." He took a sip of beer, then added, "A pro would also take a front view and rear view."

"What's the rule about touching?"

"Look but don't touch – unless you're given permission."

"Where am I supposed to stand?"

"Either side, but never behind."

"Do Thoroughbreds kick?"

"All horses kick. Of course, some are more combative than others. Stallions are the most aggressive and will sometimes bite. Fillies are the most temperamental. Geldings are usually well behaved, but a little detached."

"What's a gelding?"

"A castrated horse."

"No wonder they feel detached."

McVey gave him a forced smile. He spoke slowly, hoping it would help Gold keep up with the flow of information. "A majority of stallions are castrated, and for good reason. You see, some horses are like people. They get easily distracted by females, they can be difficult to handle, and they don't run to their full potential due to behavioral issues. A gelding won't have these problems."

Gold laughed nervously. "Don't get any ideas."

Looking through his binoculars, McVey surveyed the track and then checked his watch. Thirty minutes to post time. "You'd be smart to keep your eyes on the prize."

"What prize?"

"The claim you're investigating."

"What do you think I'm doing?"

McVey lowered the binoculars and looked directly at Gold, amused by the puzzled look on his face. "I think you've gotten off track – no pun intended."

"What do you mean?"

"You seem to be more concerned about the claimant than the claim."

"Ah, Miss Dupry. The belle of the ball. You think I might be smitten?"

"Wouldn't be the first time."

Gold had been accused of many things in his time, but being a fool for love wasn't one of them. "You needn't worry. Melanie Dupry is just another pretty face. I'm only trying to kill two birds with one stone."

"I hope that's the case."

"You're starting to sound like Kaminski."

"She's worried, too?"

"Worried, angry, and a little bit jealous."

"Why is she angry?"

"Dupry keeps calling, demanding that we pay the claim. Irene doesn't like to be pushed. She's starting to smell a rat."

"Irene's got a good nose for that sort of thing."

Gold nodded. "Irene's got a lot of good parts."

"Yes, I've noticed."

"I'm sure you have."

McVey looked down, smiling. "She also has a temper."

"And a black belt."

"Bad combination. Dupry should watch her step."

"Hell hath no fury like a woman scammed."

"Or scorned."

"Amen, brother."

McVey sat back with his fingers laced behind his neck and stared at the crowd that was gathering below. "Do you really think she's jealous?"

Gold had been asking himself that same question. "She pulled the same routine when I told her about Sungila Taylor."

"Huh. Maybe she's hormonal."

"You know Irene. She's very controlling. It's a German thing."

"She's Austrian."

"Whatever."

"If I were you, I'd mind my Ps and Qs."

"I might do that, if I knew what they were. What the hell are Ps and Qs?"

"I have no idea. I thought you would know."

"No clue."

"Well, if you don't know what they are, then you don't have to mind them."

"I'm glad that's settled."

McVey glanced at his watch again. "Almost post time."

Gold reached for the binoculars and looked at a group of horses that were standing in the paddock. He noticed that several wore bandages. When he asked about that, McVey told him that with the advent of year-round racing, most horses were over-raced and, despite anti-inflammatory medications, suffered from chronic soreness and a variety of infirmities. He went on to explain that there were two kinds of bandages – rundowns and front wraps. Rundowns were usually small and wrapped tight around the back ankles. They were meant to protect a horse's ankles from the bottom of sloppy or sandy tracks. Front wraps, as the name implied, went around the front legs and often indicated some sort of weakness in a tendon or ligament.

"You won't see any bandages at the auction," McVey said. "None of those horses have been on a track."

"Haven't they been in training?"

"Some of them, but if they had a problem they wouldn't be at the auction."

There was something else on Gold's mind, an unpleasant subject that had come up during his meeting with Irene Kaminski. The subject of painkillers. He was wondering if they were allowed, and if so, which ones were used. There was only one way to find out. He lowered his voice, just a notch. "Which drugs are legal?"

McVey told him that the list varied from state to state, but most states allowed Lasix, phenylbutazone, and corticosteroids. These were used to alleviate bleeding in the lungs, reduce inflammation, and diminish pain.

There were a long list of illegal drugs, some of them habit forming and most of them still in use. Back in the bad old days, some trainers actually injected their horses with heroin.

"Hard to fathom," McVey said. "But that's why heroin is known as 'horse.' Before you ask, it's no longer used."

"Too expensive?"

"Too easy to detect. Keep in mind that every horse that wins a race is tested. They take blood and urine samples. If they find anything that's banned, the horse is disqualified."

"Any punishment?"

"Depends on what they find. If a trainer uses something like dermorphin, a Class 1 drug, they could be looking at a fine and suspension. The racing commission determines the penalty."

Gold rubbed his chin in a thoughtful fashion. "What's dermorphin?"

McVey smiled. "Remember the time you were shot with a blow gun?"

"How could I forget it?"

"The arrow was dipped in curare, which grows wild in Central America and South America."

"So?"

"Dermorphin is found in the skin of a South American frog. It happens to be 30-40 times more potent than morphine, but less likely to become addictive."

"Horses can become addicted to drugs?"

"Absolutely."

Gold adjusted the binoculars and followed the horses from the paddock to the track, watching the post parade and then the warm-up jog . One by one each horse jogged down the backstretch, stopping at the first turn, and then walking back to the starting gate. Like human athletes, they were a little stiff at first, but after some gentle exercise they were ready to run.

The tote board favored a Bay-colored horse, but Gold was drawn to a gray-colored stallion that was listed as a long shot in *The Racing Form*. He was 16 hands tall and carried himself in a regal manner, trotting past the grandstand with his head held high. Both front legs were bandaged, but Gold decided to play a hunch and put some money on him. Not a huge bet, but enough to pay for their day at the track.

"I'll be right back," Gold said. "Get me another beer."

McVey frowned. "Where are you going?"

"To place a bet."

"Save your money."

"I've got a hunch."

"Ah, yes, the famous gut feeling. Who do you like?"

"Number seven – the gray horse."

"What's his name?"

Gold stood motionless for a moment, then said, "Kentucky Bound."

CHAPTER TWENTY-TWO

Jubal Morgan, alias Jesse James, finished his complimentary breakfast and then went outside to smoke a cigarette. The Rhett House Inn did not permit guests to smoke indoors, and that was fine with him. There was too much chatter in the breakfast room anyway. Outside, on the veranda, he could be alone with his thoughts and enjoy the view of Waterfront Park.

The Rhett House Inn was right out of the set of *Gone with the Wind*, something a person would expect to find on the cover of *Southern Living* magazine. The white, Greek revival mansion was nearly 200 years old, originally the home of the Rhett family, who lived there until the Civil War. Thomas Rhett, the family patriarch, built the 6,000-square-foot mansion with a two-story wrap-around piazza overlooking the Beaufort River. During the war, the home served as a hospital recovery building, and after surviving the Great Hurricane of 1896, it changed hands several times before becoming one of the best bed-and-breakfast hotels in South Carolina.

Staring across the manicured grounds of the park, Morgan could have passed for a tourist, although in truth he was a man on a mission. He'd recently learned that his business partner – Tyrone Teague – had been killed during an attempted robbery. First he would attend his friend's funeral, and then he would track down the scumbag who killed the only man he'd ever trusted.

Lost in thought, Morgan almost forgot that he had to be at Eddings Point Cemetery at nine o'clock.

In less than thirty minutes, Tyrone Teague would be laid to rest on St. Helena Island.

Gone but not forgotten.

Not by a long shot.

Raynelle Teague, the mother of the deceased, had given Morgan the bad news over the phone, imploring him to come to St. Helena Island as soon as possible. By tradition, Gullah bodies were quickly interred, the actual burial beginning with a drum beat to inform people that someone in town had died. Mirrors were turned to the wall so the corpse could not be reflected. When the family was together, a funeral party conveyed the body to the cemetery, pausing at the gate to ask permission of the ancestors to enter.

Morgan arrived just in time to witness the "breaking of the chain," a graveside ritual in which participants danced around the grave, singing and praying, before smashing bottles and dishes over the site. The clutter piled up quickly, but it was part of a longstanding tradition meant to ensure that no one else in the same family would soon die.

Morgan stood in the shadow of an ancient black oak, waiting for the ceremony to end. After a while, the mourners began to drift away, allowing Raynelle Teague to grieve in private. When she finally stopped crying, Morgan walked over and sat beside her, patting her hand in a show of sympathy. There was a short silence, then he turned to her, his voice barely a whisper, and said, "I'm sorry for your loss, Mother Teague."

Though she answered in a small voice, the Gullah accent was unmistakable. "I know'd you come, mistuh Morgan. I know'um in my heart that you would come. Tyrone was your fr'en'."

"I came as quickly as I could."

"Yes, I know dat."

Morgan, his mouth set tight, let a long, slow breath out through his nose. "Tyrone was more than a friend, Mother Teague. He was like a brother to me. I loved him very much."

She fixed him with a sorrowful look. "He was my only chil'."

Showing a hint of anger, Morgan leaned closer and said, "And my only real friend."

She rubbed her chin thoughtfully for a moment, then said, "You was the best man at his wedd'n'."

"Yes, ma'am."

"You kept my boy out of trouble."

"Well, I gave it my best shot. Tyrone was a good man. He always tried to do the right thing."

That assessment made her smile. But not for long. "Some folks talk'um mean about my boy. They say dat Tyrone was a tief." She made a dismissive gesture with her hand. "Let he b'dout sin cast dat fus' stone."

"Amen, Mother Teague."

"Ain't nobody perfect."

Morgan nodded and tried out a comforting smile on her. "Tyrone hit a few bumps, but he tried his best. In the end, that's all a man can do."

"Praise the Lord, Brudduh Jubal. I b'leew hat he was on the path to Salvation."

"No question about it."

Another little smile. "I'm so glad you comeyuh. I'm so 'fraid to be alone."

This was going to be difficult, but manageable, as Morgan had expected. "You're not alone. I'm staying at the Rhett House in Beaufort. I'll be around if you need to talk."

She sat with her arms crossed over her chest, her eyes focused on the freshly dug grave, now covered with dirt. From time to time she'd draw a breath, then sigh. There was resignation in her weathered face, but no anger. "You know dat twenty-third psalm?"

Morgan's mouth tightened in concentration. "I, uh, seem to have forgotten the words."

"You a churchgoing man?"

"Yes, ma'am, but I can't think straight today."

Mrs. Teague bought that excuse, but then she went on to recite the entire psalm, sobbing as she spoke. "The Lord is my shepherd," she repeated at the end. "What a comforting thought."

Morgan couldn't keep the emotion out of his voice. "I remember the first time we met. I was selling cars and trucks at a Ford dealership in Atlanta. Tyrone had just been drafted by the Falcons, and he was anxious to spend some of the money that was burning a hole in his pocket. Well, he decides to buy a new pickup, but when he sees the price, he gets sticker shock. Thirty thousand for a truck? That's highway robbery!" He felt the impulse to laugh, but resisted it. "We spent about an hour haggling over the price, but we finally reached an agreement. You know Tyrone, though. He always had to have the last word. After he signed on the dotted line, he told me that when he was a boy, his momma would send him down to the corner store with a dollar and he'd come back with five potatoes, two loaves of bread, three bottles of milk, a hunk of cheese, and a dozen eggs. I didn't believe it, but I told him that you couldn't do that nowadays. He agreed. He said there were too many security cameras!"

Mrs. Teague lowered her voice to an all-but-inaudible whisper. "That's my boy. Always makin' jokes."

They sat in silence for several minutes. Morgan felt emotionally drained. Part of him wanted to go back to the hotel and get drunk. But there was work to be done. A score to settle. He put his arm around Mrs. Teague and said, "Tell me what happened, Mother Teague. How did Tyrone die?"

"They kill my baby boy."

"Who killed him?"

"Two mens in Chaa'stun. The police say it was self-defense, but I know'um it was murder."

"How do you know that?"

"'Cause I know my boy. Tyrone would nebbuh rob no store. He wasn't raised that way."

Morgan pulled himself up straight in his chair, his attention now riveted. "They told you he robbed a store?"

"Dat what the report say."

"The police report?"

"Yes, suh." She reached into her handbag and pulled out a wrinkled sheet of paper. "You can read it for yoself." She handed him the paper. "They wrote it all out. But it ain't nutt'n' but a pack of lies."

Morgan read the report slowly, noting the day, date, and time of the incident. Anguish crossed his face when he read the details of how Teague had met his end. He continued reading, shocked to learn that the long, steel blade had severed a coronary artery before piercing the left ventricle of the heart. Due to the severity of the wound, Teague never had a chance of surviving, and had, in essence, drowned in his own blood.

For a long moment, Morgan said nothing, and it was clear he was turning things over in his mind. Finally he lit a cigarette, leaned back, and exhaled. He tilted his face skyward and took in the warmth of the sun. His mind raced, but he kept his thoughts to himself. A long time passed. Finally he said, "I don't get it."

"Get what?" she asked.

"Why the report was redacted."

Mrs. Teague didn't respond, just sat there staring at the grave. Then ever so slowly, her eyes went to Morgan and stayed there. "Redacted? What dat mean?"

"They removed some important details. I don't see the name of the store, the owner's name, or the name of the person or persons who killed Tyrone."

"Don't matter. That report ain't nuttin' but a pack a lies."

Morgan sighed. "Maybe the case is under investigation."

"I already know the trute."

He tried a smile that mostly failed. "Something's not right with this picture."

"Dey can't fool me. I wasn't born yistiddy. I know who killed my boy. The witch done'um!"

"The *witch*?"

"Dat daa'k-hearted debble'ub'uh a woman who lives on the salt pond. She the one dat killed Tyrone! I know she done it!"

Keeping his voice under control, Morgan took a drag on his cigarette, then said, "Calm down, Mother Teague. Too hot to get overexcited."

"You mark my words. Dat witch put a hex on my boy!"

Morgan cleared his throat and frowned. "Does this witch have a name?"

"Sungila Taylor."

"Why would she put a hex on Tryone?"

"She say he stole from the Gullah. Took things from the graves of the dead. Dat girl the daa'tuh of the debble himself!"

For the briefest moment there was no response. Then, as if visited by a revelation, Morgan's eyes sharpened, his shoulders came back, and he sat upright once again. "Wait a minute. I think Tyrone mentioned her. Is she the one who works at the Penn Center?"

"One and the same."

"Tyrone said she was a troublemaker."

"She make nothin' but trouble."

"Yeah, that's what I heard."

For a long moment, her eyes glazed over and she sat utterly still. Finally, a small tremor passed through her body, she blinked, and a tear ran down her cheek. She looked at Morgan, her lip quivering. "She conjured up the Boo Hag, and dat creetuh got after my poor chil'. Dat be the God's honest trute."

Morgan's eyebrows went up in surprise. He knew that the oldtimers believed in witchcraft, which they called *wudu*, *wanga*, or *juju*, but he'd forgotten about their obsession with evil spirits. Thinking back, he remembered that Teague had once told him that many of the Gullah papered the walls of their houses with newsprint or put a folded sheet of newspaper inside a shoe, believing that an evil spirit must read each and every word before taking action. The custom was derived from the common West African practice of wearing a protective amulet containing a written passage from the Koran.

Morgan didn't buy any of the mumbo jumbo associated with black magic, but he thought it might be worthwhile to have a little chat with Sungila Taylor. Maybe she knew something about Teague's death, but if nothing else, it would be fun to slap her around for badmouthing his friend. "How do I get to Taylor's place?"

She looked at him in the long, contemplative, deliberate way Morgan had noted before in many of the older Gullah. "Why do you want to know that?"

"I'd like to pay her a visit."

Her mouth tightened, the lips conveying a mild distaste. *"Pay her a visit?"*

"She might know something about Tyrone's death. Something the cops don't want you to know. For instance, the name of the store."

She squirmed a little, reached up and pinched her ear as she thought about it. "Oh, Lord, she's a 'ceitful woman. A bad cullud person. If I were you, I'd keep my distance."

"I'm not afraid of her."

"Well, you should be. She might put a hex on you, too."

"I'll take my chances."

Mrs. Teague stopped protesting, sat a moment, and thought about it. She reluctantly gave him directions, but insisted on adding a caveat. "Be careful and watch what you drink. She brews up some wicked potions. I hear she turned a Yankee feller into a frog!"

Morgan filled his lungs with smoke and exhaled. All this talk about hexes and witches was far beyond his tolerance level. He calmly folded the police report and gave it back to her. A thought occurred to him. "The man was a Yankee?"

"So they say."

"Hmm, big improvement."

CHAPTER TWENTY-THREE

Saint Helena Island has a land area of about 64 square miles, and is surrounded by expansive marshes, particularly along the eastern side of the island. Due to the flat terrain, there is only a handful of orientation points, making it easy to get lost. When Morgan drove out of the cemetery, he made a wrong turn and found himself in unfamiliar territory. He turned around and tried to find his way back, but soon was on a winding road he'd never been on before. He began to wonder if he was going around in a huge circle. He stopped beside a fruit stand and asked a Gullah farmer for directions to the Penn Center, a well known landmark close to Sungila Taylor's house.

Finally, after ten more minutes of driving, he found US-21, and from there, it was only a short drive to his final destination. Pulling off the main road, he gazed out at the salt pond – a gray, unreflecting sheet, like a mirror of his own dark soul. It was forbidding, but at the same time curiously mesmerizing.

A man could easily get lost out here, he thought.

So could a body.

Morgan thought about that for a while. Never look a gift horse in the mouth, he told himself. If Sungila Taylor gave him a hard time, and he had to get rough, he would dump her body in the pond. Nobody would think of looking there, but even if they dredged the pond, there wouldn't be a lot left to find. The crabs would see to that.

Lighting up, he studied the property carefully, planning his next move. He was tense with anticipation. His eyes, clear and penetrating, searched for the best entrance and exit points. There was intrigue here – maybe she would know something about Teague's death he didn't, or at least something that could help.

Truth was, the police report was almost worthless. It was plain to see the cops had redacted it because they were still investigating the case. An ongoing investigation could mean a number of things, but to Morgan it meant that the authorities weren't buying the story they were told. Long familiar with how the game was played, he figured that the witnesses had been questioned, and now the cops were running down leads and examining the forensic evidence.

In all likelihood, the cops had produced a half-assed report simply to placate the victim's family. Under normal circumstances the stalling tactic might have worked, but the cops had forgotten to redact the part about the sword, a very important clue as to the identity of the person claiming self-defense.

How many merchants would defend themselves with a sword?

Who keeps a sword at their place of work?

What type of store did Teague try to rob?

Shit, Morgan was thinking. *Maybe it was an antique store.* That possibility hadn't occurred to him. Now it made perfect sense. He felt his stomach go hollow. He caught his breath, cleared his throat, tried to retain his composure. He would come back to that later. Right now he had to focus on the job at hand. He stepped out of his car and walked toward the salt pond, dawdling like a tourist admiring the view. For a full five minutes he stood on a footpath leaning against a tree, hands thrust deep in his pockets, listening to the sounds of nature.

For a moment, his thoughts drifted back to the antique store, then he remembered why he was there.

It suddenly occurred to him that he could probably just walk up the front steps and kick in the door, right this minute, and locate the lady of the house without much trouble. The idea sent a shiver through him, thinking how easy it would be to tie her up and rape her, but he rejected the impulse. He didn't come all this way to just screw some broad. Maybe later, after he got what he wanted, there would be time for fun and games.

But not right now.

Now it was time to go to work.

After fishing out another cigarette and lighting it, Morgan exhaled a cloud of smoke, then calmly walked toward the house. When he knocked on the front door, a woman's voice told him to meet her in the backyard.

Morgan was cautious, not knowing what to expect. When he saw Sungila, his mouth fell open and he smiled. It took a moment to get his tongue in gear. "Sungila Taylor?"

Barefoot, pant legs rolled up, tight T-shirt untucked, and looking as fresh as a daisy, she folded her arms across her chest and stared at him. "How can I help you?"

Morgan studied her, comparing the actual person to the image he had formed. He had pictured an unattractive woman with a hairy mole and a large nose. The woman standing in front of him was young and beautiful, and devoid of any witchlike features. Flashing the smile he relied on to disarm, he whipped out a fake badge. "Lieutenant Mannion. Charleston Police Department."

She hesitantly offered her hand. "Nice to meet you, lieutenant."

"I'm sorry to barge in like this, but I need to ask you a few questions."

She was quiet for a moment. "What's on your mind?"

"The usual mayhem. I'm working on a high profile case. A homicide investigation. You might have read about it in *The Post and Courier*. A black man, named Tyrone Teague, was recently killed by a white merchant. Some folks think the killing was racially motivated. Others say it was self-defense. It's my job to uncover the truth, and I sure could use some help." He forced another smile. "I, uh, understand that you work at the Penn Center."

"Yes, that's right."

"What do you do there?"

"Museum docent."

"What is that, a tour guide?"

"Similar."

"How long have you worked there?"

"Seven years."

"Hmm, you must know everyone on the island."

"Eight thousand people live on this island."

Morgan, smoke pouring from his nostrils, said, "How many played for the Atlanta Falcons?"

A tiny smile appeared on Sungila's face. "Are you asking if I knew Tyrone Teague?"

"Yeah, I suppose so."

"He lived a few miles from here."

"You don't seem surprised by his death."

"I'm surprised that he lived as long as he did."

"Do I detect a note of hostility?"

"The man was a worthless son of a bitch. Ask around. Nobody liked him."

"Why don't you tell me how you really feel?"

She chuckled contemptuously. "I don't usually speak ill of the dead, but in Teague's case I'll make an exception. The man was no good. He was a bully, a cheat, a liar, and a grave robber."

Morgan stared at her for a long moment. She quickly grew uncomfortable. "Those are serious allegations."

"Those are proven facts."

He wiped his mouth with the back of a beefy hand and said, "I knew that Teague had a record, but I had no idea that he was a grave robber."

"The worst kind."

"What do you mean?"

"He robbed the graves of his own ancestors."

"You gotta be kidding me."

"Last summer, Teague and his buddy, a man who introduced himself as Robert Freeman, came to the Penn Center and tried to sell us some stolen Gullah artifacts."

Morgan was digesting this, but not comfortably. "Did you report them to the police?"

"No, but I should have. By the way, Freeman's real name is Roger Fremont. He operates an antique store in your neck of the woods."

Morgan felt hairs bristle on his arms and neck. "How do you know his real name?"

"I have my sources."

He laughed derisively. "I'd like to know who they are."

She didn't feel comfortable mentioning Gold's name, so she told him a little white lie. "I found Fremont's card in the parking lot."

"Lucky find."

She lowered her voice to an all-but-inaudible whisper. "Was Fremont the one who killed Teague?"

"I'm not at liberty to discuss the details on our investigation."

"I understand. You need to dot the i's and cross the t's. Is that it?"

"Something like that. Did you ever run into Fremont and Teague again?"

"No, but after I threw them out, things went from bad to worse. Teague began to harass and threaten me. I told him to back off, but he wouldn't listen to reason. I finally had to teach him a lesson."

"What did you do?"

Sungila's face showed something like sympathy. "I put a hex on him."

"A *hex*?"

"A magic spell."

"Yeah, I know what it means. Do you think that was nice?"

"He had it coming."

"If you say so."

"I wasn't going to mention it, but he almost killed a friend of mine." She told him about Adam Gold, without mentioning Gold's name – or the fact that he'd spent the night under her roof. Her story was received with mounting irritation. "My friend is lucky to be alive."

Morgan leaned forward and with a suave smile said, "Your friend have a name?"

"I'd rather not say."

Another smile. "We have ways of making you talk."

"I'm afraid I'll have to invoke the doctor-patient privilege."

"Are you a doctor?"

"No, but I practice folk medicine, and my friend was a patient. I was the one who provided emergency care. If not for me, the police would be investigating another murder."

"Why would Teague want to kill your friend?"

"Maybe you should ask Roger Fremont that question."

"I intend to."

"While you're at it, ask him if he intends to stop robbing graves."

"I've made a mental note."

"Good. The last thing we need on St. Helena Island are a bunch of grave-robbing ghouls."

Morgan almost groaned out loud. "Teague had his faults, but I wouldn't refer to him as a ghoul."

"Are you serious? The man was a monster. I'm glad he's dead, and I hope he rots in hell."

Morgan's face went a shade darker. "Tyrone Teague was far from perfect, but he was still a human being. Still somebody's son. Someone's friend. It wouldn't hurt to show a little remorse."

"*Remorse?*" Her eyebrows furrowed in puzzlement. "Surely you jest. If I had the time, I'd throw a party."

Morgan let that register for a moment before saying anything. "You really did hate him, didn't you?"

"More than you can imagine."

"Mrs. Teague was right about you."

"I beg your pardon?"

"You're nothing but a cold-hearted bitch."

Sungila stood silent and motionless, starting at Morgan, trying not to look offended, but knowing she wasn't pulling it off. She suddenly responded in anger. "How dare you talk to me like that!"

Morgan let out a humorless laugh. "What are you going to do, file a complaint?"

"I might just do that."

"I doubt it, sweetie. Sounds like you're too busy casting spells."

Sungila decided she had had enough. Holding up a palm, she said, "I'd like you to leave."

Morgan watched Sungila's eyes grow large and fearful as she processed what he'd said. There was now a growing look of panic in them. "Just one more question." He stepped closer, much too close for comfort. "How deep is that salt pond?"

"I…I wouldn't know."

"Take a guess."

"I'm not in the mood for games, lieutenant."

"Are you in the mood for love?"

"What the hell is wrong with you? Have you lost –"

She never finished the sentence. Morgan's fist brought it to a premature conclusion. Sungila fell to her knees, her hand pressed against her face, tears in her eyes. Morgan punched her again, this time on the side of her head. The blow knocked her unconscious, but only for a couple of minutes. When she regained consciousness, Morgan clamped his hand over her mouth and told her to keep still. She bit down on his palm.

"Owww!" Morgan shouted. "You bit my fucking hand!" He shoved a clump of grass in her mouth and pushed her lips together. She began to gasp for air and choke. He pulled himself directly on top of her and pinned her shoulders to the ground. Sungila thrashed her head and twisted back and forth, but he maintained his grip. "Stop squirming, bitch!"

Sungila mumbled something incomprehensible, and then tried to butt her head into his face. She was too slow, and the next thing she knew his thick fingers were around her neck. He began to squeeze her windpipe. She managed a muffled scream, but a moment later her eyes began to flutter and she drifted toward death.

The last thing she saw was her killer's face, but it registered not the faintest hint of emotion.

Nothing.

CHAPTER TWENTY-FOUR

It was almost midnight by the time Morgan pulled up in front of The Gender Bender. Although the lights were still on inside, there were only four cars parked in the lot. And just as Morgan had hoped, one of them was Roger Fremont's Mercedes. Outside, a summer storm was abating, the thunder and lightning fading in the distance, the rain little more than a drizzle. A light mist still hung over Charleston Harbor, but it seemed to be moving east, toward the ocean.

Morgan made a mental note of the street signs and traffic lights, then drove into the lot, parking directly behind Fremont's vehicle. After checking the time, he extracted a silencer from his overnight bag, fitted it over the barrel of a pistol, and screwed it tight. He had no intention of using the weapon – unless he had to – but it was better to be safe than sorry.

Keeping an eye on the front door, his thoughts began to drift on a stream of consciousness. For the next thirty minutes, he sat there, on autopilot, reminiscing about the good old days with Tyrone Teague. They had raised a lot of cain together, and for a while, it seemed like the party would never end. But looks can be deceiving. For some strange reason, Teague had decided to rob a store, and now he was dead. What in the world had come over him? Why rob a fucking store when they were on the verge of a big payday?

Goddamnit, Morgan thought. None of this made a lick of sense. He shook his head as if trying to free a jumbled thought. *Que sera, sera,* he told himself. Whatever will be, will be. There was no use crying over spilled blood.

All he could do now was even the score.

Morgan was about to light a cigarette when three people staggered out of The Gender Bender walking arm in arm down the street toward the parking lot. They were self-absorbed, laughing, half-dancing to the music that could still be heard inside the club. When they reached the lot, they exchanged hugs and kisses, and then two of the men drove off together, leaving their older companion to fend for himself.

Morgan got out of his car and walked up behind the man, watching him fumble for the key fob, then struggling to find the entry button. The man was having trouble standing erect, and the darkness wasn't helping.

Losing patience, the man slapped his free hand on the roof of the car, baring his teeth in a snarl. "Where the fuck is that button!"

Morgan took a moment deciding whether or not he should laugh, finally deciding against it. "Good evening," he whispered. "Having a problem?"

Roger Fremont dropped his head, lifted it, shrugged. "Too fuckin' dark."

"Let me give you a hand." In one swift move, Morgan grabbed the keys and found the right button. "There you go, Roger."

Fremont felt hairs bristle on his arms and neck. He recognized the voice and even in his present condition, he knew he was in trouble. He stood still for a moment, breathing hard, fighting down panic. When he turned around and saw Morgan's face, waves of dizziness and nausea nearly buckled his knees. He kept his head down, waiting it out, trying to keep calm. Fear made his mouth go dry. He slumped in despair, then said, "Jesus Christ, what are you doing here?"

Morgan jammed a cigarette into a corner of his mouth, but he didn't light it. He glared at Fremont, then glanced around to make sure they were alone. "What's wrong, Roger? You look like you've seen a ghost."

"I ... didn't know you were in town."

"One of those last-minute things."

"When did you get here?"

"Yesterday."

"You should have called. We could have gone out."

Morgan put his finger to his lips, signaling Fremont to lower his voice. "I wasn't in the mood to celebrate."

"Something wrong?"

"Yeah, I'm afraid so."

"What's up?"

Morgan shook his head, almost in admiration. Fremont was a good actor, even when he was drunk. "You know why I'm here?"

Fremont was shaking, his face dead white, breath coming in short gasps. "I ... I guess you want a status report."

"A *status report*?" The light died out of his face. "What the fuck are you talking about?"

"General Jackson's arm? I should have brought you up to date." He tried to sound upbeat, but the news didn't lend itself much to that. "The company hasn't paid the claim. I think they're stalling for time."

Bristling, Morgan said, "I don't give a shit about the money. I've got more important things on my mind."

"More important than half a million dollars?"

"There are some things money can't buy."

"I can't really think of any."

"That's because you're a blind motherfucker."

Careful, Fremont warned himself. Don't get the man angry. He breathed deeply and felt a thick knot in his stomach. "So what brings you to Charleston?"

"I came to say goodbye to a friend."

Fremont's heart did a little flip in his chest. He'd already had one heart attack – a few years before – and though this was a different type of pain, he placed his hand over his chest and sucked in a quick breath. "I … I guess you heard the news."

Morgan's scowl deepened, his voice grew harsh. "What news, Roger?"

Fremont was thinking as fast as he could, trying to find a way to give Morgan as little information as possible. He gave him a garbled version of the incident, sounding confused, and at times, incoherent. "I should have called you, but I've been eating my heart out."

Morgan smiled coldly. "I can tell you're heartbroken."

Fremont opened his mouth, but no words came out. Rather, tears began to roll down his cheeks. He didn't try to stop them. "I was afraid to contact you. Afraid you wouldn't understand. I know how close you were. I swear to God, Teague's death was an accident."

"And accidents happen, right, Roger?"

"All the time."

Morgan rolled his eyes at Fremont as if to say, "What kind of fool do you think I am?" He would have burst out laughing if the situation wasn't so serious. "You and I need to have a little chat."

Fremont watched Morgan's face, already hard, turn to stone. The eyes narrowed, the lips went tight, the jaw muscles began to quiver.

He'd seen that look before, and it scared the hell out of him. "Jubal, please, don't hurt me. It wasn't my fault. I was just a bystander."

Morgan forced another smile. He didn't feel remotely friendly. "Take it easy," he said. "You're shaking like a leaf. I just want to ask a few questions. Why don't we go to your place?"

"My place?"

"We can make some coffee and talk."

Fremont forced himself to some semblance of calm. "You … just want to talk? You promise?"

"I give you my word."

Fremont took a deep breath and decided to hold his tongue. "All right," he said at last. "I could use some coffee." He turned to leave. "Follow me."

In a heartbeat, Morgan was on top of him, his forearm pulled tight across his windpipe, cutting off his air supply. Fremont cried out in surprise, then struggled wildly.

Morgan strengthened his grip. Fremont's chest heaved as he fought for air. Morgan shifted his pressure to the carotid arteries on either side of Fremont's neck, shutting off the blood flow to the brain. Fremont thrashed and kicked, but to no avail. Morgan maintained his hold until Fremont passed out, blue in the face, but still alive.

Now came the hard part.

Dragging a limp body into his rental car.

When that chore was done, he got in, put the key in the ignition, and started the car.

Jesus Christ, he thought. *I'm getting too old for this shit.* He eased himself all the way back into his seat and slumped down low. Eyes closed, he massaged his temples. Finally, he opened his eyes. "Damn," he said out loud. "There's gotta be an easier way to skin a cat."

When Fremont awoke, he was lying face up, staring at the sky. The sun was just coming up and there were streaks of orange and yellow mixed with the blue. He wasn't sure where he was, he only knew he was not in Charleston. He touched his face; it felt tender and raw. Swollen, too. He rolled to one side, broadcasting pains up and down his spine. Never mind, he thought to himself. Maybe I'll just lie here for a while.

He wrestled with his next move for another minute or two. Finally, he turned his head to one side, and out of the corner of his eye, he saw that his left ankle was tethered to a stake. He tried to lift his foot, but a metal chain held it in place. "Good god," he muttered. "What the hell is going on?"

Morgan sidled up next to him on the grass and leaned close enough for Fremont to smell the bourbon on him, among other odors. "Good morning, Roger. Sleep well?"

"Jubal," Fremont said, tension creeping into his voice as he pronounced his name firmly. "You promised not to hurt me. You gave me your word."

"Stop whining, you fat piece of shit. You're lucky I didn't put a bullet in your ear."

As Morgan inched toward him, scrutinizing him closely, Fremont's skin began to crawl. Morgan came closer and closer, until he was just a foot away. Fremont watched him in silence, wariness gathering inside him.

A pall of impending doom settled over Fremont. He could almost hear himself saying, I *told you not to trust him*. He made a fist with one hand to stop the tremor. "Where are we?" he asked.

Morgan sighed deeply, and turned his wrist a little so he could see his watch. Seven on the nose. Plenty of time to chat. "We're in lovely Calhoun County. Just outside of Columbia." Columbia was 114 miles from Charleston, smack in the middle of the state. "Teague bought this place. Don't ask me why. Too remote for my taste. What do you think?"

"I think you're scaring me. Why the hell did you bring me here?"

"I thought you might like to get out of town for a while. Take in some fresh air. Enjoy the peace and quiet." A nasty little smile turned one corner of his mouth. "It seemed like a good idea at the time."

Fremont was agitated and confused, but he forced himself to remain calm. "Why am I chained down?"

Morgan was silent for a moment, hoping the hesitation would send a message to Fremont that he was looking to obtain information, not distribute it. "I thought you homos were into bondage?"

Fremont's mouth twitched, and he didn't respond, but he kept staring at Morgan. After a long thirty seconds, he said, "Please don't talk like that. I hate when you say ugly things."

"You think that's ugly? I'll show you ugly." Morgan's left hand came up, a small knife in it. He held it against Fremont's throat and said, "If you don't tell me what happened to Teague – what *really* happened – I'm going to cut you from ear to ear."

Fremont took a deep, steadying breath, and his voice emerged in a hoarse whisper. "I didn't kill him. I swear to God I didn't."

Morgan's voice was ice. "Who did?"

"A man named Gold."

"*Who?*"

"Adam Gold. He's a claims investigator. He works for the Anchor Insurance Company."

Morgan scoffed and shook his head. "Why would he want to kill Teague?"

"He didn't set out to kill him – it was an accident. They got into an argument and Teague tried to tackle him. Gold was holding a sword – a Civil War relic – and it ended up in Teague's chest. We lied to the police to make it look like robbery. I didn't want to do it, but Gold forced me to play along."

Morgan showed neither belief nor disbelief. He pulled back the blade and thought about it. He never believed that Fremont had killed Teague, and now he was sure of it. 'What was Gold doing in Charleston?"

"Snooping around."

"How'd he get your name?"

"Melanie Dupry."

Morgan seethed with rage. "Stupid bitch."

Fremont, reading his mind, said, "She had no choice. They're not going to fork over 500 grand without asking a few questions. I warned you about that in Richmond. These people are not as dumb as you think."

Morgan stayed silent for a full minute, then he stood up. The sun was up and it was getting hot. His palms were sweating, and he kept rubbing them on his pants. He leaned against a tree, trying to appear relaxed, but in truth he was worried about loose ends. Two loose ends to be precise. "Tell me about the argument. Who started it?"

Fremont gave him a brief recap of the events leading up to the confrontation in his store, and by the time he finished, Morgan was standing over him, his face set with contempt. "I know what you're thinking. I shouldn't have sent Gold down to Beaufort. You're right, Jubal. It was a dumb mistake. I… I didn't know what else to do. He was breathing down my neck and bound to cause trouble. What was I supposed to do, let him ruin our plans?"

"You were supposed to contact me. I would have done the job right."

"I thought Teague could handle it."

"You thought wrong."

"You're the one who recruited him."

"Not for that sort of thing."

"I'm sorry. I made a mistake. It's not the end of the world."

Morgan's scowl deepened for an instant and then, suddenly, he found himself chuckling. "Not the end of the world? Don't be so sure about that. Somebody has to answer for Teague."

Fremont looked at him, meeting his eyes for only a second, but that was long enough for him to understand the depth of his anger – and to be frightened by it. "Gold's the one you want. If you get rid of him, we'll be back in business."

Morgan snorted derisively. He seemed to be wrestling with something. Finally, he came out with it. "How did Gold force you to play along?"

"He threatened to call the police. He was going to tell them that I robbed some graves and set him up to be killed. If he turned me in, I'd go to jail and lose my store. I had to play along, and I had to give him your name."

There was a lengthy silence, and when it ended, Fremont was totally unprepared for Morgan's fury. "Holy sh--" He couldn't believe what he'd just heard. He came closer, enraged. "You did *what?*"

Fremont swallowed, but his mouth was dry as sand. "I ... gave him your real name. I had no choice." His shoulders slumped visibly as the weight of the world seemed to settle on him. "He would have stumbled upon it sooner or later. They have all sorts of ways of tracking people down."

Morgan gave the subject more reflection, then shook his head. "You know what we have here, Roger? A total screw up. I'm dealing with a confederacy of dunces."

For several moments, Fremont stared at him, a fearful expression on his face, then he said softly, as if to himself, *"I can make this right..."*

Morgan's reaction was delayed a bit. He grunted as if to laugh, but there was no humor in it. He instinctively looked over his shoulder in the general direction of where he'd parked the car. Then he stared at Fremont. He exhaled, closed his eyes tightly, and slowly shook his head. "I'm sorry, old boy. There are no second chances."

CHAPTER TWENTY-FIVE

When Irene Kaminski got back from lunch she was not in good spirits, and her mood wasn't much improved when, despite having no scheduled meetings, she was informed that two people were waiting to see her. A troubled expression clouded her face, and she looked at her secretary questioningly. "What's up?"

"They have badges."

"*Badges?*"

"Agent Evans and a gentleman with a funny accent."

Kaminski maintained a show of indifference, but inside she was worried. She had no time for distractions, not today, and the last thing she needed was a police problem. The F.B.I. agent, whose name was Kellie Evans, worked out of the New York branch and had been her TaeKwonDo instructor for a couple of years. Twenty-nine years old, personable, smart, and super-competent, Evans was, in Kaminski's opinion, destined for great things within the agency.

Every so often, the two women met for a drink, but they never talked shop. Which is to say they never mixed business and pleasure.

Until now.

"Kellie, good to see you again," Kaminski said. "How are things?"

Agent Evans said she was doing fine, exchanged a few pleasantries, and then introduced Solomon Carter. Carter stood up and reached across the desk to shake hands. "Chief Carter is the head of the Charleston Police Department."

"Long way from home," Kaminski said. "Nice meeting you, sir."

"My pleasure, ma'am."

Agent Evans noticed how Kaminski flinched when she heard where Carter was from. "The chief is conducting a murder investigation. He's asked for our assistance."

Kaminski raised her brows in a politely quizzical expression. "What does that have to do with me?"

Carter grinned to make himself look amicable. "The suspect is one of your employees."

"One of my employees?"

"Yes, ma'am."

Kaminski slumped, sitting back, and let her head rest on the cushion behind her. She heaved a great sigh, then said, "Who?"

"Adam Gold."

She looked at him as if she couldn't quite believe what she was hearing. Anger crossed her face, and she felt a knot tighten in her throat. Regaining her composure, she straightened up. "There must be some mistake. Gold is our lead investigator, and I know him quite well. He would never be involved in such a crime."

Agent Evens began to dab her face with a Kleenex. Her skin was moist and florid, and she looked as if she had just led a martial arts class. It was the first time Kaminski had ever seen the woman appear affected by the temperature or anything else. Looking solemn, she said, "The police are investigating three murders."

"*Three?*" Kaminski said, her voice little more than a breath.

"All citizens of South Carolina," Carter said. "Two men and a woman." He glanced at his notepad. "Tyrone Teague, Roger Fremont, and Sungila Taylor. Any of those names sound familiar?"

Kaminski's mouth fell open, but she recovered quickly. Struggling to maintain her poker face, she deflected the question by asking one of her own. "How did Gold become a suspect?"

"I questioned him and Fremont about Teague's death. They said it was accidental and Fremont took the blame, but I have reason to believe that Gold was the culprit." He leaned back, placing his hands together, the tips of his index fingers resting against his nose. "Lacking evidence, I was forced to let them go. Miss Taylor was murdered a short time later. She was beaten and strangled. The person who killed her dragged her body across the ground and dumped her in a salt pond. The drag marks were clearly visible. I guess the killer was in a hurry to leave the crime scene." A moment of silence passed. "Always the little things that trip these guys up."

Kaminski's face twisted into a look of confusion and annoyance. "I'm sorry to hear about her death, but what the hell does that have to do with Adam Gold?"

Agent Evans cleared her throat. "They found Miss Taylor's cell phone. I have a list of all her incoming and outgoing calls. Gold used her phone to call his wife ... and his employer." She stiffened, then smiled at Kaminski. It was a small, sad smile. "Why would Gold have access to her phone?"

Kaminski took a deep breath, letting it all out before she answered. "They spent a few days together."

"You don't say."

"Nothing like that. Gold contracted West Nile Virus and she nursed him back to health."

"Why was Gold in South Carolina?"

"He was investigating a claim."

"What sort of claim?"

"I'm afraid that's confidential."

Evans sighed again. "I could get a search warrant."

"You could try."

"Those warrant requests are hard to hide from the press. Are you sure you want that kind of publicity."

"You forgot to say checkmate."

Evans shrugged, her effort to smile halfhearted at best. "I don't have time to play games. We might be dealing with a serial killer."

Kaminski's jaw dropped again. She glared at Evans, her patience and very nearly her sanity all but at an end. "Good Lord," she breathed. "That's the most ridiculous thing I have ever heard. Adam Gold is a model citizen. Well, maybe not a model citizen, but a law abiding one. In any case, he's not a murderer."

Evans fired back. "Then why don't you help us clear his name?"

"Maybe she can't see the forest for the trees," Carter said. He ran his fingers across the top of his head, as if brushing back hair that had not graced his scalp for many years. "You know what they say. Love is blind."

Kaminski turned her head, staring at Carter as if his remark had exceeded all bounds of propriety. Which it had. "They also say it's better to remain silent and be thought a fool than to speak out and remove all doubt." She stood up shakily and glanced at Agent Evans, then turned her attention back to Carter. "I can assure you that I have 20/20 vision."

Agent Evans moved quickly to cover the awkward moment. "Let's get back to the claim."

Kaminski rummaged through a wire basket and withdrew a manila folder, handing it to Evans. "Here's the claim file. Knock yourself out."

Evans went through the file, reading and rereading the initial report, making notes on a separate sheet of paper. Every once in a while she would make a face or shake her head, but she kept her thoughts to herself.

Carter remained still, mesmerized by an oil painting depicting the city of Vienna covered in snow. He seemed to find it appealing, although it was difficult to know what he was actually thinking.

Kaminski sat down and gently massaged her temples. Her head had been aching before her visitors arrived, now it was splitting. Feigning nonchalance, she leaned back and folded her arms over her chest. "Find anything interesting?"

Evens met her eyes, but only briefly, then passed the folder to Chief Carter. Without answering the question, she abruptly got up and walked over to the windows that ran along one side of the room. She stood there for a few seconds before nodding to herself and turning around. "Let me get this straight. Your insured, Melanie Dupry, filed the claim and is asking you to pay a half million dollar ransom for the return of Stonewall Jackson's arm. Is that right?"

"Sad but true," Kaminski said.

Carter opened his mouth to speak, but Evans cut him off before he could say a word. "Why didn't Dupry contact the F.B.I.?"

"You'll have to ask her that question."

"Have you paid the claim?"

"No."

"Do you intend to?"

"I doubt it, but that depends on the outcome of the investigation."

"Gold's investigation?"

Kaminski resented being quizzed but had better reasons for answering than staying silent. She didn't want to give them the impression that she had something to hide. "Gold should be finished shortly. Two or three days at the most."

Chief Carter opened the folder and riffled the pages like a deck of cards. Almost instantly something caught his eye. "Teague and Fremont are involved in the claim?"

Without providing too much detail, Kaminski explained that Teague was one of the grave robbers and Fremont was a ransom negotiator. "The third man – the one who calls himself Jesse James – is still at large."

A dry chuckle caught in Carter's throat. "Two down, one to go."

Squeezing at her temples, she sighed deeply, then looked across at him. "What happened to Fremont? I mean, how was he killed?"

Carter set his mouth, drew a determined breath. "Somebody tied him up and cut his throat. Odd timing, don't you think?"

Reeling from this latest grisly revelation, Kaminski struggled to control her voice. "What are you implying?"

"Well, I hate to rush to judgment, but it looks like your investigator has his own way of declining a claim. All the parties just disappear."

Kaminski looked contemptuously at him, thinking that if she were in his shoes she might be thinking the same thing. "I hate to rain on your parade, but it wouldn't be worth the trouble. Reinsurance covers most of the payment. Besides, our claimant is alive and well."

Agent Evans pasted on a tolerant smile, keeping any anger out of her voice. "I wouldn't go that far. Your handwritten notes tell a different story."

Kaminski shifted uneasily in her chair. "What do you mean?"

"How do you explain her injuries?"

"She's involved in a dangerous sport."

"Horseback riding?"

"That's right."

"I ride, too. As a matter of fact, I've been riding since I was a teenager. And I've never had a single injury."

"You're a lucky woman."

"Sometimes people create their own luck — by the choices they make."

"What are you getting at?"

"Maybe Gold is more dangerous than you think."

"I don't think he's dangerous at all. You're the one who's worried about him."

"You're right. I am worried about him. I'm also worried about you and your company. I guess you don't realize it, but there could be a full-scale investigation by the Justice Department. Aren't you wondering why the F.B.I. is involved in this matter?"

"I figured you were having a slow month."

Evans ignored the flippancy. "Think about the murder victims. A black man, a black woman, and a gay person. Are you familiar with hate crimes?"

"I was under the impression that all crimes were hateful."

"Some more than others. I don't know how they do things in Austria, but here in the states we have something called hate crime laws. Current statutes permit federal prosecution of bias crimes, which are crimes committed on the basis of a person's race, religion, ethnicity, nationality, gender, and sexual orientation. Do you see where I'm heading with this?"

Kaminski tried a brave smile. "Like I said, I have 20/20 vision."

"I strongly suggest that you give us your full cooperation."

"What do you think I'm doing?"

Evans looked around the office, indicating that she wasn't impressed with Kaminski's performance. She returned to her chair, crossed her legs, and made a great show of looking at the clock on the wall. She sighed and said, "We spoke to Gold's secretary. She said he was out of town."

"No wonder he hasn't returned my call."

"You didn't know he was gone?"

"I don't keep track of his every move."

"Got a lot on your plate?"

"More than you know."

"Where do you suppose he went?"

"I wouldn't know."

Chief Carter slumped back in his chair, leaning his head into the leather and swiveling from side to side. This couldn't be happening. "Jesus Christ," he growled. "I just flew six hundred miles. What am I supposed to do now?"

Evans coughed, thinking hard. She hadn't anticipated this problem, and she felt suddenly like an F.B.I. cadet abruptly called on to answer a question. She finally found her voice and said, "Time for Plan B."

Carter made a face. "Plan B?"

Evans stood up. Her tone was businesslike. "Where does Gold live?"

Kaminski sighed. "Long Island."

"Where on Long Island?"

"North Woodmere."

"Nassau County?"

"Close to JFK."

"That's where we landed," Carter said. His expression remained sour, but he seemed mollified.

"I'll need an address," Evans said.

"No problem." Kaminski wrote it down on an index card, and handed the card to Evans. "Are you planning to drive out there?"

"That's the general idea."

"Seems like a waste of time."

Maybe, maybe not, Evans thought, but she kept her opinion to herself. Because it was late, and they were both tired and stressed, she decided to hold her tongue. No sense saying something she might later regret. "Maybe his wife knows where he went."

"Could be worth a shot."

Evans locked gazes with her and, in a steely voice, said, "Remember one thing. Phone calls can be traced. I wouldn't try to contact Mrs. Gold. You might be charged with obstruction of justice. Catch my drift?"

"Aye-aye, Captain."

CHAPTER TWENTY-SIX

Ten minutes later, still deep in thought, Kaminski was told that she had a telephone message from Samantha Wong. Ms. Wong had left her office in Greenwich Village, and she was on her way downtown. She wanted to meet at the Pearl Diner, and whatever she had to say couldn't wait. With the day already half-gone, and her head still aching, Kaminski decided to knock off early. She told her secretary to hold her calls, and then she leaned back, put her feet on the desk, and closed her eyes. Before long, she began to envision her favorite hideaway, the tropical island of Saint Martin. In her mind's eye she could see the Caribbean Sea, marbled blue and green, darker in the troughs, lighter and more colorful on the surface. Shallow depth and light-colored sand reflected the sunlight, giving the water its distinct blue color, the blue of watercolors.

The dog days of summer were starting to get to her.

So was work.

One of these days she was going to hop on a plane and get the hell out of Dodge.

But not today.

She was going to spend today putting out fires.

An urgent call usually spelled trouble, but for the life of her, Kaminski couldn't guess why someone from the MIB needed to talk with her. The Anchor Insurance Company was a property and casualty carrier and did not sell health or life insurance. Thinking back, she couldn't remember a single time when she had needed to call on the services of the Medical Information Bureau, and that made her even more worried.

From the outside, the Pearl Diner on Pearl Street near the East River looked like a typical Greek diner, but the menu was rather eclectic. Anything from souvlaki to filet of sole, and the best cheesecake in the financial district. Sammy Wong was sitting in a booth, facing the entrance. She was twirling her cup around in its saucer, biting on her lower lip. Eventually she raised her eyes. "Hello, Irene. Thanks for coming."

"Your message said it was urgent."

"It's about Adam Gold."

Kaminski eyed the younger woman. She had a sinking feeling in the pit of her stomach. "What about him?"

"I've been trying to reach him all morning."

"He's out of town."

"Yes, I know. Did he tell you about our meeting?"

"He said you had been very helpful."

"He was just being kind. I wasn't much help at all. As you know, the MIB keeps track of medical conditions, but we don't collect or store medical records. I'm not sure how much Adam knew about us, but I told him that we didn't have any examination reports, physician statements, lab test results, x-rays, or underwriting files."

"What's the problem?" Kaminski pressed. This time her voice had an impatient edge.

Wong beckoned her closer. "Melanie Dupry. There were four codes attached to her profile." She ticked off the various codes on her fingertips: high-risk sport, sustained drug use, sexual deviation, and criminal history. "Not a typical profile. Not by a long shot."

Kaminski's mouth dropped open. "I should say not."

"You look surprised."

"Gold didn't mention the last two codes."

"There were no details. Simply a mention of past involvement."

"Wonderful."

Wong sat brooding for a half-minute and finally said, "That's not why I asked you to come. I thought he told you everything." She looked down, her bottom lip quivering slightly. "I found something else. Something disturbing."

Kaminski frowned. "Sounds serious."

"I had some free time so I kept digging. I thought I was doing a good deed."

Kaminski, clearly nervous, leaned even closer. "What did you find?"

Wong pulled out her notebook and a pen, arranged them next to her drink, and hunched over, speaking softly. Her words, though spoken calmly, stunned Kaminski. Getting right to the point, she explained that the sexual deviation code was the result of her insured's first marriage, a union between a seemingly red-blooded woman and an openly gay man. "Your insured married a man who came out early, shortly after their honeymoon. He was arrested two times. Once for prostitution and once for indecent exposure. She posted bail on both occasions, which might explain how she got tainted with the same brush as her spouse."

"Sounds plausible. Do we know the husband's name?"

Wong glanced at her notes. "Roger Fremont."

Kaminski glared at her and literally spat out the name, "*Roger Fremont?*"

"He lives in South Carolina."

"Charleston?"

"That's right."

Kaminski's jaw went slack. She blinked a couple of times, then eased back. She opened her mouth to speak but found she had no words. Finally she shook her head and said, "Son of a bitch."

"What's wrong?"

"Everything. How does he earn a living?"

"Retail merchant. Buys and sells antiques."

"Shit, that's our man."

"Excuse me?"

"How did you discover this information?"

"Old-fashioned snooping. Marriage records are usually stored with the clerk of the town or county where the bride lives. In this case I contacted the Division of Vital Records in Kentucky and Virginia. You'd be surprised what you can find in marriage records." The list included the ages and full legal names of the bride and groom, date of marriage, name of the minister or priest, names of the witnesses, occupations of the bride and groom, and the residence of both parties. "Web sites are another good source, but not as reliable."

"Find anything else?"

"Fremont has a lengthy MIB file. All sorts of codes, typical and otherwise. You might be interested to know that he was the victim of a hate crime – or what appears to be a hate crime."

There was that term again.

A long silence ensued.

"Do you have any details?" Kaminski asked.

"The incident occurred at a gay pride event. He was severely beaten and hospitalized, but no charges were ever filed."

"I wonder why."

"The incident occurred in South Carolina."

"So?"

"Well, I'm no expert, but from what I remember from law school there are several states that don't have hate crime statutes. South Carolina is one of them."

"Interesting."

Wong momentarily toyed with the idea of sharing her own experience as an Asian-American, but some things were better left unsaid. Instead of elaborating about her past, she said, "Hate crimes are a problem everywhere. Most of them are motivated by racial bias. Over half, if I remember right. Religious bias ranks second, then comes sexual orientation and ethnic bias."

Kaminski was clearly impressed. "Where did you go to law school, Samantha?"

"Columbia University."

"I used to live near Morningside Heights."

"I commuted from Chinatown."

"Long commute."

"I had an apartment on Pell Street. It was all I could afford at the time."

"Did you ever practice law?"

"Two years. I was a health law attorney. My firm represented patients, clinics, insurance companies, and physicians. Long hours, little pay. I hated every minute of it. Working for the MIB is more rewarding and much more interesting."

"You'd make a good investigator."

"Speaking of investigators…" She brought a hand to her forehead, then closed her eyes for a long moment. "I don't know if you're aware of it, but your insured has a criminal record. Three arrests. All misdemeanors. DUI, shoplifting, and trespassing."

"Another thing Gold forgot to mention."

"I don't think he forgot. I don't think he knew about the crimes. Her record was expunged." Expungement is the process by which misdemeanor charges may be sealed, or in some cases, permanently erased from a person's criminal record. "I got lucky and stumbled upon a 'Petition for Dismissal.'"

"People make their own luck," Kaminski said. "Gold should've dug deeper."

"It wouldn't have made a difference."

"I beg your pardon?"

"The petition wasn't filed under the name of Melanie Dupry."

"Huh?"

"The crimes occurred before she married and divorced her second husband, Ronald Dupry."

"What name did she use, Melanie Fremont?"

"No, it was some other name. Give me a moment and I will look it up."

"I wonder why they agreed to dismiss the charges."

"She was relatively young when the crimes occurred."

"Yes, but she committed three misdemeanors."

"If you find a lenient judge – and grease a few palms – all can be forgiven."

"Is that the way the system works?"

"In many places."

"Sad."

"To see what is right and not to do it is want of courage, or of principle."

Kaminski did a double take. "That sounds like something Victor Wong might say."

"My uncle loves to quote Confucius."

"I've noticed. I guess it runs in the family."

"Great minds think alike."

"How is your uncle?"

"He's doing fine. I spoke to him yesterday. He's still in Hong Kong."

"Business or pleasure?"

"A little of both. We have relatives in the city of Kowloon. He's been making the rounds, visiting with family and friends. Catching up, as we say in the states. He leaves for the mainland at the end of the week."

Kaminski raised an eyebrow. "He's going to the mainland?"

"Business trip."

"I thought your uncle was persona non grata in China. Because of Tiananmen Square."

Wong looked away, slightly embarrassed. "Well, that was a long time ago. Things have changed in recent years." She lowered her voice, just a little. "Wong is a common surname. Hopefully he'll be able to fly under the radar, if you know what I mean."

"Yes, I understand. Send him my regards."

"I certainly will."

"Did you find Dupry's other name?"

"Just a moment." She reached for her notebook. "I remember writing it down. I thought you might need it for something." She flipped through some pages. "Here we go." She smiled broadly. "Melanie Morgan."

"Come again?"

"The name she used was Melanie Morgan."

Every hair on the back of Kaminski's neck stood up and her skin actually goose-pimpled for the first time in years. "Her last name was *Morgan?*"

"Yep."

"Oh my God."

Wong glanced up at her. "You all right?"

The color had drained from Kaminski's face. Her eyes flitted to the corners of the room as though she hoped to find some answer there. She brushed a strand of hair from her forehead and steadied herself by placing a hand on the table. A long silence stretched between them. Eventually she slumped back in her seat, suddenly looking like an old woman. "Melanie Morgan," she muttered. "I've got to warn Gold."

Wong sat stiffly, her back pushed up tight against the booth. "What's wrong?"

Kaminski rose out of her seat, visibly unsteady. "I have to leave."

"Right now?"

"Something's come up."

"I don't understand."

"I don't have time to explain."

Wong was frowning, shaking her head from side to side, wondering if she'd said something wrong. "Where are you going?"

Kaminski looked at her for a moment and then pulled her phone out of her waist clip and started dialing. "I've got a plane to catch."

CHAPTER TWENTLY-SEVEN

Agent Evans was startled by Kaminski's abrupt departure from the Pearl Diner. She assumed that Kaminski and her companion were having a late lunch and would be there for several hours. Scratching her head, she wondered whatever happened to the three-martini lunch. My, how things had changed since the last recession. Looking through her binoculars, she watched Kaminski walk up Pearl Street and then turn left at John Street. She checked her watch, then nudged the person sitting next to her. "Bird on the wing."

"What's that?" Chief Carter said.

"Kaminski just left."

Carter looked highly skeptical. "So soon?"

"I don't get it either."

"Maybe she's on a diet."

"She seems to be in a hurry."

"Where the hell is she going?"

"Back to her office."

"What about the Asian woman?"

"Still inside."

"Do you think we should question her?"

"If we do, Kaminski will hear about it, and she'll know she's being followed."

"So what do we do now?"

"We park ourselves on John Street and wait. If I know Kaminski, she'll try to contact Gold as soon as possible."

Carter didn't respond at first, but then he spoke as if something had just occurred to him. "She could just call him."

"Why do you think I mentioned the phone trace?" She shook her head impatiently, as if a phone call were out of the question. "No, I know this woman. She's the protective type, a real mother hen. She'll contact him, but she won't take any chances."

"I hope you're right."

"Would you rather call it a day?"

"No, I'm just bored. We don't do a lot of surveillance in Charleston." "How do your numbers look?'"

"Our numbers?"

"Crime stats."

Carter phrased his answer carefully, not wanting to sound smug. He described Charleston as a safe city, with a crime rate that was substantially lower than the national average. When pressed for details, he recited the numbers, and they were surprisingly good. Year after year Charleston was ranked as safer than 60% of the cities in America. The chances of becoming a crime victim were only 1 in 38. The chances of falling victim to a violent crime 1 in 551. "Last year we had seven murders, 29 rapes and 72 robberies. Not bad, considering we're one of the top tourist destinations in the country."

Her lips twisted into a lopsided smile. "When was the last time you had a triple murder?"

"Last year. Three gang bangers were gunned down in Myrtle Beach."

"During the Atlantic Beach Bikefest."

"Yes, ma'am, that's right."

"They were members of the 'Town of Lincolnville,' or the TOL, one of your local gangs."

Carter stared at her with an incredulous look on his face. "The shooter is still at large."

"Yes, I know."

"Do you mind if I ask *how* you know?"

Smiling grimly, she told him that she'd had some experience with the FBI's Gang Intelligence Unit, the group that kept an eye on the nation's 33,000 violent street gangs, motorcycle gangs, and prison gangs. These gangs had about 1.4 million members throughout the country. "I spent five years with the GIU. Four of them in your state."

"You worked in South Carolina?"

"Columbia."

He looked as shocked as if she'd slapped him. For a moment he was silent. Then he said, "Damn. Small world."

"Violent, too."

"You run into some trouble down there?"

She reminded him, albeit reluctantly, that from 2000 to 2010, Columbia, South Carolina, was plagued with one of the deadliest gang feuds in history. The feud involved three of the most notorious gangs in the state, the Gangster Killer Bloods, the Gangster Disciples, and the Insane Crip Nation. During this 10-year period, the state ranked first in violent crime, surpassing even California, Illinois, and New York. "We busted up the hierarchy and put some thugs in jail, but as I'm sure you now, gang activity is still a problem."

"Well, I'm sure you gave it your best shot."

"And I'm about to give it another."

"What do you mean?"

"When I saw your request, I asked to be assigned to this case. I don't doubt that Gold had something to do with the deaths of Taylor and Teague, but I'm not so sure about Roger Fremont. I think his death might be gang related."

Carter's expression indicated that this was the last thing he wanted to hear. "What brought you to that conclusion?"

"Well, as far as the public knows, Fremont killed Teague. The newspapers are calling him a hero, and the story has been broadcast across the state. If I were one of Teague's friends, I'd be pissed and I might seek revenge."

"Just one problem," Carter said. "Teague was a rotten son of a bitch, and as far as I know, he didn't have any friends."

"What do you know about his gang connections?"

For a moment, Carter's weary brow furrowed again. He sank back into his seat, then brought his hand up to his temples and squeezed them. "Teague was in a gang?"

"No, but he did some business with the Killer Bloods."

"What sort of business?"

"The type of business that gets you banned from the NFL. Thanks to the Bloods, Teague had a nonstop supply of anabolic agents. Are you familiar with performance-enhancing drugs?"

"Well, I'm no chemist, but I know a thing or two about them. Which ones were being peddled?"

"Everything from A to Z." Which meant, she told him, everything from Adderall to Zilpaterol. "Teague had access to anything and everything."

"I'm familiar with Adderall, but I've never heard of Zilpaterol."

"It's sold under its trade name, Zilmax. The players use it to add bulk, but it was formulated to increase the size of cattle."

"*Cattle?*"

"Tyson Foods banned Zilmax-fed cattle three years ago. Would you like to know why?"

"Go on."

"Cattle began arriving at their processing plants with missing hooves."

Carter shook his head in disgust. "I'm sorry I asked."

"So am I."

"Did you ever bust Teague?"

"We never got the chance. He injured himself before we could pounce. After he left the game, he fell off the radar."

"Too bad."

"He had quite an operation. Very profitable. He made a lot of money for himself and his gangster friends."

"So you think one of his buddies whacked Fremont."

His comment was a statement, not a question, but she responded anyway. "I think it's possible. After all, Teague was a good customer. A celebrity. He was also from the hood, so to speak. These gang bangers don't need much of a reason to take someone out."

Which Carter was forced to admit, was true. But he still had doubts. "Sounds farfetched to me. I don't believe in honor among thieves."

"Let me ask you something. Where did they find Fremont's body?"

"In a dumpster."

"Which town?"

"A place called Saluda."

"Where's Saluda?"

"West of … Columbia."

"Fifty-two miles away. Easy drive for a gang banger with a car."

"Yeah, you're right."

She started the car, pulled out slowly, and parked on John Street, one block west of the Anchor Insurance Company. After a five minute silence, she let the other shoe drop. "There's something else you should know. When Teague's name popped up, I took a peek at his estate. I was curious to see what he left behind. I was surprised to find he owned three properties – a house, an apartment, and some farmland. The house is on St. Helena Island, the apartment in Charleston, and the farmland in Calhoun County."

"*Calhoun County?*"

"South of Columbia."

"Thirty-five miles."

"Another easy drive."

"Damn."

"All you have to do is connect the dots."

Carter considered this for a long time and then nodded. "How do you think it went down?"

Agent Evans was frowning deeply, sitting all the way back in her seat, her hands on her lap, her legs straight out and crossed at the ankles. She scrunched her face, puzzling it out. Hesitantly, the words started to come. "Some thugs saw an opportunity to enhance their reputation, so they drove down to Charleston, abducted Fremont, and brought him back to Teague's place. I haven't seen the autopsy report, but Fremont was probably beaten and tortured before he was killed. That's the way those bastards operate. The body was dumped in Saluda to throw us off the trail."

"Sounds like you've got it all figured out."

"We sent down a CSI team. Hopefully they'll find enough forensic evidence to move forward. Until then, Gold remains our number one suspect."

Carter finally asked the question that had been nagging at him. "Why would he kill the woman?"

"I was wondering the same thing."

"Seems like a random target."

"What's her story?"

"Single black female. Mid-thirties. No criminal records. Lived on St. Helena most of her life. She worked in a museum."

"Which one?"

"The Penn Center."

"The Gullah museum?"

"Volunteer docent."

"Was she Gullah?"

"Through and through."

Evans turned, a look of irritation on her face. "What does that mean?"

Carter's mouth turned upward briefly in a parody of a smile. "I was told that she practiced witchcraft. Some sort of mumbo jumbo brought over from Africa. Magical herbs, hexes, Hoodoo. That sort of thing. Sounds satanic, if you ask me."

"I wonder how she got mixed up with Gold."

"The Beaufort police are working on that."

"Let me know if you hear anything."

"Will do." As Chief of Police, Carter was forced to attend an endless series of ceremonial functions, most of them having little or nothing to do with actual police work. Lots of breakfast, lunch and dinner meetings, usually followed by a speech. Tracking down a real criminal – like Adam Gold – was something he rarely did anymore, and it was damn exciting to be back in the line of fire. He wondered if Agent Evans felt the same way. He also wondered about *her* story. He was tempted to get personal with her, but he got the feeling that she was all business, so he took a pass. Just as well, he thought. It was too damn hot to play *Twenty Questions*. The conversation seemed to be stalled, so not knowing what else to say, he defaulted to the old standby. "Kind of warm today."

"Summer in the city."

"I sure could use a cold drink. Why don't I …"

Evans held up her index finger, cutting him off. "Hold that thought."

"What's up?"

"Kaminski just came out."

Carter's face took on a puzzled look. "What's she doing?"

"Waiting for her ride."

"Where do you think she's going?"

"She's a mother hen."

"So?"

Evans broke the hint of a smile. "Time to protect her flock."

CHAPTER TWENTY-EIGHT

On the flight from New York's LaGuardia Airport to Blue Grass Airport in Lexington, Gold found himself thinking about the horsey set and the exclusive world they inhabited. In a few short hours he would be part of this world, surrounded by buyers, sellers, trainers, and agents. He would also be rubbing elbows with the big money boys, represented by syndicates from Ireland, Russia, Japan, and the United Arab Emirates. A typical person might have been worried about fitting in, but for some strange reason, Gold found the whole thing amusing. That and a bit silly. So instead of eating his gut out, he nudged McVey and asked him if he remembered Abbott and Costello's "Mudder" routine.

McVey frowned, evidently surprised by the question. "Yeah, I remember it. Why?"

"I was just thinking how funny it would be if we did some shtick at Keeneland."

McVey heaved a great sigh. "Please don't ask if I scratched my mudder."

"Actually, I was going to ask if you fed your fodder to your mudder."

"You're hopeless."

"Where's your sense of humor?"

"I need a drink."

"I think we'd be a big hit."

"Two drinks."

"You have to admit it was a funny bit."

"Funny in the Catskills, not in Bluegrass Country."

"Laughter is the best medicine."

"I'd settle for a glass or two of wine."

"You drink too much."

"You talk too much. Why don't you get some rest?"

"I'm not tired."

"It's going to be a long day."

Gold shrugged. "Twenty-four hours. Just like the rest of 'em."

"Ever the optimist."

"You worried about something?"

"Your upcoming performance. I'm not sure you're ready for prime time."

"I'm as ready as I'll ever be."

"That's comforting."

"Jesus, you worry more than Kaminski."

"You're giving both of us gray hair."

Gold searched for something to read, but there were no magazines in the seat pocket in front of him. "What's wrong with this airline?"

"What's the problem?"

"No *Sky Magazine*."

"They went bankrupt."

"When?"

"Last year."

"Why am I always the last to know?"

"Why do you care? You never order anything."

"Where am I supposed to put my chewing gum?"

McVey ordered a glass of wine. "You got any last minute questions?"

"Yeah, why did I ever leave underwriting?"

"Questions about the mission."

Gold gave it some thought. "Are we going to use our real names?"

"Why not? Nobody knows who we are. Just remember, you're the buyer, I'm the trainer. Do you understand what trainers do?"

"I imagine they train horses."

McVey's voice dropped to a whisper. "You'd better know exactly what they do."

Gold studied the serious look on McVey's face and said, "What is it? What's wrong?"

McVey sighed heavily, closing his eyes. When he opened them, he took another weary breath. "Morgan may be a psychopath and a pyromaniac, but he's not stupid. He didn't survive this long by being careless. Trust me, he'll be listening for false notes, and if he hears any, he'll either take off or try to take you out. You need to be on top of your game. Do you understand what I'm saying?"

There was something subtly pedantic in McVey's voice, but Gold listened carefully as he explained the role of a trainer. He began with the old axiom that good trainers run their horses in races they had a chance of winning. The odds of winning were greatly improved f the trainer understood that racehorses were fragile creatures, susceptible to many ailments, some manageable, some not. Any of the yearlings at the upcoming auction could become a bleeder, or suffer chronic confirmation problems.

From the trainer's point of view, bleeders were a chief concern. These were horses that suffered from exercise – induced pulmonary hemorrhaging. Why horses bleed was still debatable, but it was a widespread problem and a topic that was sure to come up at the Keeneland auction.

McVey told him that some horses shed blood from the nose, but most bled from the lungs, which was commonly detected in the windpipe or trachea. Studies suggested that 50-60% of horses experienced bleeding after a race, and in some states, like California, more than seventy percent of all racehorses were bleeders.

Gold muttered something under his breath, then said, "So, that's the reason they use Lasix."

"Yeah, but most owners have switched to Salix, which is basically the same thing. Both are diuretics, used to treat fluid in the lungs and kidney disease."

"What do I need to remember about conformation?"

"As much as you can. Conformation is what trainers worry about the most – how a horse is built physically. If you keep your ears open, you'll hear a lot of talk about a yearling's structure. A real owner would know what that meant, and he would know how to converse with a trainer."

Gold smiled. "I'm not a real owner, I just play one on TV."

Another sigh. "If you know what's good for you, you'll follow the script. Try to remember that conformation is very important to the soundness of a horse, from his feet on up."

"What would I be looking for?"

"Physical faults. Toed-out feet, offset knees, crooked legs. That sort of thing. I don't think we'll see many poorly built yearlings, but you never know. Every once in a while a bad one will show up."

"Did you see any nags when you worked at Belmont?"

"More than a few. I was hired as a groom, but I did the same chores a trainer would do. In other words, I spent a lot of time with the horses. I was usually the first one in the barn. It was my job to check each stall and make sure that every horse was still standing." Though he laughed when he said that, McVey was being serious. "If a horse is lying down, it's a bad sign. The first thing you have to do is get him up. If a racehorse can't stand, you've got a serious problem. That's when you call the vet." He pulled down his tray, in preparation for his wine. "I also had to monitor their feed. A healthy horse will eat every drop of their evening rations. A horse that's off its feed might be getting sick."

Gold looked questioningly at him. "Time to call the vet again?"

"After you take the horse's temperature."

"How do you get a horse to open wide?"

"You don't."

"I don't understand."

"Other end."

A slow smile crossed Gold's face. "I see said the blind man."

"I was also responsible for taking care of all the riding equipment. The saddles, reins, bits, and blinkers. The last thing you need is for a strap to break during a race. You could end up with an injured rider or an injured horse. Either way you'd be out of a job."

"Sounds like there's a lot of pressure on grooms and trainers."

"You can say that again."

"My summer job was stressful, too."

"What the hell did you do?"

"I was a lifeguard at the Valley Stream pool."

"How was that stressful?"

"Too many bikinis."

"Okay," McVey said, after the flight attendant had poured his wine and moved on. "Enough talk about how I spent my summer vacation. Tell me about the game plan."

Gold told him that Kaminski had contacted the Kentucky State Police. She'd had a telephone conversation with a Colonel Smith in

Frankfort, and during the call, she got an earful about Jubal Morgan. Smith told her that Morgan was currently under investigation for a number of crimes, including arson, insurance fraud, racketeering, and animal cruelty. Hoping to end Morgan's reign of terror, the colonel offered the services of an undercover officer – a man who knew all the bad actors at Keeneland. The officer would introduce Gold to Morgan, building Gold up as a rich investor looking to make a quick buck.

"After that," Gold said, "I'm on my own. I'll have to figure out a way to gain Morgan's trust."

"That won't be easy."

"Nothing comes easy in my line of work."

"I know the feeling. Did you remember to bring a gun?"

"Nah, I've become a pacifist."

Glaring at him, McVey said, "You'd better be kidding, or I might have to pass a fist across your face."

Gold broke the hint of a smile. "I brought a Beretta."

"Which model?"

"Tomcat."

"If you have to use it, get close. The .32 ACP cartridge has marginal stopping power."

"Hopefully, it won't come down to that."

"Semper paratus, my friend. Always be ready for trouble."

"Do you still carry a Glock?"

"No, I joined the Beretta club."

"Why the switch?"

"Travel brings wisdom to the wise."

"Meaning?"

McVey lowered his voice and explained that he'd taken a detour after their last adventure in France. Instead of flying directly back to the states, he rented a car in Marseille and drove to Gardone Val Trompia, a picturesque town in northern Italy. The town, located in the Lombardy region, hard by Lake Garda, was known as the home of the world's oldest arms manufacturer – the Beretta *fabbrica*.

"Long drive?" Gold asked.

"Four hundred miles."

Gold looked at McVey with a quizzical expression in his eyes. "You drove all that way just to see a factory?"

"They've been around for five hundred years, and they've been making weapons in the Valle Trompia for more than two thousand years."

"I hate to break the news to you, but they have a factory in Maryland."

"I know. That's where they make the M-9 for the police and military. Believe me, it's not the same ambience."

"I'll take your word for it."

McVey was a gun enthusiast and a collector, and in his opinion the Beretta factory employed the best engravers and gunsmiths in the world. He didn't need any encouragement to launch into a disquisition on the subject. Realizing that he had a captive audience, he went on and on about the thirty or so custom engraving workshops, known to gun aficionados as ateliers. Each room was occupied by a craftsman, surrounded by the tools of the trade, the holy triumvirate of the hammer, the chisel, and the *bulino*.

"What's a bulino?" Gold asked.

"An ancient hand chisel. They use it for the creation of shadow."

"That must be a painstaking process."

"Everything's done by hand. There are no assembly lines."

"Uh-oh, that sounds expensive."

"You get what you pay for … but you do pay dearly."

"How dearly?"

"Depending on the engraving and the walnut stock, a commission for a premium gun can run to a hundred grand."

Gold stared at him for a long moment, then shook his head. "I guess you didn't buy one."

"Slightly beyond my means."

"Mine, too."

The pilot announced that they were beginning the descent into Lexington. McVey finished his wine, lifted his tray, and said, "Where do you meet the undercover cop?"

"He should be at the gate when we land. Hopefully he got us a room at the Hilton."

"*Us?*"

"I thought you'd want to stay at the same hotel."

"I don't think so."

"Why not?"

"I'm supposed to be watching your back."

"So?"

"How can I watch your back if I'm standing beside you?"

Gold smiled. "You just keep thinking Butch, that's what you're good at."

CHAPTER TWENTY-NINE

An undercover cop was supposed to blend in and not call attention to himself, but Eduardo Perez, Gold's contact, failed on both counts. He was a short man, barely five feet tall, impeccably groomed, dressed in a white silk suit. A red carnation was pinned to his lapel. His cologne arrived a few steps before he did. He was also the nervous type, one of those fellows who blinked a lot and bit his nails down to the quick. Gold couldn't place the accent, but he guessed it was from either Central or South America.

After a few minutes of aimless chitchat, Gold asked, "Where are you from, Perez?"

"Venezuela," Perez said. "A small village near Caracas. And you?"

"New York City."

"I spent a few years up there."

"Whereabouts?"

"Aqueduct Racetrack. I used to be a jockey."

Gold took a moment to figure out a diplomatic reply. "You look like an athlete. Not an ounce of fat."

Perez told him that trainers looked for jockeys who weighed less than 113 pounds to saddle up. Most riders ranged in height from 5-1 to 5-5. Interestingly, most of today's Thoroughbred jockeys were men from Spanish-speaking countries. Like Perez, they came from humble beginnings, eager to live the American Dream. They had surnames like Dominguez, Velazquez, Rosario, and Garcia.

And like Perez, they all grew up on horseback.

"You got any luggage?" Perez asked.

"Just my overnight bag."

"Follow me."

Before Gold could ask where they were going, Perez told him that there had been a slight change of plan regarding their accommodations. Due to the auction, and record attendance, there were no rooms available at the Hilton. Figuring that Gold wouldn't mind, he'd booked adjoining rooms at the Hyatt Place Hotel – five miles from the city center.

A pang of disappointment went through Gold. "What about Morgan?"

"What about him?"

"Do we know where he's staying?"

"It doesn't matter. I've already set up a meet."

"Where and when?"

"My old stomping grounds. Keeneland Racecourse. Two hours from now."

Gold glanced at his watch, then looked around to see if he could signal McVey. There was no sign of him. He made a mental note to call him as soon as he got settled. "Well, I guess we're off to the races."

By and large, undercover cops only opened up to other cops, or their significant others, but Perez was an exception to that rule, too. He had no problem sharing his life story with a complete stranger, and not surprisingly, it was quite a story. Eduardo Perez, who used to be known as Fast Eddie, had once been ranked as one of the best jockeys in the country. He was a rare breed, a jock that could ride a horse with a kind hand or a heavy hand, depending on what was needed to win. During his heyday, nobody got a mount out of the gate faster, and he was capable of running fast on the front end or coming from behind. He was also capable of telling a trainer to fuck off if they suggested that he "strangle" a horse at the gate, bunch up, or burn the horse on the front end.

A nasty spill at Santa Anita Park abruptly ended a brilliant career, but by then, Perez had already come to the conclusion that there were easier ways to make a buck. Truth was, life was hard for most jocks. There were about three thousand licensed riders in the United States, and of these, fewer than half made a living at it. In fact, the average jockey only earned $30,000 to $35,000, which meant that many of them needed a second job to makes ends meet.

After climbing down, he was offered a position at the Kentucky Horse Racing Commission, a natural fit for somebody with his background. He spent the next three years with the Division of Licensing and Enforcement, and was then recruited by the Kentucky State Police. While working undercover, he'd been involved in investigations at Keeneland, Churchill Downs, Turfway Park, and Ellis Park.

Those operations had netted some low-hanging fruit, but not the one rotten apple he wanted the most. In his view, Jubal Morgan was public enemy number one, and he was anxious to put him behind bars.

"Morgan's at the top of my short list," Perez said. "No pun intended."

"I'd like to get my hands on him, too."

"Sounds personal."

Gold didn't have to think about it too long. Right or wrong, he took every case personally. Of course, some cases were worse than others, and this one was right up there with the Presley tapes, Captain Kidd's treasure, the Gutenberg Bible, and the Gobelin tapestry. Leaving the terminal, they walked along in silence, each man occupied with his own thoughts. Finally, when they got to the car, Gold said, "How does one become a jockey? Is there a school for that sort of thing?"

Perez, perhaps struck by the abruptness of the question, cocked his head to the side. "I like a guy who does his homework."

"Knowledge is power."

A slow, knowing grin spread over his face. "Most of us learn to ride when we're young, but there is a school. Only one, as far as I know."

The school, which was an indeed one of a kind, was called the North American Riding Academy. Begun in 2006, the academy was part of the Kentucky Community College System, and was the first and only accredited racing school in the United States. In the beginning, the emphasis was strictly on professional riding, but nowadays the school also produced licensed grooms, assistant trainers, trainers, and breeding farm managers.

Perez had come up the old fashioned way, through trial and error, but he was not entirely dismissive about learning to ride in school. "Either way," he said flatly, "it's a hard row to hoe."

Gold was curious about that, but he didn't ask Perez to elaborate until they were in the car – and the AC was pumping. "I know what it takes to be a cop," he said. "What's so hard about being a jockey?"

Perez smiled. "More homework?"

"No, I'm really curious. You're the first jockey I ever met."

"All right, I'll give you the abbreviated version." The smiled widened. "Pun intended."

Keeping his eyes on the road, Perez admitted that he began his career in the worst possible way, by developing a reputation as a "long shot" rider – a jockey who rode only long shots. Riding poor horses was a hard way to get ahead, and when a jockey wasn't near the top of the standing, they seldom got a "live mount," racetrack vernacular for a good horse.

The process of getting a live mount – and moving up in the standings – began with the morning workout. Every day, at 6:00 a.m., Perez got to the track and volunteered to work a horse. He did this because of an unwritten rule that said when you work a horse in the morning, you ride him in the afternoon.

But like most rules, this one was made to be broken.

Financially pressed trainers, trying to reduce exercise costs, often took advantage of young jockeys by having them exercise their horses for free in the morning, and then bumping them in the afternoon races.

Perez put up with this nonsense for several years, but even when things got better, he barely made a living. The problem was the pay scale, which in his view was grossly unfair.

"What do you consider unfair?"

"The split," Perez said. "Regular riders have agents, and they get twenty-five percent of a jockey's earnings."

Gold raised his eyebrows. "Jesus, that's a hefty fee."

"Almost as bad as the mob."

"No agent, no ride?"

"You got it."

"Some racket."

"You don't know the half of it." He let out a short, aborted chuckle. "Jockeys are paid a minimum fee of sixty dollars, regardless of whether any purse money is won, but after the agent gets his cut, the Jockeys' Guild takes twenty percent and the rider's valet gets ten percent. The only time a jock sees any real money is when they win a stakes race, but to tell you the truth, even the best jockeys win only one of out every six races."

"Lousy odds," Gold said.

Perez nodded emphatically. "A jockey has to finish in the first three positions to make any serious money." He examined his fingernails for a moment, and then turned his attention back to the road. "That's why a typical racing career lasts only five to seven years." Out of the corner of his eye, he saw a change in the expression on Gold's face. It was small and subtle. A look of sadness and surprise. "Some jocks give up the profession because of problems making their riding weight, but I gave it up because of a serious injury."

Gold had once read that, minute for minute, being a jockey is the most dangerous athletic profession in the world. In fact, over the past thirty years, on average two jockeys have died each year, and there were currently fifty riders who were permanently paralyzed as a result of racing injuries. When he mentioned this to Perez, the ex-jock shrugged, as if it such risks came with the territory.

"Horse racing is dangerous," Perez said calmly. "There are no seat belts, no air bags, and no impact bars. If you fall off a horse at 40 miles per hour, you're gonna get injured or killed, and that's all there is to it."

"Simple as that," Gold said sarcastically. "Let me ask you something. Are you some sort of thrill seeker?"

"Excuse me?"

"You went from racing horses to chasing criminals."

"Racing to chasing," Perez said. "Very amusing." He laughed as if to prove it. "Don't worry, I don't have a death wish."

"Neither do I, so why don't we go over the game plan?"

The plan was simple. Perez would introduce Gold as an owner with some financial problems and some problem horses – horses that were past their prime, but heavily insured. Morgan would be asked to arrange their demise, and in return, he would be generously compensated, meaning ten percent of the insurance settlement.

"That's the going rate," Perez said.

"What if he balks?"

"Bump it up to fifteen percent."

"And if he asks for twenty?"

"Tell him to fuck off."

"Really?"

"Nobody would pay that much. He'll smell a rat."

"All right, so let's say we come to terms. Then what?"

"Then you shut up and let him suggest the time, the place, and the method of execution. Listen carefully, but don't ask too many questions. When he's done talking, tell him you need a day or two to think it over. If I know Morgan, he'll give you twenty-four hours, and demand that you bring a down payment. My office will supply the money. Once Morgan takes the bait, we'll swoop down and bust his sorry ass. Any questions?"

"Just one," Gold said. "Do you think he'll be armed?"

"Armed and dangerous."

"Swell."

"What did you expect? A welcome bouquet?"

"I was hoping to avoid any ... unpleasantness."

"*Unpleasantness?*"

"Gunplay."

Perez smiled an indulgent smile. His matter-of-fact voice made the whole thing seem more ominous. "Look, you know how stings work. We'll move in fast, but there are no guarantees. The man is an unpredictable psychopath. He might overreact."

Gold's face abruptly drained of all color. "How the hell does a guy like Morgan get a weapon?"

"Surely you jest."

"That easy?"

"Yep."

"Don't they have background checks in Kentucky?"

'I can't speak for others, but I always try to check the background before pulling the trigger."

"Gallows humor," Gold muttered. "Just what we need."

"Look, we'll do our best to protect you, but you know what they say. There are no sure bets."

CHAPTER THIRTY

Right after leaving the airport they got caught in crosstown traffic, and Perez realized that if they continued on their present course, they would be late for their meeting. They were headed from the west side of the city to the east side, and it was slow going. He suggested that they go straight to the Keeneland sales pavilion and check into their hotel later.

"Everything's set," Perez said. "We've got a guaranteed reservation."

"Good deal. Let's not keep Morgan waiting."

"The son of a bitch might get cold feet."

"Not worth the risk."

"I agree."

A quick turn brought them back to Keeneland Racecourse, and five minutes later, they were in the thick of things, watching an endless stream of skittish yearlings being coaxed out of their stalls. Perez explained that colts and fillies were identified at auction by a hip number, a round adhesive sticker affixed to the yearling's hip. All a buyer had to do was request a horse by number, and a groom would lead the horse out for inspection.

248

Perez was happy to demonstrate how the system worked. He walked over to the barn and caught the attention of a groom. "We'd like to see number fifty-two, please."

The groom glanced at their credentials and then jogged off, promptly returning with a sleek bay colt. "Here you are, sir."

Now that's a racehorse, Gold thought. *A champion through and through.* A buyer would need deep pockets to purchase a horse like that. Very deep pockets.

Perez strolled up to the animal and studied his withers – the nape of the colt's muscular neck "Good lines," he muttered. "All the way from the neck to the front of the shoulders. He'll have some reach. Legs are a little skinny, but he's not fully formed." There was nothing in his tone. Gold wasn't sure whether he was pretending to be happy, or displeased. "What do you think, boss?"

A faintly amused smile flitted across Gold's face. "Certainly a possibility."

"I don't think he'll be the session high horse, but a lot of people are going to bid on him."

Not missing a beat, Gold said, "He's a good- looking animal."

Perez was about to give the groom a tip when another man intervened and handed the groom a twenty dollar bill. "We're done with this one," the man said quietly. "Bring out hip number sixty." After the groom left, the man's eyes took on a furtive cast. In a quick pass, they scanned the length and breadth of the barn area, then came back to them. He threw a questioning glance at Perez and, getting a quick nod of approval, turned toward Gold. He studied Gold's face for a long moment with a keen, assessing look. "Your friend is right. The bay had skinny legs."

Gold folded his arms across his chest and just stared at him. He thought that maybe the man was a racetrack tout. On second thought, he realized that the man was too well dressed to be a tout. He was wearing a suit and tie. Well-pleated sharkskin, not the usual Seersucker garb. The most striking thing about him, other than his rudeness, was his eyes. They were cold and dark, animalistic. "Are you buying or selling?" he finally asked.

The man smiled to be polite. "Neither."

Perez started to say something, and stopped himself.

A moment later, the groom returned, and this time he was leading a chestnut colt, groomed to perfection. The man, who had yet to introduce himself, marveled at the proportions of the horse. He was genuinely impressed with just about everything, especially the sturdy legs and well formed hips. "If I was bidding, this would be my number one horse."

Gold smiled an indulgent smile. "Thanks for your advice."

Perez murmured, "We'll keep him in mind."

Reading between the lines, the groom led the handsome colt back to its stall.

The man waited until the groom moved out of earshot, and then walked over to Perez and stuck out his hand. "You're right on time."

Perez reluctantly shook the man's hand. "Time is money."

"Some say that money is the root of all evil. Not in my book."

Unable to fake even a stab at levity, Perez simply said, "I'm glad we're on the same page." He turned to Gold. "Say hello to Jubal Morgan."

Gold had been expecting this, but now that the moment was here he still didn't know quite how to play it. Finally he gave the murdering bastard his very best, ultra-friendly smile. "Nice to meet you, Morgan."

"Pleasure to meet you," Morgan said matter-of-factly, though his expression said something altogether different. "I don't think I caught your name."

Gold took what he hoped was an invisible deep breath, stepped forward, and held out his hand. "Adam Gold."

In a couple of seconds, Morgan's face went through a range of expressions. Initially, he seemed shaken, but he recovered quickly, realizing that this was a set-up. *Now there is an idiot*, he thought. It was a careless thing for Gold to use his real name. Of course, Gold had not spoken with Irene Kaminsky since leaving New York, so he didn't know about the murders of Sungila Taylor and Roger Fremont. Nor did he know that *he* was the prime suspect. For a moment Morgan stared unbelieving, trying to digest his luck. Then he said, "I can't place your accent. Are your people from the South?"

Proving that ignorance is bliss, Gold continued to bury himself. "Yeah, my people are from the South. The south shore of Long Island."

Morgan laughed lightly. "I thought I detected a Yankee accent."

"Call it a speech impediment. I've had it my whole life."

"Have you tried bourbon?"

"No, but that seems like a good idea."

"Kentucky bourbon can fix just about anything."

"I'll give it a shot."

"If I were you, I'd try several shots."

"Sounds good to me."

"Say, I've got an idea. Why don't we stroll over to the clubhouse and get ourselves a drink?" He looked at Perez, forcing himself to smile politely, but secretly wanting to crush his head into a bloody pulp. "Would you mind if we talked in private?"

Perez studied him for a moment and registered his look as completely sincere. "No, I don't mind. You two have a lot to discuss." He turned to Gold, his voice barely a whisper. "I'll meet you back at the hotel."

On the way to the clubhouse, Gold kept up the charade, pretending to be a newcomer to the sport of kings. Figuring that an owner might be curious about the Bluegrass Region, he asked if there was something special about the Kentucky landscape that accounted for the production of great Thoroughbreds. Morgan told him that, in his opinion, it was the limestone in the soil and in the water. The large concentration of minerals was good for the horses' bones. He said as an aside to Gold, "Some folks think our water has magical properties."

"What do you think" Gold asked.

"Well, I'm not sure, but that might explain why we produce the world's best whiskey."

A slow, skeptical grin spread over Gold's face. "When it comes to whiskey, I'm from Missouri."

Morgan stared at him, uncomprehending. "What's that supposed to mean?"

"Missouri is the 'Show Me State.'"

"Funny, I thought that would've been New York."

"Common misconception."

The clubhouse was cool and dark, the perfect place to be on a hot summer day. Morgan requested a corner table, then excused himself to make a phone call. Gold sat with his back to the wall, his green eyes sweeping the room, taking in every detail. Pictures of Thoroughbreds were on every wall, and behind the bar stood a gold trophy urn, inscribed with the names of the horses that had won the Kentucky Derby. When Morgan returned, he ordered two glasses of bourbon, Blanton's, served neat.

"Sorry about that," Morgan said. "I had to return a call."

"No problem," Gold said. "Must be a busy week."

Morgan sipped at his bourbon. "Very busy."

"I can only imagine."

"I guess I shouldn't complain." He looked at Gold, his head cocked to one side. "What do you do for a living?"

Gold made up some bullshit about being the owner of an insurance company. Due to a soft market, profits were down, but expenses were on the rise. To make matters worse, he'd made some lousy investments, including the purchase of two unhealthy Thoroughbreds. "The horses are draining me," he complained. "I'd love to get rid of them."

"Have you tried to sell them?"

"I'd lose most of my investment."

"That would be a big hit."

"One that I can't afford."

"I assume they're insured?"

"Over-insured."

"That must be costing some money."

"The premium is killing me."

"I'd be thinking about killing the horses."

Gold nodded slowly, his face projecting discomfort. He looked, Morgan thought, like a man at the end of his rope. It was a fine acting job. "I've been thinking it over," he said quietly. "I'd like to cut my losses. Collect the insurance benefit."

Morgan seemed not to hear him. "How do you like the bourbon?"

Gold stared at him in bewilderment. "What?"

"Do you like the bourbon?"

"Yeah, it's wonderful."

"One of my favorites."

Gold lowered his voice artificially. "Do you understand what I'm trying to say? I'm anxious to cut my losses and collect some money."

Morgan stared at a spot in the middle of the table, not meeting Gold's eyes. Finally, he looked up. "What does that have to do with me?"

"I was told that you could help me."

"Help you do what?"

"Get rid of the horses."

Morgan continued his act. "Are you asking me to kill them? Is that what you mean?"

Gold sighed. "That's the general idea."

Morgan knew that Gold was trying to entrap him, but he wasn't sure if he was wearing a wire, so he had to tread lightly. Since he was holding all of the cards – or most of them – he decided to play along for a while. He was curious to see how far these fools would go. "Let me get this straight," he said at last. "You're an insurance executive, but you're asking me to commit insurance fraud?"

Another sigh. "I'm not asking you to do anything you haven't done before."

"How would you know what I've done before?"

"Look, I'm willing to make it worth your while."

Morgan grinned. "Perez told me that you were a generous guy."

"Generous to a fault."

"You seem to have a number of faults."

"Nobody's perfect."

"Risky investment, racehorses. Safer to buy coins and stamps."

"Too safe. Some of us need the adrenaline rush."

Morgan gave him a little resigned smile, indicating that he understood where Gold was coming from. "When did you become an owner?"

"Two years ago."

"Why did you take the plunge?"

Test time, Gold thought. He took his time formulating a believable answer. He told Morgan that he was a horseplayer, and like most horseplayers, he'd always fantasized about owning a racehorse. He began by buying a share of a bottom-rated claimer, which he figured would be an inexpensive way of getting his foot in the door. Back then, the thought of owning colors, free clubhouse passes, and access to insider information was simply exhilarating. Of course, that was before he learned about the expenses associated with owning a horse, which quickly dampened his enthusiasm.

Trying to sound defeated, he repeated the well known fact that owners lose money on nine out of ten horses. He shook his head disgustedly, then said that he'd thought about breeding his injured horses instead of racing them. Unfortunately, nobody was willing to pay a stud fee, despite the fact that both of his stallions had won some races.

"Which brings us back to you," Gold said. "You're my last resort."

"How flattering."

"I didn't come here to flatter you, I came here to do business. Are you interested or not?"

Morgan was startled by the sharp edge in his voice. Now he's overreacting, he thought. He tried to smile, but it came out crooked. "Let's just say – for argument's sake – that a guy was willing to ease your worried mind. How much would you pay him?"

"Ten percent of the settlement."

"I'm no expert, but ten percent sounds low."

"I'd be willing to pay fifteen percent."

"You might be asked for a down payment."

"I'm willing to pay a reasonable amount."

Morgan smiled. "You're a reasonable fellow."

"Up to a point."

What happened next caught Gold by surprise. Morgan told him that he needed time to think things over and check his busy schedule. He would sleep on it and get back to him first thing in the morning. "Where are you staying?"

Dumbfounded, Gold mumbled, "Hyatt Place Hotel."

"I'll be in touch." He tossed back the rest of his bourbon, and then placed a fifty-dollar bill on the table. "Enjoy the rest of your day - and be careful who you talk to. The place is full of scoundrels."

CHAPTER THIRTY-ONE

Gold stared into his empty glass, wondering about his performance. *What the hell just happened?* Did he say something wrong? Maybe he'd been too pushy. Maybe he should have kept his mouth shut and allowed Morgan to do the talking. Maybe the son of a bitch had more work than he could handle.

Maybe. Maybe. Maybe.

Rather than make himself crazy, he walked over to the sales pavilion, just east of Keeneland's track. When he entered the lobby, he noticed that there were five clocks bolted to the wall, each bearing the name of a principle client city. The names were in bold letters, and from left to right, read SYNDEY, TOKYO, LEXINGTON, LONDON, DUBAI. The pavilion also contained a theater-in-the-round, but there was no stage, only an auctioneer's stand and, below that, the sales ring, a semicircle of turf around which the horses paraded as they were sold.

There were no seats available inside the pavilion, so Gold made his way to the show ring, a holding area of sorts, where horses were brought and walked when they came from the barns. There was even a patio bar outside, and as Gold soon learned, this is where some buyers preferred to bid. The buyers were mainly Irish, but there was also a fair number of Australians and Brits. There were spotters stationed above the crowd, and it was their job to relay bids to the auctioneer.

Gold snaked his way to the bar and ordered a mint julep.

"I'll have the same," said a woman standing beside him.

When Gold glanced sideways, he saw a tall, well-dressed brunette, wearing a wide-brimmed hat and designer sunglasses. Her voice was smooth, casual, and had a faint Southern accent. She looked vaguely familiar, Gold thought as she smiled at him in the mirror, her eyes sparkling with amusement. Doing a slight double-take, Gold said, "Jesus." His eyes widened with recognition. "What are you doing here?"

Melanie Dupry gave him a theatrical pout. "Is that any way to greet an old friend?" She giggled, then eased closer, and answered in a whisper. "I came to watch the auction."

Gold scrutinized her closely. "Long trip."

"Did you forget that I love to ride?"

"Not likely."

"What are you doing here?"

Gold hesitated, choosing his words carefully. "We insure some of the horses. I'm involved in a risk management program."

"I wish you were involved in claims management."

"I beg your pardon?"

"I haven't seen a penny from your company. What's the status of my claim?"

Obviously this wasn't the time or the place to get into a long conversation about her claim, but Gold did have a few nagging questions about her MIB file. Specifically he was curious about the codes that indicated "sexual deviation" and "criminal activity." He suggested that they find a quiet place to talk. She agreed, and after their drinks were served, they found a shaded picnic area.

They sat in silence for a few minutes, sipping their drinks and enjoying the pleasant weather. Gold let the silence extend a while longer – while he considered the best approach. Finally he decided he had to give it to her straight. He sat back, cocked his head, and spoke in a measured tone. "Your claim raised a red flag. When the flag goes up, we take a closer look at the claimant, which means a background check. Are you familiar with the MIB?"

"The movie?"

"The Medical Information Bureau."

"No, but it sounds ominous."

"They operate a database of medical information."

"Whose information?"

"Individuals who have previously applied for certain types of insurance. Health insurance, life insurance, disability insurance. That sort of thing."

"What does that have to do with me?"

"You've got an extensive file."

She looked down at her drink, lifted the glass, and took a sip, then put it down carefully. When she raised her head, her glasses were halfway down her nose. "You looked at my medical records?"

"It's called due diligence."

"I call it invasion of privacy."

"I'm only trying to help."

Dupry's glare caught him off guard, and he realized he'd hit a nerve. "Who the hell do you think you're kidding? You're just looking for a reason to deny my claim."

"I'm sorry you feel that way."

She gave him a withering look. "Did you find what you were looking for?"

Something in her tone changed Gold's demeanor. Like flipping a switch, he became angry. "Hey, I wasn't looking for anything except answers. I want to know what's going on in your life. What's with all the injuries?"

"Jesus Christ," she growled. "I told you before, I ride a lot. What can I say, I'm accident prone."

"You're full of crap," Gold snapped. "Nobody gets hurt that often."

Her face betrayed the truth. She made no effort to deny what he had said. She shook her head, tears welling up in her eyes. "Let's change the subject."

"Let's not," Gold shot back. He gently peeled off her sunglasses with a slow, measured motion and looked at her. Her left eye was swollen and there were black and blue marks above her cheek. He felt a sudden sinking sensation, now painfully clear on why she was wearing the dark shades. Without warning, he slammed a fist down on the table. Dupry almost jumped out of her seat. "What the fuck? Are you kidding me?"

Dupry pulled away, then buried her head in her hands. She was crying, he realized, her body trembled, then shook convulsively. She couldn't stop crying, and he didn't know what to do, so he just put an arm around her shoulder. The gesture seemed to comfort her. Finally, after a long five minutes, she regained her composure. "My life is a mess," she said quietly. "A complete and total mess."

Gold patted her reassuringly on the leg. "I've been down that road once or twice myself."

"I don't know what to do. Where to turn."

"If your life's a mess, you should start with taking out the trash."

Dupry drew a breath, collected herself, let the breath out. It was just possible, she supposed, that Gold knew what he was talking about. "What do you mean?"

"Look, I'm no expert, but it seems pretty clear that you're a victim of domestic violence and abuse. Somebody is trying to maintain control over you, and I'm sure you've been worn down by fear, guilt, shame, and intimidation. You shouldn't put up with that crap. You're a grown woman. You deserve to feel valued, respected, and safe."

Dupry gave a snort of laughter. "How do you know what I deserve? Maybe I've created some bad karma. Maybe this is payback."

"Maybe you should stop blaming yourself."

"Thank you, Dr. Phil."

"Wake up, Melanie. You're being manipulated."

"I'll bet you know a thing or two about manipulation."

Gold didn't like the way she said that, with a sneer on her lips, her eyes narrowing ever so slightly. He assumed she was referring to her claim, so he let it pass. "This isn't about me. It's about your freedom. Do I really need to draw you a picture?"

"A picture is worth a thousand words."

Gold gave a sad little laugh. He wasn't sure if she was reaching out to him, or just playing games. He decided to stick his neck out even further. He got a good handle on his temper and told her that, in his experience, abusers relied on a variety of tactics to manipulate a victim and exert their power. Going for broke, he ran through the list: dominance, humiliation, isolation, threats, intimidation, denial, and blame.

Dupry sat silently and listened and Gold thought she looked pale and frightened. She cleared her throat several times, then said, "No expert, huh?"

"I've done some reading. I wanted to understand the problem."

She nodded, and suddenly tears flowed from her eyes. Sobs racked her body, and she put her face back into her hands and mumbled, "Why do you care what happens to me?"

For a moment Gold hesitated, then he pressed his lips against her forehead. "I'm a sucker for a pretty face."

"Seriously, why do you care?"

Caught off guard, Gold gave it some thought, wondering how much to tell her. Like a lot of men, he had no problem asking tough questions, but he felt awkward about sharing his own feelings. Truth was, he didn't want to sound like a sap. He looked around the picnic area and pretended not to hear. She kept starting at him. Finally, he said, "Does it really matter?"

She bit the corner of her lip, lowered her head slightly, and looked out the tops of her eyes at him – her little girl look. Convincing, too. "Yes," she whispered. "It matters a lot."

Gold hesitated, struggling for an answer. "Have you ever heard of a paladin?"

"No."

"The paladins were the foremost warriors of Charlemagne's court – chivalrous heroes. One of my friends – my best friend – thinks that I have a paladin complex. You know, like a white knight riding to the rescue of a damsel in distress. I don't know if it's true, but it's the only explanation I can offer." He looked at her, apparently waiting for a reply. "Does that sound silly?"

"No, it sounds sweet. I wish there were more paladins in the world. Unfortunately, I think they're a dying breed."

"I don't know if chivalry is dead or just dormant."

"Same difference."

"Maybe you've been looking for love in all the wrong places."

"Honey, I haven't been looking for love since I was a teenager."

"What have you been looking for?"

She thought for a moment, then said, "Peace."

"Maybe I can help you out. Point you in the right direction. Would you be willing to give it a shot?"

"What do you have in mind?"

"Have you ever considered a protection order?"

"Is that the same thing as a restraining order?"

"More or less."

"I looked into it once, but I never pursued the matter."

Gold told her that all 50 states had some form of protective statutes, and even though the orders couldn't stop an abuser from stalking or hurting a victim, they did permit the victim to call the police and have the abuser arrested if they violated the order.

Typically, a protective order lasted for one to five years, but in extreme circumstances, they could apply for a lifetime.

Sensing some interest, Gold went on to explain that she could request a "no contact provision." Under this order, her abuser would be prohibited from calling, texting, emailing, stalking, attacking, hitting, or disturbing her.

"Here's the best part," Gold said. "A violation of a protection order can be treated as a felony. That's a serious charge. If convicted, a violator could be sent to prison."

Dupry frowned. "For how long?"

"Depends on the judge – and the circumstances of the case."

She recoiled from the thought. "I don't know if I could handle that – sending someone to prison."

"It's a lot easier than handling a broken arm or a black eye."

An uneasy silence lingered between them, lasting for several minutes. Dupry took a long drink from her glass, trying to think of a way to change the subject. Finally, feeling trapped, she promised to give the protection order some thought. "I'm too tired to make a decision right now."

"I understand."

"Was there something else on your mind?"

Gold still wanted to discuss her MIB file, but he could see that she was emotionally drained. Tomorrow was another day. No sense pushing her to the edge. "Why don't we enjoy the rest of the day? We can talk some other time."

"I've got a better idea. Have dinner with me."

Gold smiled. "Love to."

"We can dine at my house."

"Your house?"

"I own a place in Versailles – a few miles from here. Part of my inheritance."

"I don't have a car."

"I do. I'll take you back to your hotel after dinner."

"Sounds like a plan."

CHAPTER THIRTY-TWO

The manager of the Hilton Hotel was trying his best to maintain an aura of dignity, but with the Keeneland auction underway, he was besieged with special requests. The horsey set were a demanding lot, accustomed to pampering and TLC. Now, on top of everything else, he had to contend with an irate woman from New York, demanding to see his supervisor.

Owing to her upbringing, and Viennese background, Irene Kaminski seldom made a scene in public, but she was at her wit's end with this stubborn hotelier. The man was polite, but she refused to believe that her employee, Adam Gold, had not registered at the hotel.

What kind of joint were these people running?

The manager reiterated that every room was occupied, and despite her protestation, Adam Gold was not a registered guest. He went on to assure her that they had not experienced a computer glitch, and suggested that she contact some other hotels in the area. He waited a nervous minute, then added, "I told the other person the same thing. You might want to check with him before you run off."

Kaminski frowned and leaned over the desk. "What other person?"

"The gentleman that was looking for Mr. Gold."

Kaminski's voice took on an urgent tone now. "What are you talking about? Who was looking for him?"

The manager reached for a slip of paper. "A man named McVey. He was going to grab something to eat, and then check back with me. I believe he's in the Triangle Grille."

"Where's that?"

"Straight down the hall."

The Hot Brown Sandwich was oozing with Mornay sauce, just the way McVey liked it. He had been so hungry, and the turkey and bacon that were now his were broiled to perfection, the bread crisp and brown. The sandwich, sometimes known as a Kentucky Hot Brown, had been created at the Brown Hotel in Louisville, way back in 1926. Consumed as he was by the process of eating, he was taken by surprise when Irene Kaminski took a seat across from him, staring at the gooey concoction on his plate. He looked up, a forkful of meat poised in front of his mouth, and smiled at her. "Well, this is a pleasant surprise. What are you doing here?"

"What the hell are you eating?"

McVey put the fork down on his plate. "It's called a Hot Brown. Turkey and bacon. Cheese sauce on top. Would you like a bite?"

"No, thanks."

"You don't know what you're missing."

"Speaking of missing ...Where's Gold?"

"Hasn't he checked in yet."

"No. I just spoke with the manager."

McVey frowned. "That's odd. He should have been here by now."

"Didn't you two fly out together?"

"Yeah, but then we went our separate ways. I thought it would look suspicious if we stayed in the same hotel." He picked up the napkin from the table and wiped his mouth. "Gold met his contact at the airport. I followed them in a cab. Then we got stuck in a traffic jam and fell behind. I assumed they would show up here –sooner or later – but they should have registered by now."

Kaminski instinctively knew that something was wrong and that Gold was in trouble. "Have you tried to call him?"

"Several times. We had to shut off our cell phones when we landed, and I'm guessing that the knucklehead never turned his back on."

A worried look crossed Kaminski's face. "We need to find him. He might be in danger."

McVey drew himself up in his chair. His eyes had become slits. "What's going on?"

"How much did Gold tell you about his trip to South Carolina?"

"Just about everything."

"Did he mention Roger Fremont and Sungila Taylor?"

"Yeah, he told me about them."

"They're both dead."

McVey's face sort of expanded, his eyebrows launching up, while his jaw dropped. "*Excuse* me? Dead? You're kidding, right?"

"They were murdered – both of them. Rather brutally, I might add."

"Shit."

"Would you like to guess who the police want to question?"

McVey was rapidly trying to process the news and figure out what was happening. He then hit upon the only possible answer. "Gold's a suspect?"

"Numero uno."

"How do you know?"

"I had a visit from the Charleston police chief – and the FBI."

"*The FBI?*"

"Because of the victims. Two African-Americans and a gay person. The feds smell blood, in the form of a hate crime investigation."

"Jesus, that's all we need."

"I need this like a hole in the head."

"How did the police tie Gold to Sungila Taylor?"

"They found her cell phone. Gold used the phone to call his wife – and me. Once the FBI learned about Teague and Fremont, they had no choice but to get involved. I'm sure you can understand their position."

"Yeah, I understand, but I'm not happy about it."

"Neither am I. But hold onto your hat, it gets worse." She hugged herself, shivering. "Gold might be walking into a trap."

McVey muttered something obscene, teeth clenched, and leaned forward. "What do you mean?"

"After you and Gold flew out here, I got a call from Samantha Wong. She had something urgent to tell me, so we met at the Pearl diner. She's one smart cookie, just like her uncle. After your meeting at the MIB, she continued snooping on her own, and she discovered that Melanie Dupry had been married and divorced several times." She cleared her throat, then said, "Roger Fremont was one of her husbands."

"Fremont?"

"He was hubby number two."

"I thought Freemont was gay."

She folded her arms across her chest and nodded. "The marriage was short-lived."

"Talk about false advertising."

Kaminski gave McVey a look that told him he was being juvenile. "Mr. Dupry was husband number three."

"Who was the first sucker?"

Kaminski opened her mouth, as if she were about to answer, then shut it. Tight. Finally, she said, "Say hello to Agent Evans."

FBI agent Evans sat down and gave McVey a long and piercing look. A smiled tickled the corners of her mouth, and then slowly she shook her head from side to side. "When will they ever learn? You can run, but you can't hide. Nice to meet you, Mr. Gold."

McVey drew a breath and held it for a minute. "Well, what do you know? The long arm of the law."

"Surprised to see me?"

"Nope. You have to wake up pretty early in the morning to fool the FBI."

"I'm afraid so."

"Somewhere around noon."

"I beg your pardon?"

McVey pulled out his badge and federal identification. "Kevin McVey. Special Agent. Department of Energy."

Evans took a moment to compose herself. Her expression neutral, she looked across at Kaminski. "What's going on here?"

"You tell me."

"Where's Gold?"

"I have no idea," Kaminski said. "He never checked in."

"A likely story."

"Where's your crime-fighting partner?"

"Guarding the exit."

Kaminski looked at McVey. "Chief Carter. The pride of the Charleston Police." She turned to face Agent Evans. "Why are you following me?"

"You know damn well why I'm here. If you're smart, you'll tell me where to find Gold."

"Funny, but we were just talking about that. The manger suggested that I call some other hotels."

"I've got a better idea," McVey said. "Why don't you call the Kentucky State Police? Gold's contact might have checked in. Maybe they know where the dynamic duo are staying."

"Good idea," Kaminski said. "I'll call Colonel Smith and ask him if he's been in touch with them." She stood up. "Maybe we'll get lucky."

"Just a minute," Evans said. "Where do you think you're going?"

"The lobby. Too noisy in here."

"Grin and bear it, Irene. I'm not letting you out of my sight." She smiled, but there was no warmth or humor in it. "Before you make your call, fill me in. I want to know what's going on here. Why is Gold involved with the state police?"

Kaminski sat down and began to explain, albeit with a measure of resentment. She did not like to be ordered around like a child, but she swallowed her pride and gave Evans a thorough account of the situation. She told the agent about the insurance scam, and about Dupry's injuries, and about the MIB codes, and about Gold's undercover operation.

"Any questions?"

Evans was frowning. "Why do you think that Gold is walking into a trap?"

"Melanie Dupry was married and divorced several times. More importantly, one of her previous names was Melanie Morgan. Does that last name ring a bell?"

Evans stared at her, dumbstruck. "Are you saying that she was married to Jubal Morgan?"

"It certainly appears that way."

"So Morgan was the first sucker," McVey said. "I guess he's still carrying a torch for her."

"Or a club," Kaminski said. "I'll bet he's the one who's been abusing her."

McVey nodded. "He's probably who murdered Sungila Taylor and Roger Fremont."

"Jesus, we need to find Gold."

Evans had an odd expression as if she were trying not to laugh. "I'm not buying your theories, but go ahead and make your call."

When Colonel Smith came on the line, he told Kaminski that Perez had been unable to obtain a room at the Hilton, so he booked accommodations at the Hyatt Place Hotel on Bryant Road – seven miles away. The colonel suggested that Kaminski and her party sit tight. He would get in touch with Perez and tell him to come to the Hilton, hopefully with Gold in tow.

Kaminski thanked the colonel for his help, hung up, and then relayed the plan to McVey and Evans. They both agreed that it made sense to stay put.

Perez was on his way downtown, and just two miles away, when he received a text message from Colonel Smith. He glanced at the message, a bemused look on his face.

All Perez could think was, this should be good.

Ten minutes later Perez was standing at the entrance of the Triangle Grille, looking for the tall, blonde woman that Colonel Smith had described. When he spotted Kaminski he smiled, and she waved him over to the table.

"Where's Gold?" Kaminski asked.

"We'll get to that in a minute," Perez said brusquely. "Who the hell are these two?"

Kaminski handled the introductions, then repeated her question. "Where the hell is Gold?"

"Good question," Perez said. "I've been waiting for him to call me." He glanced at his watch. "I guess they had a lot to talk about."

"Who's *they*?" McVey asked.

"Gold and Jubal Morgan," Perez said. "I introduced them at the racetrack, and they decided to have a drink and discuss some business. I wasn't invited, so I went back to the hotel. That was the last time I saw either one of them." He looked at Kaminski, then said, "I tried to call Gold, but the dude never answers his phone. What's up with that?"

"Long story," Kaminski said. "Do you have any idea where they might have gone?"

Perez gave it some thought. Colonel Smith had once told him that Morgan had inherited some property in Versailles, a quaint community west of Lexington. He wasn't positive about the exact location, but he thought it was on Steele Pike, not far from the Rabbit Creek Bed & Breakfast. In any case, if they wanted to drive out there, he was sure he could find Morgan's place. "Seems like a good place to start."

Agent Evans nodded. "Sounds good to me."

"Let's hope we're not too late," Kaminski said.

"Better late than never," McVey said. "Saddle up, ladies. Time to send out the cavalry."

CHAPTER THIRTY-THREE

After stopping for groceries and wine, Dupry took the scenic route to Versailles, driving west on Interstate 64, and then turning south on US -62, known locally as the Midway-Versailles Road. By taking this route, they were able to view some of the most magnificent horse farms in the region, most of them containing a stately mansion and barn, surrounded by lush green pastures and a four-rail fence.

When Gold mentioned that he had recently been to the Palace of Versailles, Dupry told him that in Kentucky the name was pronounced "Ver-SALES."

"What's in a name?" Gold asked. "That which we call a rose by any other name would smell as sweet."

"How much bourbon did you drink" Dupry asked.

"Not nearly enough," Gold said. "I was quoting Shakespeare."

"Yes, I know. *Romeo and Juliet*." She smiled at him. "I used to be an English teacher."

"I took English as a second language." He smiled back at her. "I didn't learn it very well the first time around."

"Poor student?"

"Dazed and confused."

Dupry slowed down and looked about their surroundings. "Funny that you should mention roses. A lot of these horses have made a run for the roses. Lane's End, the famous breeding farm, is just down the road. Their stallion barn is filled with great horses."

"Any horse I might know?"

She swigged at a bottle of Perrier, and then ran through a short list of thoroughbreds, a list that included A.P. Indy, the son of Triple Crown winner Seattle Slew, Smart Strike, Candy Ride, Curlin, and Mineshaft. All told, their foals had earned over twenty million dollars at the races, and they were still mounting mares for $35,000 per "stand."

Her smile grew wider. "Pretty impressive, huh?"

"Unbelievable."

"God, I love it out here."

"Nice place to grow up."

"I moved out here after my parents died. My aunt and uncle had no children of their own, so they raised me like a daughter." She glanced sideways, her voice becoming softer. "That would be my Aunt Helena and Uncle Lee. I told you about them when we met in Richmond."

"Yes, I remember. They took you in after your parents died in a house fire."

"They were very kind to me. Very loving. I felt safe with them, and looking back, I realize how lucky I was. I hate to admit it, but that was probably the last time that I was truly happy."

Gold leaned forward, leveling his gaze at her. He put his hand on hers and squeezed gently, then spoke in his mildest tone. "If you're as strong as I think you are, you'll get your life back on track."

"Back on track?"

"Pun intended."

"You're incorrigible."

"Guilty as charged."

Situated halfway up a gently sloping hill, Dupry's two-story brick farm house looked like many of the others that dotted the countryside, only not as grand, and surrounded by less pastureland. Once, when her aunt and uncle had lived here, it might have been charming, but as revealed by a closer look, the years had not been kind to it. The roof was in bad shape, many of the slate tiles cracked or missing, some areas covered with sheets of rusting, corrugated steel. Weeds and vines grew wild around the house, blocking a portion of the front steps. The lawn, more brown than green, was in desperate need of raking and reseeding.

Dupry pulled into the circular driveway and parked beside a jockey statue. She managed a hollow laugh even as the sense of embarrassment she felt grew stronger. "Be it ever so humble, there's no place like home."

Gold climbed out of the car and stopped dead in his tracks. He stared at the farmhouse, failing to conceal his surprise and disappointment. "Trouble in paradise?"

Dupry seemed to find that amusing. "Nothing that a generous claim payment won't fix."

"Is that why you brought me out here? To make me feel guilty?"

"You can't blame a girl for trying."

"No, I guess not."

"Look at it this way. If I can restore my home, I might be able to restore my life." Still smiling, she added, "Isn't that what you want me to do?"

"Yeah, but two wrongs don't make a right."

"My goodness, are all you paladins so rigid?"

Suddenly serious, Gold went silent and followed her inside. The door had barely closed behind him before it was flung open again, and Jubal Morgan came rushing into the room. He grabbed Dupry from behind and pulled her close to him. "One move and you die," he told the dazed woman softly, holding a small knife to her right carotid artery. "Stay calm and nobody will get hurt."

Gold's jaw dropped, his eyes wide in terror. "What the hell are you doing here?"

Morgan waited a long time before answering. "First things first. I want you to slowly remove your gun and then toss it on the couch." They stood awkwardly, facing each other, and Morgan repeated his command. "Do it now!"

Gold's thoughts were so far ahead he couldn't keep up with them. He moved slowly and slid his Beretta Tomcat from its holster, and then tossed it on the couch. He stood with his hands at his sides, glaring at Morgan. "Why don't you let her go? This is just between us."

"Why don't you sit down and shut the fuck up."

"Whatever you say, tough guy." He eased into an armchair, struggling to remain calm. "Be careful, the gun is loaded."

"I'll keep that in mind," Morgan said. "You should, too." He nudged Dupry closer to the couch, then grabbed the gun. ".32 caliber? You gotta be kidding me."

"Deadly at close range."

Morgan grinned. "Another thing to keep in mind." He shoved Dupry away from him. "Well, this has worked out rather nicely. Here we are, all together. One big, happy family."

"Not happy, not family," Gold said.

"You're half-right," Morgan said. "You both look unhappy."

Dupry sank onto an old divan, put her face in her hands and began to weep. Gold looked over at her, a little surprised. A few moment later, she lifted her chin and stared coldly at Morgan. For a minute words evaded her. Then: "Is this why you called me from the clubhouse? So I could bring Gold here?"

Gold opened his mouth, but no words came out.

Morgan shook his head. "I don't know why, but for some reason you always run back to this dump. You're very predictable, Melanie."

Dupry's voice grew more strident. "You tricked me, Jubal."

"That I did."

"You're a sneaky son of a bitch."

"Always have been, always will be."

"And a lousy brother."

"Yeah, but I'm the only one you've got."

Gold scowled as his brain struggled with the words. Did she say *brother?* For a brief moment the word did not – could not – compute, and then it hit him, like a ton of bricks. The more he thought about it, the more annoyed he became. A disgusted look settled on his face, and he started to say something, but stopped himself. Anger spread through him, but he told himself to get the fuck over it. Time to focus on his own survival. Forcing a smile, he said, "I'm enjoying the brother and sister act, but where do we go from here?"

"This is no act," Dupry said softly. "We're fraternal twins."

Fraternal twins? Gold thought. Jesus Christ, no wonder she put up with the abuse. These two were practically joined at the hip. How the hell would she ever break away from him? "Which one of your criminal masterminds came up with the insurance scam?"

"Melanie's idea," Morgan said. "She needed money to run her stupid museum and fix up this dump."

Dupry stared up at him furiously. "You're lying, Jubal. You and that damn nigger forced me to file a claim."

"Watch your mouth," Morgan snarled. "Tyrone Teague was a friend of mine."

"Teague was a goddamn grave robber."

Morgan stared at her with an unsettling intensity, his eyes filled with hate. He took a step toward her, leaned in close, and murmured, "It's not polite to speak ill of the dead."

"What are you going to do? Hit me again?"

With raised eyebrows and a stern expression, Morgan assured her that he had no intention of hitting her. "Calm down, Mel. I've got a plan."

"You've always got a plan."

"Have I ever let you down?"

"All the time." She rose and started pacing. "What have you got in mind?"

Morgan's eyes were bright as he looked over at Gold. A bloodthirsty smile formed on his face. Slowly he reached for a roll of duct tape, and then he told Gold to put his hands behind his back. He gave the roll to Dupry, instructing her to wrap the tape around Gold's wrists. Frowning in concentration, she wrapped his wrists tightly, wondering if she might have overdone it.

"I'm sorry about this," she whispered. "I wish you would've paid the claim."

Gold eyed her thoughtfully. *You poor, naïve woman*, he thought to himself. She had no idea why he was in Lexington. "Is that what you think this is about?" he asked. "Do you think I came here because of your silly claim?" He shook his head. "I'm working with the state police. Your loving brother is under investigation. Would you like to know why?"

"Shut up!" Morgan shouted.

"No," Dupry said. "I'm tired of your games." She looked directly at Gold. "What's going on?"

"Brother Jubal has branched out. He's gone from robbing graves to killing racehorses. Business is booming."

"He's lying," Morgan said. "You know how much I love horses. He's trying to turn you against me."

Dupry ignored her brother, fixing her attention on Gold. "Jubal's far from perfect, but he would never do such a terrible thing. Believe me, you've got the wrong man."

Gold would have burst out laughing if the entire thing weren't so serious. "I've heard that love was blind. Now I realize that it's blind, deaf, and dumb."

Morgan stepped between them and hit Gold in the mouth. Right-handed, short swing, hard blow. "Son of a bitch," he shouted. "Don't you talk to my sister that way!"

Gold rocked back a step and doubled over and then came up with blood on his chin. "You're lucky my hands are tied."

"You're lucky my sister's here." He placed the barrel of the pistol under Gold's chin. "If we were alone, I might blow your brains out."

"I'd still be smarter than you."

"You think so?"

"I know so."

"If you're so smart, why did you use your real name when we met? If you ask me, that was really dumb."

"Careless mistake."

"Fatal mistake."

Gold willed himself to stay calm. "How did you know who I was?"

Morgan tsked. "Gold, please. A little respect." He chuckled contemptuously. "I've got sources, too."

Gold looked at Dupry. "Did you volunteer the information, or did he beat it out of you?"

Dupry's back stiffened as she realized what he was getting at. "I didn't tell him," she said quickly. "I swear to God."

"You're a bad liar," Gold said.

Morgan's voice rose a notch. "Don't call my sister a liar."

"It's the nicest thing I could think of."

Morgan hammered a fist into Gold's right kidney, doubling him over and dropping him to the floor. "You talk too much." He grabbed a handful of Gold's hair. "You got anything else to say?"

Dupry grabbed her brother's arm, startled, and caught her breath. "Leave him alone," she pleaded. "Please, Jubal, don't hurt him."

When his breath returned, Gold said, "He didn't hurt me." A tiny smile appeared on his face. "You punch like a sissy. If I were you, I'd stick to beating up women."

Dupry jumped between them, preventing another blow. "Enough!" she shouted. "We've got work to do. You said you had a plan. Let's hear it."

Morgan calmly lit a cigarette, puffed a tiny cloud of smoke, then held it and admired it. "I don't have time to explain. Just follow my instructions and do exactly as you're told. You and I are going to make a fresh start. With some money in our pockets." He took in several deep drags, which seemed to settle his nerves. After exhaling a big cloud of smoke, he handed the gun to her. "Keep an eye on this clown. If he tries anything cute, shoot him."

Dupry smiled nervously. "Where the hell are you going?"

"Out to my car. I'll be right back."

When Morgan left the room, she covered her face with her free hand, and words came out in a rush. "God Almighty, what's he up to now?"

"Nothing good," Gold said.

"Are you all right? Anything broken?"

"Just my heart."

"Jesus, I don't know what to say."

"I can think of a few choice words."

"Look, I know what you're thinking, but he's still my brother. What do you expect me to do?"

"Save yourself."

"How? By calling the police? Jubal's no saint, but he's the only family I've got."

"Save it for the judge."

"You're a cold-hearted bastard."

"You've got it all wrong. Your brother's the cold-hearted bastard. He's the one who's been beating you up and causing you pain. He's the one who's about to ruin your life."

She briefly closed her eyes, and took a deep breath. "God, this is so messed up."

"Snap out of it, Melanie. You've got about ten seconds to make the most important decision of your life. Do the right thing. Call the police."

Dupry exhaled deeply. She looked drained. Pale as a ghost. "I'm sorry, I ... I can't betray my own brother."

"If you betrayed me, you can betray that bastard."

She shook her head. "I told you the truth. I didn't tell Jubal who you were."

"I don't believe you."

"She's telling the truth," Morgan said, watching them intently. "Melanie has a few flaws, but she seldom lies. I seldom tell the truth. Lying is so much easier." He walked past them, holding a five-gallon plastic can. Smiling mischievously, he entered the kitchen, and returned empty-handed. "You're just dying to know the truth, aren't you, Gold."

Gold smiled without a trace of humor. "You've piqued my curiosity."

"All right, I'll be a good sport. What have I got to lose? Roger Fremont spilled the beans."

"*Roger Fremont?*"

"The Prince of Tides."

The answer came too quickly for Gold. He looked closely at Morgan's face and decided he was lying. "You're full of shit."

"The little faggot made a full confession. I had to torture him, but it was worth the trouble. Before he died, he sang like a bird." There was a moment of silence. "What's wrong, Gold? You look sick."

"You're the sick one," Gold said. "I hope you rot in hell."

Dupry closed her eyes. She desperately wanted to cry, but she had already wept too much, and now she drowned in helplessness and guilt. "How could you do such a thing?" she asked. "How could you kill such a kind, sweet man?"

Morgan hid behind a cloud of nicotine. "Did you forget what he did to you? He married you under false pretenses. You had to find out the hard way."

"Jesus Christ, you're so fucking stupid. We were young and foolish. Neither one of us knew what we were doing. We were both lost. Both virgins. I was the one who insisted that we marry."

"He should have told you the truth."

"Maybe he didn't know the truth. Maybe he had to learn the hard way, too. Did that ever occur to you?"

A mocking smile spread across his face. "Fuck Roger Fremont. We've got work to do."

"No," Dupry said firmly. "I'm through with this crap. You're on your own."

"Wait outside, Melanie."

Dupry stood her ground, shaking her head, her jaw set. "You wait outside. This is my house."

Morgan gave her a shove, then stepped back, the mocking smile now gone. "Don't make me lose my temper."

"What's that smell?" Gold asked.

They both ignored the question.

"Don't touch me," Dupry said sternly. "I've had enough of your abuse."

Morgan fumed for a few seconds, then said, "I don't have time for this, Mel. Get out of this house or –"

"Or you'll what?" Dupry stepped forward and poked him at the base of his sternum, right above his solar plexus. "Kick me? Bite me? Punch me? Break my other arm?"

Morgan retreated two quick steps and brought his hand up in case she tried to poke him again. "I said I was sorry. I won't ever hurt you again. You have my word."

"*Your word*?" She burst out laughing. "Listen to me, you son of a bitch. Once you've been beaten like you beat me, you never forget it. The bruises go away, the bones heal, but the scars remain, deep, hidden, raw. You stay beaten, and you're never the same again."

"I'm warning you, Mel. Leave while you can."

"What are you up to now? What's that smell?"

"Gasoline," Gold said. "Your dream house is about to go up in smoke."

"Shut up!" Morgan shouted.

Dupry let this register before she exploded in anger. "Have you lost your mind? Are you completely insane?"

Morgan lit another cigarette, took a long drag. "There's no other way. We burn down the house, get rid of Gold, collect the insurance. You and I live happily ever after. Simple as that."

Dupry set her mouth, drew a determined breath. "I won't let you do it."

"You have no choice."

"I've got the gun."

"You won't use it."

"I will if I have to. I love this place. I won't let you destroy it."

"You're a sentimental fool."

"No more fires, Jubal. I mean it."

"Come on, sis. Let me have some fun. I haven't burnt down a house since we were kids."

The reference to their parents pushed her over the edge. She ran forward now in a wild fury, her fists flailing at him. "You sick bastard!" She kept coming, pouncing at him, shouting obscenities, until he slapped her across the face. She stumbled backward, landing on her butt, dazed, but still conscious.

Slowly, deliberately, Morgan turned around and walked toward the kitchen. When he reached the door, he nudged it open with his elbow, and then he flicked his cigarette inside. The flames started with a quiet little whoosh, a small puff that that could be felt as much as heard. There was no heat at first, just a glowing light that kept growing brighter as the flames began to spread.

Dupry screamed.

Morgan's eyes lit up, although he tried to keep any sign of enthusiasm out of his face.

Gold stood up, looking for the nearest exit.

Suddenly two shots rang out. Dupry had fired from a sitting position, both shots hitting Morgan in the chest. She fired two more times, then dropped the pistol. Morgan staggered toward her, but collapsed at Gold's feet. An instant later, something exploded inside the kitchen. Already the flames were growing so hot he had to back off, urging Dupry to free his hands. She found her brother's knife and cut the duct tape. A thick cloud of smoke began to fill the room.

Gold picked up the gun, glanced at Morgan's lifeless body. "Let's get out of here."

"You go," she whispered. "I'm staying here."

"Are you nuts? The fire is out of control."

"I know, but I can still control my own fate."

Gold had no idea what she was talking about, but at this point he didn't care. He grabbed her arm. "You're coming with me."

She pulled away from him. "No, I need to pay for my sin. Answer for my silence. I knew that Jubal killed our parents, but I never said a word. I was too afraid. He threatened to kill me if I said anything. I acted like a coward."

"And now you're acting like a fool."

"It's payback time."

Another explosion rocked the house and shattered some windows. The front door flew open. Gold heard the sound of a siren and turned to see a line of cars coming up the driveway, a cloud of dust trailing from behind.

Crunch time.

"You'd better go," Dupry said.

"Listen to me, Melanie. We don't have time for a long goodbye. If you want to cash in your chips, that's your business. I can see you're an angel whose wings just won't unfold." He held out his hand. "Nice knowing you."

She shook his hand. "Goodbye, Gold."

"Goodnight, Gracie."

"Huh?"

Gold hated to do it, but he cold cocked her with a right cross. Her knees buckled, and she fell into his arms. He dragged her outside and down the front steps, and onto the lawn. When he looked up, he was surrounded by familiar faces – and four of them had guns drawn.

"Easy, folks," Gold said. "Everything's under control."

Chief Carter ran past him to check the house.

Agent Evans checked Durpy's pulse.

Perez called for backup, an ambulance, and a fire truck.

Kaminski and McVey tended to Gold, inquiring about his physical condition.

After the initial flurry of activity, Evans took charge. She cleared her throat and did her professional best not to look flustered. She muttered something under her breath, then said, "What happened to this woman?"

"I slugged her," Gold said.

Infuriated, Evans glared silently at Gold, and then said, "You'd better have a damn good reason."

"Do you have a list I could choose from?"

McVey was having trouble keeping a straight face. A small smile began, faded.

Kaminski punched Gold in the arm. "You forgot to turn on your cell phone."

Gold smiled. "I didn't forget, the battery died."

"No charger?" she asked.

"No time," Gold said.

Evans stood still a moment, composing herself and listening intently. The chaotic scene was overwhelming, and she could not afford to be anything less than focused. "Who is this woman?"

"Melanie Dupry," Gold said. "The homeowner."

"Former homeowner," McVey quipped.

"Over here!" Carter shouted. "There's a body inside!"

Gold nodded grimly. "That would be Jubal Morgan."

"What happened to him?" Evans asked.

"He got shot."

"This should be good," Kaminski muttered.

"Who shot him?" Evans asked.

"Miss Melanie," Gold said. "She shot him four times."

"Four times?"

"I think she was afraid of being sued."

"Survivors can be a pain in the ass," McVey said.

Not having a clue where this was going, Evans simply rubbed her chin, stalling for time. "I hate these domestic disturbances."

"They weren't married," Gold said.

Evans frowned. "They weren't?"

"They were brother and sister."

"Jesus," Kaminski whispered. "I thought they were husband and wife."

"Nope."

Evans shook her head in disbelief. "How could she shoot her own brother?"

"He started the fire," Gold said. "The son of a bitch was hoping to collect the insurance."

"He sounds like a desperate fellow."

Gold brooded about this for a while. Then he said, "Well, you know what they say. If you can't stand the heat, stay out of the kitchen."

THE END

CPSIA information can be obtained
at www.ICGtesting.com
Printed in the USA
FSOW01n1341190516
20624FS